THE *Victorian Mystery* SERIES

7

Death at EPSOM DOWNS

ROBIN PAIGE

SOUTH DOWNS CRIME & MYSTERY

First published in the UK in 2016
by South Downs CRIME & MYSTERY,
an imprint of **The Crime & Mystery Club Ltd**,
PO Box 394, Harpenden,
Herts, AL5 1XJ, UK

southdownscrime.co.uk

ISBN
978-0-85730-025-6 (print)
978-0-85730-026-3 (epub)

Typeset in 11pt Palatino
by Avocet Typeset, Somerton, Somerset TA11 6RT

Printed in Denmark by Nørhaven

ACKNOWLEDGMENTS

We are grateful to those who helped fill the blanks in our understanding of some of the complex questions involved with Victorian horseracing. Mr. Ian Nelson, a guide at the National Horseracing Museum in Newmarket, Suffolk, England, provided an invaluable service in reading the manuscript, correcting our errors, and suggesting possibilities we hadn't considered. We thank him for sharing his knowledge, experience, and enthusiasm with us. Professor Thomas Tobin, of the Equine Research Center of the University of Kentucky at Lexington, and Professor Richard Nash of Indiana University helped to clarify our understanding of the doping of racehorses at the turn of the century, while good initial leads to the toxicological issues were offered by our local veterinarian, Dr. Tom Hembree, and pharmacist and toxicologist Luci Zahray, RPh, MS. We also received helpful suggestions of possible source material from members of the Victoria list on the internet. We are very grateful to our agent, Deborah Schneider, and our editor, Natalee Rosenstein, whose belief in, and support of, Robin Paige has made it possible to move the series from paperback to hardcover.

Robin Paige
aka Bill Albert
Susan Wittig Albert

CAST OF CHARACTERS

Lord Charles Sheridan, Baron of Somersworth

Lady Kathryn Ardleigh Sheridan, Baroness of
Somersworth and mistress of Bishop's Keep

Patrick, apprentice jockey and stable lad at Grange
House

Bradford Marsden, close friend of Charles and Kate

Edith Hill, Bradford Marsden's fiancée

Albert Edward, His Royal Highness, the Prince of Wales

Lillie Langtry (aka Mr. Jersey), actress, theatrical
producer, and racehorse owner

Jeanne-Marie Langtry, Lillie's daughter

Lord Reginald Hunt, Jockey Club member and racehorse
owner

Colonel Harry Hogsworth, racehorse owner

Admiral Owen North, steward of the Jockey Club

Jack Murray, former Scotland Yard detective, now a
Jockey Club investigator

Jesse Clark, American trainer

Mr. Angus Duncan, head trainer at Grange House,
Newmarket

Mr. James (Pinkie) Duncan, assistant trainer at Grange
House and Angus's nephew

Todhunter Sloan, American jockey

Dr. Septimus Polter, veterinary surgeon

Captain Dick Doyle, Lord Reginald's racing manager

Henry Manford Radwick, moneylender

Alfred Day (Badger), bookmaker

Eddie Baggs, Alfred Day's partner

Oliver Moore (Sobersides), Alfred Day's clerk

Amelia Quibbley, Kate's maid

Margaret Simpson, Lillie's maid

1

Wednesday, 31 May 1899

At the Derby

"Epsom on Derby Day! It was a national holiday, when a vast concourse of men and women assembled on Epsom Downs to see the race for the Derby Stakes. This was still the England of old— the England in which rich and poor were united by a common love of sport. Here at Epsom, a coster in his cart could still shout a cheery welcome to a Duke in his crested coach, whilst the handsome young coachman behind, resplendent in braid and cockade, could throw a knowing wink to the young scullery maid who whistled at him from the back of a broken-down pony and trap."

The Pocket Venus: A Victorian Scandal
HENRY BLYTH

WALKING ALONG THE racecourse on her husband's arm, Amelia Quibbley thought she had never before seen such a crowd. Bookies in checked suits and green silk ties traded cries with betting men in gray overcoats.

"On the Derby, who'll bet the Derby?"

"What's the price on the favorite in the Stakes?"

"Five to Two."

"Done!"

And the half-crowns jingled in the bookies' buckets, while men in dirty white aprons filled foaming glasses from beer kegs, shouting "Accommodation! 'Commodation here!" A parson in front of a gospel tent pounded a drum, exhorting sinners to turn their backs on the Derby and wager their lives on Christ. Blind beggars cried for alms, a boy on stilts called for coins, and drunken soldiers shouted out popular ditties.

Half-deafened by the din, Amelia said, "I'm thirsty, Lawrence. Shall we 'ave a ginger beer?"

Lawrence's handsome dark eyes laughed down at his wife and his arm circled her waist. "A ginger beer ye shall 'ave, ducky, as soon as I find one o' Badger's men in the Ring and lay my bit. Badger's posted the best odds on Ricochet."

Lawrence paused to peer at a man standing behind a banner that read *Alfred Day, Commission Agent, Newmarket. All Bets Paid*. "On th' Derby!" the man was droning, like a sour bagpipe. "On th' Derby 'ere! Bet th' Derby!"

"And there's Badger 'isself, by Gawd!" Lawrence exclaimed. "Stop here, dear. I want to put down a crown." He stepped up to the banner and raised his voice over the din. "Badger! Say, Badger, wot's odds on Ricochet?"

"Sev'n to two," Badger cried. Where other bookmakers were gaudy in suits of black-and-white checks the size of sixpences, with flowing silk ties as green as May and yellow posies pinned to their lapels, he wore a dignified gray frock coat with a pale gray top hat and sparkling diamond rings on both hands. Never mind that the coat was stained and missing a button and the rings most likely paste, he looked almost as fine as a gentleman.

"Sev'n to two on Ricochet," Lawrence cried. He held up a coin. "'Ere ye are." Badger's man, a rusty little fellow with a crooked collar, held out an open satchel.

"Drop it in there," Badger directed. "Right in there, sir. And take care o'yer ticket, or some evildoer will relieve ye of it." Badger's man snapped the satchel shut and scribbled in a black book. He tore out the ticket and handed it to Lawrence.

Amelia frowned as Lawrence pocketed the ticket and fell into step beside her, jaunty and proud as a peacock, now that the long-awaited transaction was over. It wasn't so much the money she minded; they could afford to lose a crown, if it came to that, although she hoped it wouldn't, with Baby at home needing new boots. But she'd been raised by Scripture and had been taught that betting was against God's law. It was against common sense, too, as she knew for herself. At the pub where she and Lawrence stopped on their nights out, she'd seen Mr. Starkey, who earned ten shillings a week, lay down five on a horse while eight little Starkeys shivered at home for want of coal. And Mrs. Hartop, the old woman who swept Dedham High Street for nine shillings a week, was regular with her half-crown though she couldn't pay the butcher. Betting took money from the poor, Amelia did not doubt, and the parson was right to bang on his drum and shout out its evils, even though not a soul was listening.

But Lady Charles Sheridan, whom Amelia served as lady's maid, had given her a holiday today, and Amelia was carrying a ruffled white sunshade and wearing her best sprigged muslin with a blue shawl and white cotton gloves. Her own Lawrence, dressed in a fine gray coat and bright blue trousers, had been given the important job of helping Lord Charles Sheridan photograph the finish of the Derby Stakes. And since men had laid down their money since the beginning of time and would go on laying it down whether their wives wished it or not, the practical Amelia set her qualms aside and happily applied herself to the enjoyment of the Derby, counting the crown that Lawrence had dropped into the bookmaker's satchel as the price of their admission.

But behind all the revelry, above the music, beneath all the whooping and cheering of the great, noisy mob, she could hear Badger's stentorian voice behind her: "On th' Derby 'ere! On th' Derby! Bet th' Derby now!"

2

The Bookmaker

"He was dubbed the Lord Chesterfield, but a better name would be the Tallyrand, of the Ring. A list of his smart sayings would choke up the British Museum, and I never saw him nonplussed but once, and that was when a railway guard wanted two points over the odds. Well do I remember the first wager I had with him. 'Take care of your ticket, sir,' he chanted in his most dulcet tones, 'or some evildoer will relieve you of it.' The last time the chant was in the minor key. 'Here! Take your bloomin' custom somewhere else: I'm tired of payin' you!' ... When the history of this man comes to be written, it will be told how he defied the Stewards of the Jockey Club on their native heath and played the noble game of spoof with Her Majesty's police."

Edward Spencer Mott,
quoted in Old Pink 'Un Days
JB Booth

FOR HIS PART, Alfred Day, also known as Badger, was having a fine Derby. He looked well, he felt well, and Sobersides, his clerk, was holding a bulging satchel. And why shouldn't he feel well and happy with his lot in life? Over the past half-dozen years, Badger's various enterprises—some of them legal, some of them not—had prospered. The bookmaking business, which had begun as a convenient front for his other activities, had particularly flourished. In addition to his Newmarket headquarters, he had opened two other offices in London, and he now employed several men to take wagers for him at the track.

But the fact that Badger could hire helpers didn't mean that he might absent himself from the Ring. No, indeed. No matter how much money he might make or how much leisure it might buy, he preferred to be where the action was. And what sweeter action might there be in this world than wagering on the Derby, the Blue Riband of the Turf, the grandest event in racing? He raised his hand in a commanding gesture. "Bet on the Derby!" he cried. "Bet on the Derby here!"

A young gentleman stepped out of the crowd in front of him. "Ah, there you are, Badger," he said expansively, and Badger saw that he was a little drunk. "Mrs. Lillie Langtry would like to put a hundred more on Gladiator. What're the odds, my good man?"

"The odds, m'lord," Badger said, "are 66 to 1." He pursed his lips. He'd studied the form, of course, and hadn't seen any reason to offer anything more favorable on the unspectacular colt, a lazy runner who'd finished at the back of the field in all but one of his previous outings—so poor a show that one had to wonder why Lord Hunt had bothered to enter him. Even so, there had been quite a run on the outsider in the last hour. The horse's owner had bet heavily, and the stable, too, followed by several other large wagers. Badger had already begun to think that a game of one sort or another was afoot—and now came Mrs. Langtry with yet another wager. It was enough to raise a bookmaker's suspicions.

Still, it was out of the question to reject Mrs. Langtry's custom, even though she had not yet settled her losses from Kempton Park. There was the matter of her occasional cheating too, which she thought he didn't notice—this time, at least, her bet was placed before the starting bell rang. But while Badger was generally a careful man and kept a close eye on accounts, these issues were of little consequence in the case of Mrs. Langtry, for he was comfortably aware that he had the ability, any time he chose, to require her to settle—and more, too, much more. He'd only been waiting for the propitious moment, when she might feel a compelling reason to do business with him. The thought of this made him quite cheerful, and he nodded shortly at his clerk, who wrote the wager in his black book and tore out a ticket.

"Take care of the ticket, m'lord," Badger said, offering his ritual caution, "or some evildoer will relieve you of it."

Lord de Bathe, that silly young fool, took off his top hat and made a great show of sticking the ticket in the band. "And what evildoer," he asked with a tipsy laugh, "would have the galling effrontery to steal from the most beautiful woman in England?"

Badger bowed. "The odds might be high, m'lord," he said with a smile, "but one never knows."

"Well, I'll give you a tip you can lay on, Badger." Lord de Bathe jammed his hat crookedly on his head. "I'm going to ask our fair Lillie to marry me. What odds'll you give on her yes?"

"Oh, I never lay on a sure thing," Badger said, without hesitation. "But I will say congratulations and well done,

15

my lord," he added, doffing his hat with a flourish. "Very well done indeed."

Yes, it was well done, Badger thought, watching the young lord weave his unsteady way through the crowd—at least on Mrs. Langtry's part. And unless he was mistaken, her coming marriage might bode well for himself, too. Perhaps that propitious moment had arrived.

3

The Start

"It was hard to die without knowing who had won the Derby."

Lord Charles Beresford

PATRICK GATHERED GLADIATOR'S reins as Lord Reginald Hunt and Mr. Angus Duncan said goodbye to the farrier, who was still shaking his head at the difficulty of getting the horse to stand still for his racing plates, and to the veterinary surgeon. Then the two of them walked several steps away, speaking so quietly that Patrick had to strain to hear.

"I'm glad that the Stewards agreed to have him saddled at the starting gate," Lord Hunt said. "If he had to parade in the state he's in—"

"He's on his toes, that's all," Mr. Angus replied in his usual Scottish brogue. "A bit edgy, p'rhaps, but he'll smooth out by the turn."

"You don't want Pinkie to lead him on?" Lord Hunt seemed increasingly anxious. "He's a bundle of nerves. What if he breaks away from the lad?"

Mr. Angus's nephew, whom everyone called Pinkie, stepped forward eagerly. "Be glad to take the horse in, Uncle."

Without answering, Mr. Angus turned to Patrick. "We'll be off, then, lad. Mind ye keep him steady, now. His lordship and I'll make way, but the crowd's apt to push."

The May afternoon had gone cloudy, and a light mist brushed Patrick's face as he gathered the horse's reins and prepared to follow the two men through the milling spectators between them and the starting gate, where Gladiator was to be saddled. He paused for a moment, laying a hand on the sweating, quivering shoulder and whispering a steadying "Quiet, now." But the horse began a nervous dance, and Patrick's earlier apprehension—that Gladiator might not be able to do himself justice today— grew even sharper. He frowned, thinking that perhaps that stuff in the veterinary's bottle might have something to do with the way the horse was behaving.

But Gladiator was known to be erratic. The powerful colt, by the great Ballyhoo out of Brindlebay, had already showed that he had the heart of a Derby champion and the power to match it. At his best, as in the Bedford Stakes the previous autumn, he demonstrated tremendous acceleration, a remarkable finishing speed, and a wonderful maneuverability. At his worst, he was lethargic and dispirited, as at the Two Thousand Guineas at Newmarket in April, where he finished at the bottom of a field of eight. He could also show a sour, savage temper. Once, before Patrick came to apprentice at the Grange House Stable, he had bitten a thumb from an unwary stableboy. And just the week before, out on the Limekilns for trial gallops, he had thrown his rider and raced wild and free across the Newmarket Heath while Mr. Angus and his nephew Mr. James watched helplessly, fearing that he might injure himself. It had been Patrick who finally caught the rebellious horse and returned him to his box, for though the boy was still several months away from fourteen, he was the only lad in the Grange yard whom Gladiator could tolerate.

From Patrick's point of view, the bond was a natural one. He saw in the horse an unruly spirit much like his own and loved him for it, and the horse, as far as he was able, returned him a certain affection. Seeing this, Mr. Angus had made him the horse's traveling lad, responsible for helping Pinkie with his care during the railway trip to Epsom and for leading him through the Derby crowd to the starting gate. It was enough to make a stable lad's head swim.

But Patrick was not an ordinary lad. Some two years before, he had found himself one of the players in a grand adventure at Rottingdean, a village on the south coast of England, through which he had been introduced to His Royal Highness and two other gentlemen, Lord Charles Sheridan and Mr. Rudyard Kipling. In gratitude for his services, the Prince had granted Patrick a stipend sufficient to guarantee his education, and at Mr. Kipling's suggestion, he had gone off to school at Westward Ho!, on Bideford Bay, in Devonshire. Lady Charles herself had taken him to the school and had even shed a few tears when she kissed him and said goodbye.

Westward Ho! was an unconventional school, and as long as the boys paid the requisite attention to their studies and attended chapel with some regularity, they were free to bathe in the Atlantic beyond Pebble Ridge and wander the Devonshire countryside. But while Patrick was gifted with a shrewd intelligence and a maturity far beyond his years, he was hardly a disciplined scholar, and whatever academic enthusiasm he might have felt was poisoned by

19

an odious master who took a sadistic pleasure in inflicting corporal punishment upon those in his charge. Patrick and his friends Turkey Bates and Jake Shanks sought sanctuary in the furze thickets above the cliff. There, smoking pipes and reading aloud from Surtees's racing novels, they plotted to run away and become apprentice jockeys. It was a scheme dear to Patrick's heart, for he loved horses more than anything else in the world—more than books, certainly, or games, or the prospect of taking the Army examination and embarking on a military career.

But those lazy golden days in the furze came to an abrupt end, and so did Patrick's education. Turkey drowned one September day in the sea, and a fortnight later Jake was sent home to India because his father had failed to pay his tuition and board.

His friends gone, his heart broken, Patrick paid even less attention to his studies, and the master's floggings consequently grew less restrained. The boy tried to hang on, if only to please Lady Charles, who wrote him the most marvelous letters and promised that he could spend the holidays with her and Lord Charles at Bishop's Keep. But a month after Turkey's death and Jake's departure, and a day after the most severe beating yet, Patrick could endure it no longer. He left without saying goodbye, without even writing to Lady Charles, whose kindness he could never repay. How could he confess that he had failed? How could he tell her that he wasn't worthy of her concern, or her love?

Leaving Devonshire, the boy struck out eastward across the Downs to Rottingdean and to Harry Tudwell, in whose stable he had once worked. Harry set him to doing morning and evening stables and exercising the string on the Downs, and at midwinter, impressed by the boy's understanding of horses and his firm determination to ride, he prevailed on his old friend Angus Duncan at the Grange House Stable to take Patrick on as stable lad and apprentice jockey. That was how he had come to be here on this day, at this race of all races, the Blue Riband of the Turf, the Derby Stakes, with the horse he loved.

Following the men, Patrick led Gladiator into the paddock near the start, where they were joined by Captain Dick Doyle, Lord Reginald's racing manager and quite the fattest man Patrick had ever seen, and Johnny Bell, the jockey, who rode often for the stable and usually in Lord Hunt's rose-and-green colors. Johnny was a pleasant, even-tempered young man, warm-hearted and kindly toward the stable lads and with none of the arrogance displayed by other winning jockeys. Over the past few months, Patrick had come to love him dearly, in part for his gentle way with both horses and boys and in part because Johnny somehow reminded him of his lost friend Turkey.

Now, Johnny Bell came to Gladiator, running his hand along the sweating flank. "How is he?" he asked Patrick, speaking low.

"Nervy," Patrick replied, feeling the horse trembling against him as Pinkie attempted to throw on the saddle. Gladiator half reared, and as Patrick struggled to gentle him down, he added, in a breathless warning, "Wilder even than the day he got loose on the Heath." Johnny had been there that day, and had seen what happened.

"Don't like the looks of him," Johnny said, stroking the quivering flank, and Patrick heard the nervousness in his voice. But quite apart from the condition of the horse, it was no surprise that Johnny was nervous. It was his first Derby too, and Patrick knew how desperately he wanted to do well.

Patrick was considering telling Johnny about the

21

business with the bottle, when they were joined by Lord Hunt and Captain Doyle. "He should run well today," the captain remarked with a jovial confidence, pushing his betting book into the pocket of his frock coat and adjusting his waistcoat around his enormous girth. To Johnny, he said, "You have your instructions, my boy?"

Johnny cast an apprehensive eye at the horse, who was clearly unhappy with his saddle. "Don't go for an early lead," he muttered, "but keep in touch with the front runners. After Tattenham Corner and into the straight, show him the whip and come hard on the outside."

"And keep clear," Lord Hunt warned. With a glance at the horse, he hunched his shoulders and added, unnecessarily, "He's spirited today."

Maniacal was a better description, Patrick thought, for Gladiator was behaving as though the very devil was in him. He glanced uneasily at Johnny. His friend was not the strongest of the two or three jockeys who rode for the stable. He was known to be at his best with novice or reluctant runners, handling them lightly and expertly, knowing instinctively when and how to bring them on. Patrick wondered uneasily how he would fare with Gladiator, who seemed to be growing wilder by the moment.

"The more spirit, the better," Captain Doyle said emphatically. "He stands at 66 to 1." He grinned at Lord Hunt. "Shades of last year's dark-horse Derby, eh, my lord? Jeddah at 100 to 1. Those with something on that horse went home wealthy." From Captain Doyle's sly look, Patrick felt that he must have gone home wealthy too. He wondered how much the captain had bet on Gladiator.

Brightening, Lord Hunt clapped the jockey on the shoulder. "Bring him home the winner, Johnny, and I'll see there's a handsome present for you."

Nervously, Johnny touched his cap. "I'll do my best, sir."

"Right," said the captain, and he and Lord Hunt left hurriedly for the stands, making a detour through the crowded betting ring for a last-minute wager.

The field was collecting and the starter called the preliminary warning. Patrick held Gladiator's head while Mr. Angus gave Johnny a leg up. The horse reared angrily, snorting and pawing the air, and Patrick leaped out from under the flashing hoofs. But Johnny had found his seat and managed to keep it, and after a moment he seemed to be in control. But the start was not propitious. It took ten minutes and several false starts to get the runners to the line and pointed in the right direction, but finally the flag came down and they were off. The starting bell tolled, the men shouted, and Patrick watched, his heart in his mouth, as the horses grew smaller in the distance.

He could not have guessed that the end of it all would be much worse than the beginning. Gladiator would disgrace himself, and his friend Johnny Bell would die without knowing who won the Derby.

4

The Finish

"On Epsom Downs when racing does begin,
Large companies from every part come in,
Tag-rag and Bob-tail, Lords and Ladies meet,
And Squires without Estates, each other greet..."

1735 racecourse ditty

"In this world there are only two tragedies. One is not
getting what one wants, and the other is getting it."

Lady Windermere's Fan, 1892
OSCAR WILDE

"KATE!" JENNIE CHURCHILL exclaimed excitedly, turning
from a conversation with a fashionably dressed
lady. "How delightful to see you!" She leaned forward
to brush a kiss on Kate's cheek, then glanced around. "Is
Charles with you?"

Kathryn Ardleigh Sheridan was no racing enthusiast,
but the Derby was as much a national holiday as a race,
and since she now called England her home, she had
begun to think she should attend the race one of these

years. Then the Jockey Club Stewards had invited her husband, Lord Charles, to set up a camera that would automatically photograph the finish. The Prince of Wales extended an invitation to her to watch the race from the Prince's stand, and the question of her attendance was settled. Not that Kate was especially impressed by royal invitations, or had any personal interest in the social circus that surrounded HRH. But she had recently embarked on a writing project—an ironic novel featuring the racing set, written under her usual pseudonym of Beryl Bardwell—and she was on the lookout for ideas and material. She also knew she would encounter a few special friends at the race, Lady Randolph Churchill among them. Kate and Jennie—both Americans, both married to Englishmen—had been close friends since the preceding autumn, when Charles had helped Jennie and her son Winston deal with an ugly blackmail scheme.

"Charles is down on the course, setting up a camera to record the finish," Kate said in response to Jennie's question. She stepped forward to be introduced to the other lady, who was costumed in an elegant wine-colored silk and a fur wrap against the spring chill, her large hat trimmed in fur and feathers. She was smoking a cigarette in a long ivory holder and observing Kate with a supercilious air.

"Lady Charles Sheridan," Jennie said, "I should like to present Mrs. Langtry, whom you have undoubtedly seen on the stage." She gave Mrs. Langtry a restrained smile, and Kate thought that perhaps Jennie did not really like the woman. "Here at Epsom," Jennie added, "you will hear Mrs. Langtry spoken of as 'Mr. Jersey,' the name under which her horses run."

Kate turned with real interest to Mrs. Langtry: the Jersey Lily, once known as the loveliest woman in

25

England, beautiful enough to capture the Prince of Wales as her lover and clever enough to keep him as a friend and sponsor even after he had transferred the royal affections to the Countess of Warwick, and more recently, to Mrs. Keppel. Now in her forties, Mrs. Langtry was still almost beautiful, Kate thought, her chestnut hair gleaming, her movements graceful, her figure ripely mature, if perhaps rather too abundantly endowed. But she had an actress's self-assured awareness of her beauty, and her calculating glance and the cool, half-amused curl of her lips gave her an arch, disdainful look.

Kate was immediately intrigued. "I have indeed seen you perform, Mrs. Langtry, some years ago in New York, in *Agatha Tylden*. I thought the character of Mrs. Tylden perfectly suited to you." The title role had been that of a powerful, energetic woman who inherited a shipping business and became so fully engaged with it that she rejected a worthy lover—only to marry him after her business failed and he rescued her from bankruptcy. At the time, Kate had admired the play but thought that she would have put a different ending to it. Surely a woman of Agatha Tylden's power and resourcefulness could have arranged her own financial recovery without having to rely upon marriage to save her!

At Kate's compliment, Mrs. Langtry thawed slightly. "Ah, *Agatha Tylden*," she said in a reminiscent tone. "A very satisfying play. Every performance sold out, and the crowds made it difficult for me to reach the Holland House, where I was staying. 'Langtry fever,' the newspapers called it." She gave a tolerant chuckle. "It was all quite amusing, I must say, and very flattering."

Kate started to reply, but Mrs. Langtry, disregarding her, went on. "One does so enjoy roles that are written exclusively for one, of course, with one's experiences in mind. The next will be that of Mrs. Trevelyan in Sidney Grundy's *The Degenerates*—quite a daring play. No doubt some will be scandalized by its picture of modern smart society." She smiled and flicked her cigarette ash.

Jennie Churchill gave an ironic cough. "Lady Charles also has another name," she remarked dryly, "one that I'm sure you'll recognize. Her novels and stories are read both in England and America. She writes under the pen name of Beryl Bardwell."

Kate smiled inwardly. As Beryl Bardwell's work gained in popularity, her identity had become more widely known, but she doubted that Lady Randolph would have mentioned it just now had she not wanted to put Mrs. Langtry in her place. The strategy seemed to have succeeded, for Mrs. Langtry's large blue-gray eyes—those smoky lavender eyes that had held princes in thrall—widened perceptibly.

"Beryl Bardwell!" she exclaimed, her manner warming. "My dear Lady Charles, I am quite speechless! I must confess myself to be one of your most devoted followers. You write with such sensibility, such passion. Your characters are so *real!*" Kate might have spoken, but Mrs. Langtry did not give her time. "I was deeply impressed by a story of yours, *The Duchess's Dilemma*. I thought when I read it that it might be easily adapted to the stage, and that the role of the duchess would be marvelously suited to me. What do you say to that?"

Taken aback, Kate saw that Mrs. Langtry's instinct for characterization was chillingly accurate. The main character of *The Duchess's Dilemma* was the imperious, autocratic Diana Radcliffe, Duchess of Wallingford, who staged the theft of her own jewels to conceal the fact that she had pawned them to cover her racing debts. Then, when they were stolen in earnest, she tracked down the thief and successfully achieved their return. It didn't require more than a moment's acquaintance with the actress to be sure that Mrs. Langtry would play the role perfectly.

But Kate was not at all certain that she wanted Mrs. Langtry to adapt her story to the stage, for it was one thing to work quietly behind a pseudonym and quite another to take on the far more public role of playwright. What was more, she suspected that working with Mrs. Langtry on the project would involve endless trials and frustrations.

"Thank you for the compliment, Mrs. Langtry," she said. "However, I really do not feel—"

"The idea is new to you, I see," Mrs. Langtry said confidingly. "I shall have to persuade you. But persuade you I shall." She placed her gloved hand on Kate's arm, her laugh melodious. "I always get my way, Lady Charles. Any of my friends will be glad to tell you that. 'Lillie Langtry always gets her way,' they'll say."

Kate was grateful that a stir at the entrance kept her from answering. His Royal Highness had arrived, accompanied by a boisterous entourage beribboned with the royal colors—and by Mrs. Keppel, smiling and elegant in ivory satin and a feather boa. Jennie, Mrs. Langtry, and Kate made their curtsies and the Prince extended his pudgy, ringed hand and greeted each of them in turn.

To Kate, he said in a guttural, accented voice, "Lady Charles. Delighted, my dear, delighted. Is Lord Charles still down on the course?"

"Until the finish, sir," Kate replied.

"Ah, good, good!" the Prince exclaimed. "He and his camera will sort it all out for us." He paused thoughtfully. "I am so glad that Persimmon's great finish in '96 was caught on film. He won by a neck, you know?"

Kate rose as the royal party pushed forward to the rail.

She was eager to have her first good look at the course where the Derby would be run and the crowd that had come to celebrate it.

And such an incredible crowd it was! Kate thought as she gazed out at the vast throng—a quarter of a million people, by some estimates—which completely covered the racing area and all the Downs beyond. There was the grandstand, with its flag-draped boxes and the enclosure below, crowded with top-hatted men in morning dress and women in silks and laces, white gloves and parasols and great flower-heaped hats wound with tulle. There was the Ring, with its frenzied pack of plungers, punters, bookmakers, tipsters, and touts—and the ever-present pickpockets. On the other side of the U-shaped course, coaches and carriages were drawn up wheel-to-wheel, with cigar-smoking men and a few intrepid ladies lounging on the roofs, lunching out of their picnic hampers. Behind them marched a row of smartly striped regimental marquees where champagne and oysters and other delicacies were served, and around and among all this mob swarmed smock-clad country folk, black-frocked City men, soldiers in scarlet tunics, check-suited men with ties of brilliant green and yellow, flirtatious girls in pink dresses and rosy cheeks, and a ragged rabble of East Enders, glad to escape for a day the dirt and despair of Shoreditch and Spitalfields. All these were entertained by a riotous carnival of hawkers and dark-skinned gypsies, black-faced clowns, conjurers and costermongers, fire-eaters and acrobats and thimblemen with their polished patter. And if these amusements palled, there were the wagons and tents and booths flung like handfuls of dice across the slopes of the Downs—dancing booths, sparring booths, fortune-telling booths, booths that staged *tableaux vivants* or dispensed food carted from the gargantuan kitchens beneath the grandstand, where an army of cooks prepared mountains of lamb, beef, lobsters, oysters, and chickens, together with bushels of salad and immense tubs of dressing and towering pyramids of bread loaves.

Kate was still gazing in awe at this vast and energetic hubbub when Mrs. Langtry appeared at her side, her race card in her kid-gloved hand.

"Whom do you fancy, Lady Charles?" she asked, and then, as Kate hesitated, added archly, "Which of the runners, that is." She laughed. "One always keeps one's other intimate attachments secret, of course."

"I'm afraid I don't follow the horses, Mrs. Langtry," Kate said. "Is there one I should watch especially?"

Mrs. Langtry's brows lifted slightly, as if to convey surprise at Kate's ignorance. "The Duke of Westminster's Flying Fox is favored at 5 to 2. But a friend was kind enough to give me a tip, so I've put a few shillings on Gladiator, at 66 to 1." She gave Kate an encouraging smile. "There's still time to make a wager, Lady Charles. Do put a little something on Gladiator. It's always great fun to see a dark horse win."

A handsome young man with waxed mustaches came up behind Mrs. Langtry and put his hands familiarly on her shoulders. He bent down and kissed the back of her neck. "Lillie, my sweet," he murmured.

Mrs. Langtry turned, raising her hand to the young man's face—a possessive gesture, Kate thought. "Where have you been, Suggie?" she demanded, making a reproachful moue. "Off drinking somewhere with your rowdy friends? I was afraid you'd miss the start."

"Not a chance of it. I was in the Ring, following your instructions, my dear. I put another hundred pounds on Gladiator for you, with Alfred Day." He took off his hat, pulled a ticket from the band, and handed it to her.

Turning, he looked inquiringly at Kate, his eyes bold and admiring. "I don't believe I've had the pleasure," he said thickly, and Kate saw that he was quite drunk.

"Oh, so sorry," Mrs. Langtry said gaily, taking the young man's arm and pressing herself against him. "Lady Charles Sheridan, may I present my *very* dear friend, Hugo de Bathe, whom everyone calls by the delicious name of Suggie—because he is so sweet, of course."

"Delighted, Lady Charles," Lillie's friend murmured, taking Kate's hand and holding it rather longer than necessary.

"You'll be even more delighted," Mrs. Langtry said conspiratorially, "when you learn Lady Charles's secret."

Hugo de Bathe raised both eyebrows. "Ah, secrets!" he exclaimed with a smile. "Every beautiful lady should have a dozen trunks full of secrets, and should share them as generously as she shares her kisses. Tell all, Lady Charles."

But Mrs. Langtry didn't give Kate the chance to share her secrets. "Would you believe it, Suggie? Lady Charles is *really* the author of The Duchess's Dilemma—that story I so much admire. What's more, I've undertaken to persuade her to adapt it for the stage. I'm to play the duchess, of course." She looked up at Hugo de Bathe with a meaningful smile. "She's not quite keen on the idea, but I've warned her that I always get what I want. Tell her it's true, Suggie."

"Oh, it's true, all right," Hugo de Bathe said nonchalantly. "Our Lillie gets what she wants, whether it's good for her or not."

"There, you see, Lady Charles?" Mrs. Langtry was triumphant. "You shall adapt your play to the stage and I shall make your duchess immortal."

Kate's quick protest was drowned out by a cheer from the crowd. A line of blue-uniformed constables was moving without urgency or apparent force across the track, the crowd ebbing obediently before it. When the course was clear, seven magnificent horses, riders vivid in their silks, began parading out of the paddock and down to the starting post on the other side of the course.

Distracted by the cheering, Mrs. Langtry turned to look, then frowned down at her card. "Only seven runners? But eight are listed as starters. Who's missing?"

"It's Gladiator," Suggie said, taking a pair of field glasses from a leather case. "He's suffering from nerves and has been given permission to join the field at the start." He raised the glasses to his eyes. "By Jove, Flying Fox does look fine."

"And so does Ricochet," Jennie said excitedly, coming up behind Kate and pointing. "Look there—isn't he a beauty? My money's on Ricochet."

The track was clear now, and as Kate watched, the throng grew quieter. The carriage crowd paused over their picnic luncheons, the rowdies ceased their loud singing, the preachers left off their haranguing, and the hawkers and criers among the booths were silenced as all eyes turned toward the track. Only the bookies and touts in the Ring and the pickpockets in the crowd continued to ply their trades, relieving the unsuspecting of their money. The suspense grew, moment by breathless moment, as the starter attempted to get the field in order. It was not a clean start, by any means, but at long last the flag came down and the crowd ceased to hold its breath and gave one great shout, "They're off!"

Afterward Kate reflected on the unimaginable effort, the enormous cost, the soaring excitement, the anxious anticipation—all spent in something like three minutes. Even from the vantage point of the royal box, she was scarcely able to see the actual start, and she had not got the horses sorted out before they rounded the first turn toward the top of the hill, then swung around Tattenham Corner. Something happened there that she couldn't quite make out, a melee of horses and riders and the surprised shouting of onlookers, but the field was still coming on, pounding into the half-mile straight in front of the stands and on to the winning post. A few moments later, the numbers were up on the board.

"It's Flying Fox," Hugo de Bathe said, and put down his glasses. "There was some sort of trouble at the Corner, Lillie. Gladiator didn't even finish."

Mrs. Langtry made a disappointed face. "But Reggie seemed so *sure*."

"Reggie is always sure," de Bathe replied with a sour chuckle. "Poor unfortunate Reggie. He had a great deal on that horse. After the loss he took on Tarantula last year, this may be the end of him. Radwick may just swallow him up, estate, stable, and all."

Those around the Prince were jubilant. "Well done, Westminster!" the Prince exclaimed to a tall, thin man with a large nose, who seemed unmoved by his good fortune. "Flying Fox is a superb horse. You'll have another Triple Crown before the year is out, I'll wager."

"As you say, sir," the man replied laconically, as if that did not matter, either.

Next to Kate, Jennie, who may have bet more on Ricochet than she was willing to admit, was looking downcast, while Mrs. Langtry was still wondering out loud about Gladiator's defeat. But he wasn't the only horse that failed to finish. As the runners flew down the straight in front of her, Kate had counted. There were only six.

She tugged at Hugo de Bathe's sleeve and pointed toward Tattenham Corner. "Can you see what's happening down there?"

He raised the glasses again. "There's one horse down

and another loose in the infield—Gladiator, I think." He added, for Kate's instruction, "The Corner is quite a dangerous turn, you know, there are often spills."

"I suppose it was too much to hope that an outsider should win two years in a row," Mrs. Langtry muttered, vexed.

And then the throng—the winners and losers, the well known and the nameless, the rich and the ragged— began to melt away. The stands emptied, the carriage crowd stowed its picnic hampers and took to the road, and the Prince went back to Marlborough House to host the traditional Derby Day dinner he gave to his fellow members of the Jockey Club the evening after the race. Mrs. Langtry strolled off on her Suggie's arm and Kate took leave of Jennie and made her way back to the Royal Grand Hotel on the Epsom High Street, where she and Charles had booked rooms for the night. It wasn't until that evening at dinner that she learned the details of the disaster at Tattenham Corner, and why two of the horses failed to finish the race.

5

The Stewards

"Having ridden at Epsom many times, I think I ought to know the course pretty well. It is very bad, as well as dangerous. What is known as Tattenham Corner is one of the worst bends I ever rode round or saw. It is not only down a very steep incline, but on a side hill, as well as a very sharp turn; and it is wonderful to me it is not productive of more accidents."

Riding Reflections and Turf Stories, 1894
HENRY CUSTANCE

"The word 'doping' first appeared in an English dictionary about 1899, defined as a mixture of opium and narcotics used for horses."

Drugs and the Performance Horse, 1981
THOMAS TOBIN

THE RACE HAD been over for not quite an hour when Lord Charles Sheridan went up to the second floor of the Jockey Club stand and knocked at the door of the Stewards' Room. At a gruff "Come in," he entered, to find three men sitting in high-backed leather chairs pulled close to a coal fire, coffee and brandy at their elbows. One—a brown-haired man with neatly trimmed side-whiskers, his face slightly florid, his frame tending toward stoutness—rose and held out his hand with a ready smile.

"Ah, Sheridan. Kind of you to join us."

"Thank you, Admiral," Charles said. Admiral Owen North was an acquaintance and a Fellow, as was Charles, of the Royal Photographic Society. He was also an avid amateur entomologist with an outstanding collection of photographs of rare arachnids taken on his travels around the world. As well, he was a prominent member of the Jockey Club and a Club Steward, responsible for the orderly running of the races and for hearing objections filed against jockeys or owners.

The admiral gestured at the other two men. "You're perhaps acquainted with Sir Joshua Granville and Lord Richard Longford. Gentlemen, Lord Charles Sheridan. At my request, he set up the automatic camera that photographed today's finish. All went well with the experiment, I take it, Sheridan?"

"It did," Charles said. "My assistant should have the photographs ready within the hour. If you intend to continue the practice, he proposes to train the Epsom staff and work out some method of rapid development and printing, so that if the finish is in question, there can be a timely resolution."

Charles did not offer a detailed technical report, for he knew that Granville and Longford had little interest in the intricacies of stop-action photography. It had been one of his passions since he had heard Eadweard Muybridge speak on the subject at the Royal Institution in 1882. Muybridge's photographs of animal locomotion had impressed Charles with the idea that in addition to accurately documenting what the eye could see, photography might also reveal things that happened too fast for the eye to see and the mind to grasp. Over the last two decades, the sensitivity of emulsions and the speed of lenses had improved markedly, allowing him to conduct his own stop-action experiments. And just a few years ago, the Thornton-Pickard Company had introduced a revolutionary focal-plane shutter. This device, which resembled two roll-type window shades joined by a length of chain on each edge, allowed the exposure to be reduced to one one-thousandth of a second—a speed more than adequate to freeze a galloping horse. But none of this was of interest to these worthy gentlemen. All that concerned them was that single, frozen instant when the first horse crossed the finish line, and *that* Charles could guarantee to give them.

"Good show, Sheridan!" Sir Joshua exclaimed. He had rheumy eyes and a bulbous red nose that seemed almost to glow, and he stood and shook hands eagerly with Charles. But Lord Richard, a gaunt, bent old man of some seventy-odd years, remained slumped in his chair, peering suspiciously through his pince-nez.

"Somersworth, isn't it, rather?" he asked. "Fine old name. I knew your father, the third baron. A damn good stable he had. And your brother too, of course. Somersworth," he repeated, with emphasis. "Fine old name."

"I prefer Sheridan, sir," Charles said firmly, and took the remaining chair.

Upon his brother's death several years before, Charles had reluctantly assumed Robert's responsibilities: the management of the family estates in England, including those at Somersworth, where his mother still lived; and the family peerage in the House of Lords, where his liberal leanings had earned him few friendships. But while Charles was prepared to make accommodations to duty, he held firm on three counts. He would not play more than a minor role in Society, which he considered a tedious, trivial enterprise. He would not abandon his interests in the natural sciences, photography, and the new forensic technologies. And he would most definitely *not* assume the title of Somersworth when he had a perfectly serviceable name of his own.

"Hem," Lord Richard remarked critically, making a tent of his fingers. Sir Joshua cleared his throat and put on a neutral expression, but said nothing. North signaled to a footman waiting in the corner, who brought Charles a cup of steaming coffee and a brandy. When he had left the room, the admiral spoke again.

"Afraid it's not just the photography that we wanted to discuss with you, Sheridan," he said soberly. "We have a rather significant difficulty before us, and we hope you'll agree to lend a hand."

Charles raised his eyebrows. "An objection's been filed, then, I take it?"

"Exactly!" Sir Joshua cried in some agitation. He sat forward in his chair, his hands on his knees, and his nose seemed to glow more brightly than before. "Exactly so, sir. An objection."

North sighed. "It's the tragedy at the Corner, as you might have guessed. Objections have been lodged against both Gladiator and Flying Fox by Squire Mannington, owner of Ricochet."

"But Ricochet didn't finish," Charles said. "And neither did Gladiator. I couldn't see what happened at the Corner, but only six of the eight starters came home."

"Gladiator jumped the rail and bolted into the crowd, just at the top of the straight," North replied. "His jockey was killed outright, and several spectators were injured, one seriously. Ricochet broke a fetlock and had to be destroyed."

"A bad business," Lord Richard said gloomily, tapping his lips with a shriveled finger.

"A very bad business indeed," the admiral said, returning to his chair. "Those who witnessed the affair are agreed that the objection has a certain validity. But Gladiator's jockey is dead and a penalty can scarcely be entered against him. And since Ricochet had to be destroyed, it seems pointless to take the win from Flying Fox."

Charles pursed his lips. "I wonder what the squire intends to gain by his objections."

"No good, I'll tell you that!" Sir Joshua exclaimed, growing still more agitated. "Go on, North. Go on."

"We fear," the admiral said, "that Squire Mannington may mean to use the objection as a preliminary step in a lawsuit against Lord Reginald Hunt, the owner of Gladiator, and against the Duke of Westminster, Flying Fox's owner." He smiled dryly. "As you might surmise, the Stewards are not anxious to be called to testify in such a suit." He glanced at the others. "Have I summarized the situation adequately?"

Lord Richard gave a curt nod. "Oh, indeed," Sir Joshua said nervously. "Very well said, Admiral. Well said indeed, sir."

Charles reflected that a lawsuit was the very last thing the Jockey Club ever wanted, but he only said, "The reports I've heard were vague and confused. What actually happened?"

Admiral North rose once more and went to stand before the fire, lifting his coattails to warm himself. "They were running clear into the Corner, Flying Fox and Ricochet in the lead by several lengths, Count Bolo trailing, Gladiator on the outside. Gladiator began coming up fast and crossed in front of Count Bolo toward the rail, forcing Flying Fox into Ricochet. Flying Fox recovered, but Ricochet stumbled and went down. Gladiator jumped the rail, throwing his jockey. The boy's neck was broken."

"Dead on the spot," Sir Joshua muttered. He touched his nose tenderly. "Pity. A fine young rider. Won the Cambridgeshire for me on Fairfax. Was hoping he'd do the same on Haycock."

"These youngsters don't know how to manage a hard puller," Lord Richard remarked in an acid drawl. "Easy rides, that's all they want."

The admiral pursed his lips. "Squire Mannington asserts that young Bell was riding aggressively, and that he let the horse get out of control." He sighed. "It's a pity your camera wasn't trained on that particular situation, Sheridan. A few photographs would undoubtedly show the right of it."

Lord Richard scowled. "There's something here that doesn't quite meet the eye," he growled. "Study the form book, and you'll see that Gladiator's a damned lazy horse. Done poorly in every race he's run save one. Hunt shouldn't have thought him worth entering."

"But the tipsters had him hot," Sir Joshua put in quickly, "and there was a great deal of money laid on at the last moment. I myself saw Alfred Day put down Lord Reginald for two thousand pounds just before the off. If the horse had won, as he looked like doing—"

"My point exactly," Lord Richard snapped. "At 66 to 1, Hunt would have no more need to borrow from Henry Radwick, would he? Family fortunes recouped and all that."

Hands behind his back, Admiral North pursed his lips and looked up at the ceiling. "None of us likes to speak at hazard, for we all know what harm gossip can do to a man's reputation. But today's situation is complicated by rumors that Gladiator was visited last week, at the request of his owner, by Jesse Clark. Not," he added obliquely, "that there is anything necessarily improper about the visit." He glanced at Charles. "If you take my point."

Charles picked up his brandy. "I do indeed," he said. Although his father and brother had been racing men, the Turf had never attracted Charles. However, he had certainly heard enough London gossip to understand the admiral's concern. Jesse Clark was an American trainer who had come to England with another American, Enoch Wishard. Wishard was financed by a Chicago hotel magnate, John Drake. Drake and his racing partner, William Gates— Bet-a-Million Gates, as he was known in America—had established quite a large stable at Newmarket. Members of the Jockey Club were scandalized by the huge amounts these men bet on Wishard's horses, and they snubbed the Americans whenever they could.

But over the past two years, Wishard's stable had demonstrated an interesting pattern. A horse would follow a string of losses with a surprising victory at long odds, upon which Drake and Bet-a-Million had happened to lay a large wager. If this had happened once or twice, it might have been sheer good fortune; but it occurred with increasing regularity, and people began to whisper that Wishard was doping horses with some sort of stimulant that made them run like the wind. Charles had heard that some members of the Club were anxious to declare doping contrary to *The Rules of Racing*, but that others refused, perhaps because they themselves wanted to give it a go, or because they weren't convinced that it was the doping that made the difference. In any event, the Club had not as yet acted.

Doping was legal and the situation showed no signs of being altered.

Still, the Stewards ought to do *something*, Charles thought. An uncontrollable horse was a danger to all the horses and riders in the field, as today's Derby had demonstrated, and artifically manipulating a horse's performance was unsportsmanlike and wreaked havoc with the form book. There was a good deal of resentment among owners and trainers about the practice—and especially among the bookmakers, who were at risk of losing substantial sums of money. Having paid out more than they could afford, some now refused the Americans' bets—when they could, for the wager was often delivered by one of Bet-a-Million's strongmen, whose persuasion was hard to resist.

The room was silent except for the hissing of the coal fire in the grate. Admiral North's gaze had returned to the ceiling. Lord Richard's eyes were focused on his tented fingers. Sir Joshua was staring at the fire.

At last, the admiral spoke. "Since you see our problem, Sheridan, perhaps you would be so kind as to help us further its resolution. What do you say to undertaking an inquiry for us?"

Charles put down his snifter, frowning. "I am here today to set up a high-speed camera, which is entirely within my field of expertise." He spread his hands. "I don't know enough about Turf practices to be of much help to you, Admiral."

"Don't add modesty to your other faults, Somersworth," Lord Richard said gruffly.

"Anyway," Charles went on, "you have your own investigator. Jack Murray is a good man. Why not use him?"

The admiral gave Charles a dry smile. "We have sounded HRH's feelings on this subject, Sheridan. As you might guess, he's concerned to stave off any possible scandal connected with racing."

That came as no surprise, Charles thought. It was only ten years earlier that Sir George Chetwynd, once a Senior Steward of the Jockey Club, had been hauled into court by the Earl of Durham, accused of instructing his jockeys to pull horses—hold them back from winning. The messy libel suit resulted in a great deal of notoriety in the press, something the Club, and Society itself, utterly abhorred. This humiliation had been followed not long after by the Tranby Croft affair, which took place at the running of the St. Leger and resulted in yet another accusation of cheating, this time at baccarat. Everyone involved, including the Prince of Wales, made an extraordinary effort to hush up the scandal, but the Tranby Croft affair, too, went to court. The press rubbed its collective hands in glee when the Prince was called to the witness box, and the Queen, when she read the papers, was said to have flown into hysterics. From that time on, every scandal in any way associated with the Turf had been hushed up as quickly as possible, no matter what the cost to individuals. Even the whisper of unsportsmanlike conduct, especially when money was involved, was enough to send a shiver through the entire Establishment, from bottom to top.

Admiral North was going on. "His Majesty, in fact, is the one who suggested that we ask you to undertake an inquiry for us, Sheridan. He tells us that he has every confidence in your investigative abilities, and in your discretion, as well. As for Jack Murray, he cannot make his way among the owners. You have—if you will pardon my saying so—the appropriate credentials. And Murray will be available to you for, shall we say, the dirty work."

"But of course," Sir Joshua put in hurriedly, "there won't be any... dirty work. After all, we're dealing with gentlemen."

Lord Richard gave a contemptuous snort. "Gentlemen! These Americans may be rich as lords, but they're common as dirt. We want them out of English racing, Somersworth. Send them back where they came from, or pack them off to France. But do it on the hush. We can't afford any scandal."

The admiral frowned. "I don't know that we have to go quite so far as that, Lord Richard. HRH does suggest, however, that we find some way to keep the American practice from spreading to English stables, without attracting undue attention to it with an outright ban. All very quietly, of course," he added delicately. "Out of view of the press. To that end, we hope to keep Squire Mannington from pressing his objections, if at all possible." He turned to Charles. "I would take it as a personal favor, Charles, if you would be so kind as to help us."

Damn and blast, Charles thought, more in resignation than anger. Owen North was a cagey strategist. He knew that a suggestion from the Prince of Wales was tantamount to a royal command, and that Charles would find it almost impossible to refuse. He sighed. He wasn't eager to undertake the Herculean task of cleaning out the Jockey Club's stables, for he suspected that the corruption was already widespread. But there was no good reason to postpone the inevitable. And he might as well put the best face on it.

"Very well, Owen," he said. "Tell His Highness that I'll do what I can."

The admiral's profound relief showed on his face. "Very good. Very good indeed." He rubbed his hands together. "What can we do to help?"

"I should like to examine Gladiator immediately," Charles

44

said. "I shall require the assistance of a veterinarian. One who can be trusted," he added.

"Done," the admiral replied promptly. "And I shall ask Jack Murray to be in touch with you. Use him in any way you see fit." He held out his hand. "We're grateful, Charles, and we wish you Godspeed in your invesigation. I suspect that more hangs on this than we know."

It was a prophetic statement.

6

The Moneylender

"It is the borrowers who seek the moneylender, and not he who goes to them. If they think his terms too high, they can decline them and go elsewhere. The usury laws have long since been abolished, and if the moneylender is not generous, it must be recollected that he is carrying on business at very considerable risk, and must exercise care in the way he thinks best suited to his own interest, which of necessity precludes any great regard for the interests of others."

Reminiscences of the Turf, 1891
WILLIAM DAY

HENRY RADWICK HAD no intention of jostling his way through the London-bound mob on the railway. He had taken a room at the Red Horse Hotel just off the Epsom High Street, a small and exclusive accommodation which served exceptional food and excellent wine and whose proprietress, Mrs. Stanley, was possessed of considerable personal attractions. After the hurly-burly of the afternoon—the noisy crowds, that dreadful fracas at the Corner, and the disaster that had taken out Ricochet—Henry was looking forward to a hot bath, a quiet dinner, and Mrs. Stanley's company. He would return to Mayfair at a decent hour tomorrow, where no doubt those who found themselves unable to settle their accounts at Tattersall's would already be waiting for him.

In the century shortly to come, people would look back at Henry Manford Radwick, in his heyday, as one of the most successful men of his time. By choice and by circumstance, he was a member of a group known as the Sixty Per Schenters, the notoriously predatory London moneylenders. But Henry Radwick stood apart from the group, a self-assured, self-made man who lived well and proudly at Number 4 Hill Street, Berkeley Square. His house was large and as opulently appointed as any marquis's, and he enjoyed a fine table and an equally outstanding cellar. And although Henry (whose father had been a hatter in Horsham) was not invited to the homes of the aristocracy, his own generous hospitality was much enjoyed by their younger sons, and occasionally by the fathers and mothers and sisters as well (although these latter sought him out secretly, by a door that opened into the back garden).

Henry was of middle age and height, with brown hair, carefully but not ostentatiously dressed, by temperament congenial and affable, and by manner courteous and charming—until he was pushed into a corner or until something he valued was threatened, in which case his fiery temper had been known to get the better of him. But in most circumstances, Henry managed to hold himself in check. He had built his successful enterprise upon his charm, his congeniality, and his ability to mix easily with the rich young gentlemen of the Turf, who often rather freely anticipated their fortunes. He offered them friendship and advice, rejoiced in their victories, sympathized with their losses, and smiled gently at their follies. Accordingly, when these young men found themselves financially embarrassed, it was the most natural thing in the world for them to call at Number 4, drink a glass of Henry's Madeira, and confide the latest scrape. For his part, Henry was always ready to offer a little something until the tide turned, so long as the security was acceptable.

Of course, Henry relied for his business success on the fact that the first "little something" would not be the end of it, for once begun, the habit of borrowing became an addiction, as sure as opium. An advance of a few thousand pounds, and then perhaps ten, and after that fifteen, would eventually be multiplied by accumulated interest and expenses into a staggering sum; and in time, the title deeds of an ancestral estate would pass from the hands of the luckless borrower into Henry's personal account.

In this way, Henry Radwick had gained hold of Mansfield Park, one of the loveliest estates in Northampton, and how many equal to it, no one would ever know. Not that he cared for these estates for their own sake, or for the countless works of art, jewels, and other valuable considerations that had come into his hands over the years. And not that he cared for the money, either, beyond what was needed to maintain his way of life. Simply put, Henry Radwick, bitterly conscious of his low birth and resentful of the social rejections he continually suffered thereby, was a man who kept score. Each famous estate, each fabulous painting, each fine horse that came into his possession was one more evidence of his incontestable superiority over the weak, muddled aristocrats who couldn't hold on to their fortunes. He felt much the same about his women, as well, and once he had selected one for his attentions, he felt a kind of jealous passion for her, not because he loved her, but because she was his, and a mark of his achievement.

Henry's pleasure in his preeminence over weak-minded fools was fueled by the widespread acknowledgment of his astuteness and sharp dealings. While he could have made most loans out of his pocket, he preferred to use other people's capital, offering ten percent when the current interest rate stood at one or one and a half. He could afford this attractive rate, for his charge to strangers was sixty percent, rising occasionally to five hundred percent. To friends, on the other hand, he was willing to extend a not unreasonable twenty, and sometimes, depending on the relationship, much less. Henry had many friends, of course—and not a few enemies. While his business arrangements began in friendship, they had a way of ending in acrimony, for when people did not fall in with his plans, he had a tendency to give in to his temper.

Just now, however, nothing untoward disturbed him. He had accomplished both his bath and his dinner and was awaiting Mrs. Stanley's return to the Red Horse's private drawing room, his hands folded over his slightly stout middle. This agreeable anticipation was interrupted, however, by someone's clearing a throat and a tentative "Er, Radwick, old chap." Henry looked up to see Lord Reginald Hunt standing in the door, his hat in his hand and a hangdog look on his face.

Henry did not show his annoyance at this intrusion, or demand to know how the devil Hunt had sniffed him out here. At the moment, he felt only contempt for the man standing before him, who had so obviously had a bad day. He smiled and gestured to the chair Mrs. Stanley had left.

"Sit down, Reggie, dear fellow," he said affably, "and join me in a brandy." He lifted the decanter and poured.

"Why aren't you feasting at Marlborough House with the rest of the Club?"

"Couldn't face it," Lord Reginald muttered, slumping dejectedly in the chair. His frock coat was marked with dusty creases and his shirt cuffs were dirty. He wiped a bleary eye. "Too low."

"A pity about Gladiator," Henry said consolingly. "When he came storming round the Corner, he looked like a dead cert." He paused. "I suppose you had a great deal on. Had the horse been mine, I would've emptied my pockets on him." It wasn't true. Henry always hedged his bets.

"All I had, and more, was on that horse." Lord Reginald tossed off the brandy and pushed his glass forward, summoning a wan smile and making an attempt at bravado. "But he'll run again. And I have Alabaster in the Gold Cup at Ascot, and Tarantula in the Ascot Stakes. I'll get it back."

"That's the spirit." Henry poured again. Mrs. Stanley appeared at the door; then, seeing that Henry was doing business, gave a little wave and vanished.

Lord Reginald sipped more slowly this time. "I'll be brief, Henry, old chap," he said. "I need thirty thousand to settle."

Henry leaned back in his chair, folding his hands and pursing his lips. He had been at this point before, with any number of desperate clients, and he knew his lines very well. When the right amount of time had ticked by, he said quietly: "Thirty thousand is a very great deal, Reggie. In the circumstance, that is." Henry did not have to say what that circumstance was. Lord Reginald understood perfectly that this large addition to his already enormous indebtedness entitled Henry to take part of the security he had pledged: the estate of Glenoaks, in Cambridgeshire, several dozen works of art, and half his stable.

The silence had lengthened almost intolerably when Lord Reginald cleared his throat. "Damn it all," he growled, all show of pleasantry abandoned. "Take the bloody estate, then. I never go there anyway. Just give me the thirty thousand."

"The estate," Henry said quietly, "and Tarantula."

"Not the horse!"

Henry shrugged and was silent.

"Oh, all right, then," Lord Reginald said angrily. "He's a loser, anyway. Have him, and be done."

Henry smiled. "*Well* done, Reggie." He leaned forward and placed a pacifying hand on Lord Reginald's arm. "All of us come to these difficult hurdles now and again, but it's the true sportsman among us who knows how to hold up his head and have a go at the jump." His smile just missed being patronizing. "You're an excellent fellow, Reggie. You'll have the money first thing on Monday morning. And Ascot is only a fortnight away. You'll feel better after a win."

Lord Reginald brightened, forgetting his rancor. "Oh, indeed," he said. He pushed his chair back and stood. "Thank you, Henry," he said, picking up his hat. "I know I'm safe with you. You're the best friend a man ever had."

Henry Radwick smiled. He was already thinking of making a trip to Glenoaks, just to see what Lord Reginald Hunt had lost.

7

At Bishop's Keep

"Paradox though it may seem—and paradoxes are always dangerous things—it is none the less true that life imitates art far more than art imitates life."

The Decay of Lying
OSCAR WILDE

IT WAS AFTER eleven on a glorious June morning, and Lord and Lady Charles Sheridan were sitting on the terrace overlooking the gardens and the little lake, its wild banks tumbled with ferns and briar-rose. Charles was reading the *Sporting Times* in an effort to educate himself to the intricacies of horseracing and Kate was sorting the morning post. She opened an envelope and gave a discouraged sigh.

"I'm afraid that the headmaster at Westward Ho! has nothing new to report," she said sadly. "It has been almost seven months since Patrick ran away from school, Charles. And not a word, not one single word. Something dreadful has happened to him, I'm sure of it."

Charles hardly knew what to say. He knew how much Kate cared for Patrick. He'd been fond of the boy too, and had hoped that perhaps he might help fill the place of the son whom he and Kate would never have. It was hard to find words that would comfort Kate when he felt the loss as deeply as she. He rattled his paper and affected a careless air.

"You know the boy," he said. "Free as a breeze, with not a shred of responsibility. It's a wonder Patrick stayed at school as long as he did, Kate. No doubt he's gone to sea, and will come back to astound us with exaggerated tales about the South Pacific."

Kate made an impatient noise. "Patrick is a free spirit, but I don't believe that he has no sense of responsibility. He left school for a good reason." She laid the headmaster's letter aside. "I think I'll place another round of advertisements in the newspapers. Someone is bound to have seen him." She took up another envelope, slit it, and gave a surprised exclamation.

Charles lowered his newspaper. "Something else?"

"It's a note from Mrs. Langtry," Kate said, scanning it. "She's invited me to stay with her at Regal Lodge, at Kentford, near Newmarket. She writes, 'Since I've decided to go forward with the stage adaptation of your story, I believe our time together could be most productive. My cottage is small, but I am delighted to share it with you. Come as soon as you can.'"

Charles was nonplussed. He wasn't aware that his wife knew the actress. "Lillie Langtry? A stage adaptation? *What* story?"

Kate frowned at him over the top of her reading glasses. "I suppose you've been too engrossed in that racing business to recall that I met Mrs. Langtry at the Derby and that she expressed an interest in producing *The Duchess's Dilemma*."

"Good Lord," Charles said, abashed at not remembering. "Isn't that the story about the stolen sapphires? The one you so indelicately modeled after the so-called theft of Lady Marsden's emeralds?"

"Yes," Kate replied ruefully. "In the story, the duchess needed money to pay her debts, so she pawned her jewels, then staged their theft to conceal what she'd done. When a thief actually did steal them, she tracked him down and got them back." With a smile, she added, "The duchess is quite a strong character. Mrs. Langtry, of course, wants to play her."

Charles chuckled. Lillie Langtry's range as an actress was notoriously limited, and she was known for choosing roles that allowed her to play herself—or rather, to play herself as she imagined herself, which was not at all the same thing. "I'm surprised that she doesn't find your fiction a little too close to the facts," he remarked.

"Really?" Kate asked curiously. "In what way?"

"Just about the time you came to England, Mrs. Langtry's jewels—forty thousand pounds' worth—were taken from the vault at the Union Bank. The thief presented a note bearing her name. The signature subsequently proved to be copied from the Pearl Soap advertisement that carries her personal endorsement. It wasn't even a very good forgery, as it turned out."

"Then why in the world," Kate exclaimed, "would she have anything to do with *The Duchess's Dilemma*? It's a story of course, a fiction—but some people might take it for truth and believe that she took the jewels herself!"

"Why would she want to stage it?" Charles shrugged. "Perhaps because she wants to profit from her own notoriety."

"Well, there's certainly plenty of that," Kate said in an ironic tone. "The woman is featured in the newspapers almost every week. A few years ago, there were all those reports about her American divorce, and then there was Mr. Langtry's mysterious death." She looked back at the note, her pretty face drawn into a frown. "Why *do* you suppose she's interested in my story?"

"Who knows?" Charles said. "As Oscar Wilde says, 'we live in an age where people use art as a form of autobiography.'" He knew his wife, and he knew that she didn't seek public attention. "Do you want her to stage the story?"

"I'm not at all sure I like the idea," Kate said thoughtfully. "But now that I've heard about the theft of her jewels, I must admit to being curious about Mrs. Langtry and her interest in *The Duchess*. Perhaps I'll accept her invitation after all. I've just been asked to write an article for *The Strand*, and she would make a fascinating subject. If she'll allow me to write about her, that is."

"*Allow* you to write about her? I'm sure she'll be thrilled at the prospect of seeing herself in print one more time, especially with Beryl Bardwell's name on the piece." Charles raised an eyebrow. "But you and Beryl should perhaps be a little careful, Kate. Mrs. Langtry's sporting friends are not quite as well-mannered as she. I suggest that you take Amelia. She might keep you from getting into trouble."

He had meant the remark as a joke, but Kate took it seriously. "I shall certainly ask Amelia to go with me," she said, "and I'll write to Mrs. Langtry and ask if she will give me an interview for publication." She slanted him a look. "I hope you don't mind that I go."

Charles grinned wryly. "Would it do me any good?" Then, seeing her face, he added hastily, "I don't mind in the slightest, my dear. I myself must go to Newmarket, on the racing business I told you about. I shouldn't like to intrude on your stay with Mrs. Langtry, but at least I'll be in the vicinity, if you need—" Charles broke off at the sound of a motorcar clattering up the drive.

Kate turned her head, listening. "That must be Bradford and his friend, come to luncheon." She stood up and went to the parapet as Bradford Marsden's new yellow Panhard pulled into view. "I wonder what she looks like."

Smiling at his wife's curiosity, Charles laid his newspaper aside and joined her at the parapet, watching as the Panhard jolted to a stop and its passengers began to disembark. "She's a little dusty," he said critically. "Could do with a wash. And that front left headlamp—"

Kate swatted his arm. "Not the motorcar—the girl, silly. Bradford's fiancée. Her name is Edith Hill."

"Oh, that one," Charles said. He peered over Kate's shoulder. "Looks like a regular girl to me. Not too much hat, I'm pleased to—" He stopped, staring intently. "Is that an ankle I see? By Jove, it's an *ankle!*"

"It is!" Kate exclaimed, her eyes sparkling. "Bradford Marsden has engaged himself to a woman who wears rational dress!"

"So he has," Charles muttered with rueful irony, shaking his head. "And we all know what comes of rational dress. Women earning their way in the world, insisting on managing their own property, and—heaven help us—claiming a right to the vote."

Kate smiled archly. "Well, I've achieved two of the three, and the franchise *will* come, like it or not. There are some things, my dearest love, that you shall simply have to get used to." She smiled to show that she was teasing and tugged at his sleeve. "Now, come away from the parapet. We'll have plenty of time for inspection during luncheon."

Affectionately, Charles watched Kate return to her chair, admiring the shining russet hair pinned in loose twists around her head, her firm-featured face, the confident lift of her chin, the frank, open smile whose radiance invariably dazzled him. She was a lovely woman, he thought, grown even more lovely now that she was past thirty. But what he most admired about her could not be seen at first glance: her literary talent, of course, which never ceased to amaze him; but also her stubborn Irish-American desire for independence, so at odds with the English woman's acceptance of her place; and her zealous determination to help other women achieve what independence they could. And, not least, her ability to tolerate the unhappy situation his mother's bitter intolerance had created.

The thought of the dowager Lady Somersworth made Charles sigh heavily. He had recently made one of his regular visits to the family estate in Norwich, where his mother lived—or rather, where she was dying of a cancer in her breast. Having outlived a husband and elder son, the third and fourth barons of Somersworth, she emphatically reminded the fifth baron each time she saw him that she did not intend to die until he had produced an heir. During the last visit, Charles had finally told her the truth: that Kate's first pregnancy had also been her last. There would be no children.

At this, Lady Somersworth set her mouth. "Well," she said bitterly, "what did you expect? She's Irish, and the Irish are always sickly. No constitution at all."

"Mother—" Charles began, in a warning tone.

"I'm not disappointed," Lady Somersworth snapped. "Ever since I learned that hers is the pen behind those dreadful Bardwell fictions, I've been too humiliated to hold up my head in Society. If you take my advice, Charles, you will seek an immediate divorce from this person, whatever the cost."

"Divorce?" Charles tried for a joking tone. "But think of the scandal, Mother."

"Scandal?" Lady Somersworth's laugh was bitter. "The scandal of divorce is pale as a ghost in comparison to the scandal of your marriage, Charles. Free yourself from her and choose a woman of your own class. Then you can pass Somersworth to sons who are not part"—her nostrils flared and she turned her head aside, as if from a disagreeable odor—"Irish."

At that, Charles had stalked out and taken the next train home to Bishop's Keep. The bitter old woman could die alone, as far as he was concerned, and the Somersworth title with her. And when she was gone, he had an entirely new plan for the family estates—one that would send his dowager mother spinning in her grave.

The French doors opened, and Hodge, the butler, stepped onto the terrace. "Lord Bradford Marsden," he announced, "and Miss Edith Hill."

8

Kate and Edith

"In the late 1890s, a growing number of women began to consider agriculture as a career. In 1898, the Countess of Warwick opened a horticultural college which eventually enrolled 146 students, a quarter of whom had small holdings of their own. Lady Warwick hoped to establish cooperative settlements of 'unmarrying women' who would share a cottage and manage their market farm as a partnership."

"Country Women in Victorian England"
SUSAN BLAKE

LUNCHEON HAD BEEN quite interesting, Kate thought, as she waited for Edith to return from freshening up. Bradford Marsden's fiancée was radically different from the other ladies he had brought to Bishop's Keep. For one thing, she earned her living as a private secretary. For another, she was not only effervescent and strikingly attractive, but obviously bright and energetic and practical, with a strong sense of direction and perhaps (although this was hard to gauge on a first meeting) an equally strong sense of personal ambition. While Bradford's other companions had aspired to become the mistress of Marsden Manor, Edith seemed ambitious to achieve something for herself.

"Shall we go into the garden?" Kate asked when Edith had returned. "The horticulture students are working there, and I thought you might like to see what they're doing."

"Horticulture students?" Edith asked, falling into step beside Kate. She was tall and dark-haired, with dark eyes and firm dark brows. She wore a becoming walking suit of gray serge with a white blouse, the jacket tailored, the skirt smoothly gored and pleated for easy movement, cut above the ankles, revealing handsome gray boots.

"They are enrolled in my School for the Useful Arts," Kate said, "which is organized after the model of Lady Warwick's." The school had been a dream for a long time, evolving slowly into a plan that seemed to Kate to be achievable and also to hold great promise—which didn't keep others from mocking it as idealistic and doomed to failure, of course.

They stepped off the terrace and onto the garden path, bordered by June flowers and fragrant with lavender and bergamot. "Who are your students?" Edith asked. "How many are there?"

"Just a dozen now," Kate said. "We admit only women, who come daily from the neighboring villages. But I've purchased some land from Bradford, and as soon as the cottages are repaired, we will begin accepting boarding students." She paused beside a break in the hedge and pointed toward the kitchen garden, where several women were weeding the young peas. "Mr. Humphries, the head gardener, teaches horticulture, and I've just employed a woman who is skilled in dairying and beekeeping. In a few weeks, Mrs. Grieve will come and teach a course in herb-growing. As enrollment warrants, I also plan to add a master to assist in poultry and orchard management. I'm afraid it's rather an ambitious project," she added ruefully, "but I'm determined to see it succeed. The goal is to give these women skills that will enable them to earn their own living in rural areas."

"What an exciting idea!" Edith exclaimed, her eyes sparkling. "Everyone complains that the land is going out of cultivation because there's no one to farm it, and yet there's not nearly enough fresh produce in the shops. If your graduates can gain a living by market gardening, there will be no need for them to work in the factories. Oh, Kate, I do applaud you! What a noble effort!"

Kate smiled. "Thank you—although I'm not sure how noble it is. But it breaks my heart to see the land so empty, and so many women wanting paid work. I feel I must do what I can." She paused and added curiously, "Tell me more about what you do, Edith. You said that you work for Mr. Cecil Rhodes?"

"I'm employed in the London offices of the Rhodesian Mining Consortium," Edith replied. "Mr. Rhodes is my godfather, and I am his personal secretary. That is, I handle his calendar and all his correspondence. I type and take shorthand, and I translate English into German and French where necessary. I even write letters over my own signature, with Mr. Rhodes's approval, of course." She smiled proudly.

"It sounds like a position with some very real authority," Kate remarked. She herself had come to England to serve as her aunt's secretary, and knew what a fortunate thing that had been.

"It is," Edith replied. "And of course, there's all sorts of intrigue just now, with the shameful way the Boers are treating the Uitlanders, and that ugly business about the franchise." Her chin had a determined tilt. "I hope the government will send troops and settle things quickly. The honor of the Empire is at stake. We simply must not give in to those barbaric Boers!"

Kate thought that Edith's views on the subject reflected those of Mr. Rhodes, with whom she and Charles did not at all agree. Since it was not likely she could change Edith's mind, she changed the subject. "Do you and Bradford plan a long engagement? Where will the wedding be held?"

Edith's face grew tense and there was a strain in her voice. "We mean to be married soon and simply. We had hoped Lady Marsden would be agreeable to a summer wedding at a small church near my mother's home at Newmarket. But we haven't been able to discuss the wedding with her. She dislikes me so intensely that she has not come down to dinner in the two days I've been there."

"Oh, dear," Kate murmured. She wasn't surprised. Lady Marsden intended that Bradford should marry a woman of means, whose fortune could be used to repay the family's mortgages and replenish their empty coffers. Edith was an educated gentlewoman—she had attended Girton College, Kate had learned at lunch. But that didn't alter the fact that she had to work to live. And a working woman was not the kind of wife that Lady Marsden had imagined for her only son.

Edith frowned. "I am not sorry for myself," she said decidedly. "As far as I am concerned, Lady Marsden may think as she likes. But Bradford must feel her disapproval keenly. I wish there was something I could do to change her opinion of me."

Under Edith's firm tone, Kate could hear the pain and heartache in her voice. She appreciated the girl's unhappiness, because she herself had had to learn how to live with a similarly painful situation. Thinking that

Edith might be helped by hearing about her experience, she briefly related her unhappy relationship with Lady Somersworth.

"I should make my own wedding plans if I were you, Edith," she added gently, "and let Lady Marsden make whatever peace she can with the situation. You and Bradford must please yourselves, not anyone else." She might have added that Lady Marsden had already meddled unforgivably in the lives of her daughters, Eleanor and Patsy, and that she constantly interfered in Bradford's life. It was not likely that the woman would ever be pleased.

Edith turned, her dark eyes searching Kate's face, and some of the tension went out of her voice. "Thank you," she said simply. "You've given me courage, Kate." She squared her shoulders. "I do hope that you and Lord Charles can attend the wedding."

"It will be at Newmarket, then?" Kate remembered Mrs. Langtry's invitation. "Of course, we should love to attend. As it happens, I'll be staying at Kentford myself, for two or three days. If you're at your mother's, perhaps we shall see one another."

"I'd like that," Edith said. "I'd like that very much!"

9

Charles and Bradford

"Agricultural land by itself could no longer sustain landed society in the social role which had become traditional. To secure an adequate income, other strategies needed to be adopted—including the making of advantageous marriages with social outsiders and becoming involved, in unprecedented ways, in the world of business and finance."

Corruption in British Politics, 1895–1930
GR SEARLE

"I have a country house with some land, of course, attached to it, about fifteen hundred acres, I believe; but I don't depend on that for my real income. In fact, as far as I can make out, the poachers are the only people who make anything out of it."

Jack, in The Importance of Being Earnest
OSCAR WILDE

CHARLES AND BRADFORD had gone to the small smoking room for an after-lunch smoke and conversation.

Bradford settled in one chair with his cigar, Charles with his pipe in the other. Bradford eyed his friend curiously, noticing the lines of tension around the mouth, half-hidden behind the brown beard.

"Well, what's on your mind, Sheridan?" he asked. "You could scarcely eat for wanting to talk about it, but you didn't say a word."

"I thought it might bore Miss Hill," Charles said, filling his pipe. While he tamped it down, he told Bradford what had happened at the Derby—the catastrophe at Tattenham Corner, and the death of Johnny Bell—and afterwards, with the Stewards. "I'm afraid I had no choice but to agree to look into the affair," he concluded ruefully. "Since they had already consulted HRH, I could hardly say no."

Bradford frowned. "It was Hunt's horse that's suspected of being doped to win? I shouldn't have thought Reggie would go for that sort of thing. But of course, after taking that big loss on Tarantula last year, he might be willing to try almost anything to recoup." His frown deepened. "And I had no idea, Charles, that you knew enough about racing to—"

He stopped, thinking that what he had been about to say was no compliment to his friend. But they had been acquainted since Eton and near neighbors since Charles's marriage to Kate, and Bradford knew that while Charles's father and brother had both kept horses, his own interests lay elsewhere, with fossils and bats, and such anomalous oddities as fingerprints and ballistics and X-ray machines.

Charles did not appear to have taken offense. "It's true that I don't know enough about racing to be involved with this investigation," he said pleasantly. He settled back into the leather chair and propped his boots on the hassock. "But *you* do, old chap."

"Afraid you're right," Bradford murmured ironically,

putting a match to his cigar. It was his great ill luck that he had grown up with racing: racehorses in the family stable, trainers and stablelads on the family payroll, and the Marsden Stud as the chief subject of his father's conversation. In fact, the Old Man's foolish devotion to his equine bloodlines had been largely responsible for the loss of the Marsden fortune, for he had insisted on keeping his stable—among other ruinously extravagent entertainments—until his creditors finally forced him to sell up. By the time of Lord Marsden's death, some two years before, almost the whole of Bradford's inheritance had been handed over to the banks and moneylenders. It was not a unique situation, of course: the same circumstance was occurring across England as the old landed elite, its vigor spent and its wealth wasted, dwindled into impoverishment. Almost all the sons of the leisure class were now faced with the same problem that confronted Bradford: how to find a socially acceptable occupation that yielded enough income to survive. Some, like Bradford, had gone into finance and business; others pursued American heiresses; still others pursued Lady Luck.

But the father's expensive lesson had not been wasted on the son. While Bradford might make the occasional bet, he had seen enough of racing to know how foolish it was to wager one's future on the horses. Not that his own early speculations had proved any more productive than his father's, unfortunately: he'd lost a potful of money in one of Harry Dunstable's automotive stock swindles and almost as much in a failed Canadian mining scheme. But things had definitely changed since he became associated with Cecil Rhodes and the Rhodesian Mining Consortium, on whose board of directors he served. Due to the recent gold discoveries, the Consortium stock he'd purchased looked like being worth something, enough to permit him to marry. He lingered on the thought of Edith, whom he had met in the Consortium's London office, the imagining of her like champagne in his veins. A rare and wonderful girl, vivacious and lively, and smart as a whip as well, with enough ambition and strategic good sense for the two of them. She was all this, and Cecil Rhodes's goddaughter, as well. Think of that—Cecil Rhodes's goddaughter! Bradford's mother might not think the marriage was advantageous—the poor old creature was blinded by tradition—but Bradford knew better. The possibilities made him almost giddy.

Charles cleared his throat, and Bradford came back with a start to the conversation. "Between the two of us, I think we should be able to handle the investigation," Charles said. "Admiral North has also promised to lend the Club's investigator, a retired Scotland Yard policeman." He lit his pipe and blew out the match. "I hope you'll agree to help, Marsden. You have to admit, it's a rather interesting affair. I think the admiral is right when he says that a great deal may hang on it."

"I agree," Bradford said, "and in a different circumstance, I'd join you in an instant." He'd like nothing better, in fact, than to dig up a racing scandal and drop it into the reluctant hands of the Jockey Club Stewards. But he had other important matters to attend to. "Edith and I expect to be married very soon, Mama notwithstanding."

"She doesn't approve?" Charles asked.

"Does Mama ever approve of anything?" Bradford countered. "I don't expect to bring her round to our view, so I've decided to ignore hers. For the next two weeks, I've taken temporary lodgings near Edith's mother's, at Newmarket, to make myself available for wedding consultations and the like." He paused to tap the ash off his cigar, not wanting to disappoint his friend, or to miss what sounded like an interesting game. If the investigation didn't range too far afield—"Which stable is it you'll be looking into?"

"Grange House Stable, on the Moulton Road, just outside Newmarket," Charles said. "But of course, if you—"

"Grange House!" Bradford exclaimed. "Why, that's only a mile or two from the lodgings I've taken. It's the stable where old Angus Duncan trains now. Twenty years ago, though, he trained for my father. And if I'm not mistaken, Edith's stepfather has a horse or two in training there." He studied the tip of his cigar. "How were you thinking I might help?"

"I plan to bring down two suitable horses from Somersworth to stable at Grange House. I thought that might allow me to get a look at their practices. Since you know Duncan, perhaps you would introduce me." Charles stroked his brown beard thoughtfully. "You might also go with me to the stable a time or two. It shouldn't take you away from Miss Hill, but you might find it a bit intriguing."

More than a bit, Bradford thought, feeling a flicker of excitement. "The wedding is to be a simple one, so I'm sure I could be spared for a bit of nosing around." He narrowed his eyes. "In fact, I should rather relish putting a stop to some of the ugly things that are happening in racing these days."

Charles nodded. "The issue seems to be doping, particularly the use of stimulants, although sedatives are used as well. Apparently the practice isn't much known here in England, but from the reading I've done, it seems to be widespread in America, especially on the smaller tracks."

"Doping!" Bradford exclaimed indignantly. There was no limit to the depths to which people would stoop to alter the odds. He shook his head. "A vicious business. Making the horse stupid or making him savage—either way, it's dangerous. Misjudge the dose, and the poor beast may die, or be ruined."

"Misjudge the dose and the jockey may die," Charles reminded him. "Johnny Bell was killed because he couldn't control the horse. If I read the admiral right, he'd like to obtain evidence that will convince the Club to ban doping—if that can be done without attracting too much attention."

"That's the Club," Bradford muttered. "Always eager to avoid scandal, even if it means brushing bad practice under the rug. It will have to be faced soon, though. There has been an invasion of these American jockeys and trainers, and an enormous infusion of American money. The Stewards are going to have to stop dithering and do something."

Charles drew on his pipe. "Then perhaps we can find the evidence that will prompt them to take some decisive action. Are you with me?"

"I'm with you," Bradford said. They smoked in silence for a few minutes; then he added, "Speaking of taking action, Edith and I happened to motor past the cottages on that parcel of land I sold Kate recently. I noticed that they are being repaired. Are you thinking of letting them?"

"I?" Charles asked, and both brows went up. "That's Kate's property, you know. She used her funds for the purchase. She does as she likes with it."

Bradford prided himself on his own modern attitudes, but he still had not got used to his friend's unconventional marriage. He could understand Charles's allowing his wife to purchase property, but he could not comprehend his permitting her to actually *manage* it. "Well, then," he said dryly, "what does Kate plan to do with the cottages?"

"She wants to expand her school," Charles said, "but she needs additional dormitory space. She acquired the property with the intention of refurbishing the cottages and using them to house students who come from a distance." He grinned. "There's no stopping that woman once she gets an idea, you know. Between her and the Countess of Warwick, I believe they plan to train every able-bodied woman in England to earn her livelihood from the land." He shook his head. "And by Jove, I think they might succeed."

10

Monday, 5 June, 1899

Regal Lodge, Newmarket

> "Now that Lillie was a race-horse owner, she decided
> to go in for racing in a really big way. She found a
> counsellor and guide to advise her about racing and
> pulling off betting-coups; bought a house at Kentford,
> just outside Newmarket, called Regal Lodge; and
> adopted the name Mr. Jersey as a racing pseudonym."
>
> *The Gilded Lily:*
> *The Life and Loves of the Fabulous Lillie Langtry*
> ERNEST DUDLEY

KATE, WITH CHARLES and her maid Amelia Quibbley, took
the morning Great Eastern train from Colchester east
and north to Ipswich, then west through Bury St. Edmunds
to Newmarket. There, they separated at the station, Charles
being met by Bradford Marsden and walking off in one
direction, Kate hailing a hansom and being driven off in
another. It was after eleven when the cab pulled up in front
of Regal Lodge and she got out, followed by Amelia, who
waited while the driver took down the bags.

Mrs. Langtry had written of her house as a "small

71

cottage," but it was neither small nor very like a cottage, Kate thought, looking up at it. Regal Lodge was a substantial brick house, half-timbered in the second story, with a great many mullioned windows and numerous imposing gables and chimney pots, set behind wrought-iron gates off a quiet lane. Mrs. Langtry placed a premium on privacy—as well she might, for Charles had told Kate that when the Prince visited the racing stables at Egerton House, where his racehorses were trained, he visited Mrs. Langtry as well. His Highness was not in such oblivious thrall to the Honorable Mrs. Keppel that he had forsaken his old friend Lillie.

Kate rang the bell beside the iron-studded front door and was admitted by a courteous butler named Williams, who begged to inform her that Mrs. Langtry offered her most profound regrets, but that she was engaged with her advisers and could not be disturbed.

"If her ladyship would be pleased to be shown to her rooms," he added, "the luncheon bell will ring shortly."

The rooms—a spacious bedroom and dressing room; a private bath with a water closet and a bathtub which was connected to a small gas hot-water heater; and a sleeping closet for Amelia—were more than ample. The bedroom was luxuriously furnished in blue and silver draperies, bed coverings, and carpets, and there were bowls and vases filled with roses on every table. Amelia unpacked a champagne-colored dress of embroidered linen and helped Kate change into it.

"You look lovely, m'lady," Amelia said, putting the finishing touches to Kate's hair just as the luncheon bell rang.

"Thank you," Kate said, smoothing her skirts. "If you don't mind, Amelia, I'll leave you to finish unpacking. And then you might go downstairs and join the staff at lunch."

"Yes, m'lady," Amelia answered equably, taking Kate's

leather jewelry box from the portmanteau. She gave Kate a sidelong glance. "Are there any special instructions, ma'am, especially as regards the servants?"

Kate smiled at the question. It was hard to keep secrets from one's lady's maid—and impossible to hide anything from Amelia Quibbley. The young woman—brown-haired and petite, with a pretty, open face—had been with her for several years, not just at Bishop's Keep but also at Sibley House, the London residence where Charles and Kate stayed when Parliament was in session. The house was big as a castle and as unfriendly as a mausoleum, with a large, impersonal staff supervised by an impassive butler and a tyrant of a housekeeper. Kate relied on Amelia's company and friendship and often used her as a liaison with the other, less amiable staff. Perhaps for this reason, perhaps for others, Amelia had developed an almost intuitive sense of what her mistress might require of her, as well as the ability to appraise an unfamiliar household.

Kate took the gold brooch that Amelia handed her. "I have two purposes in being here, Amelia. Mrs. Langtry has expressed an interest in staging one of my stories, and while the idea doesn't greatly appeal to me, I plan to discuss it with her." Looking at herself in the mirror, she pinned the brooch at her throat. "And Mrs. Langtry has agreed to be the subject of an article I've been asked to write for *The Strand*, and I would be glad of any insights into her true nature—the sort of insights servants sometimes share. I might not be able to use them in the article, but they would help me to better understand her character."

"Yes, m'lady," Amelia said demurely. "I'm sure people 'ud like to know wot she's really like. When she's not on the stage, that is."

Kate met Amelia's eyes in the mirror. "I'm sure they would," she replied.

"Lady Charles!" Mrs. Langtry exclaimed, rising gracefully from a sofa in the drawing room. She was wearing an elaborate dress of sea-foam green watered silk with a bodice of pleated chiffon, cut low to show the full, soft whiteness of an alluring neck and shoulders, with a circlet of impressively large pearls clasped around her throat. She held out both her hands, and she and Kate traded the inevitable social kiss on both cheeks.

"So *delighted* that you are here at Regal Lodge!" Mrs. Langtry continued. "But I shan't have any sort of ceremony. I insist that you call me Lillie, Kathryn."

"Kate, please," Kate said.

"I've played two Kates," Lillie said firmly, "and you're not a bit like either of them. If I can't call you Kathryn, I shall call you Beryl."

Lillie turned to gesture to two men, who were smoking and talking alongside what appeared to be a large tiled fish pond, sunk into the drawing-room floor. "Before you go, gentlemen, you must be introduced to my houseguest—the famous lady author. She'll be writing an article about me for *The Strand*. Lady Charles Sheridan—also known as Beryl."

As Lillie made introductions, Kate studied the two men. The elder was Captain Dick Doyle, whom Lillie presented as her racing manager, an enormous man in frock coat and waistcoat with a pale gray tie. He was round-cheeked and jovial, but there was a shrewd glint in his piggish eye. Kate felt herself being assessed and swiftly dismissed as being of no possible interest or utility. Lady authors were not, apparently, among the entities he managed.

The other man, slim and youthful in appearance, was natty in a checked tweed suit and red tie with a huge diamond tie tack. His name, Lillie said, was Todhunter Sloan.

"Tod is the brilliant American jockey who introduced short stirrups to England two years ago," Lillie said, smiling at him playfully. "They all laughed at his style when he first began to ride in this country. A monkey on a stick, they called you, didn't they, Toddie? But then he showed them how to win races, and they stopped laughing. And now they all try to copy you, don't they, dear?"

Sloan grinned and tapped his cigarette into a delicate porcelain bowl that did not look in the least like an ashtray. "Damn right, Lil, m'love," he drawled, in a broad Mid-western accent. "They all want to be just like me, don'cha know." He snorted disdainfully. "Brit jockeys don't have the sense the good Lord gave a goose. No idea how to run a race. Hang around at the start like it was a damned Sunday-school picnic and they was waitin' fer somebody to pour the lemonade." He threw back his head and guffawed, showing horsy looking yellow teeth.

"There's nobody like you, Tod, old chap," the fat man replied in an affably ingratiating tone. "You're one of a kind."

"You betch'er boots I am," the jockey said boastfully. "Can't nobody come near to Tod Sloan."

"Except perhaps for the Reiff brothers," Lillie remarked in an offhand tone, "who seem to be *two* of a kind." The corners of her lips curled upward in a slight smile. "Johnny and Lester are doing quite well, wouldn't you say, Toddie? Riding quite aggressively, scooping up the purses. I'm beginning to fear that these new American jockeys shall give us all a run for our money."

Tod Sloan's boyish cheeks grew red and his grin faded. "You don't need to be afraid of anythin', Lil. That last time out on Reliable, that was a fluke." He thought for a moment, scowling; then his voice rose and his tone became belligerent. "Say, you ain't tryin' to tell me you don't want me to ride for you no more, are you? 'Cause if that's what you want, I c'n oblige you, for certain. I got plenty o' offers. Why, Lord Beresford tells me that the Prince hisself wants me up. Think o' that, Lil! The Prince hisself!"

Lillie gave a pretty little pout and put her hand on the jockey's sleeve. "Of course I want you to keep on riding for me, you silly boy. It's just that…" She glanced significantly at the captain.

The fat man stepped forward, moving as daintily as a girl. He placed his arm across the jockey's slender shoulders. "I'm sure our lovely Lillie didn't speak to offend, old chap. Just to remind you that we have competitors, and that she's counting on you to bring home a winner, no matter what you might have to do to get it." He raised both eyebrows and opened his eyes wide. "But that's the business we're in, isn't it? We all need a challenge now and then, don't we?"

The jockey's "I s'pose" was sulky, but he brightened at Lillie's smile. She leaned over and kissed his cheek.

"I know you'll ride as hard as ever you can for me at Haydock Park on Saturday, dear Tod, and not let those other American jockeys push you around. I'm so sorry I won't be able to see the race, but I'll look forward to hearing that you and Reliable have taken a first." She turned to Doyle. "I leave it to you, Captain, to suggest a winning strategy for the race. And of course, to see that my wagers are placed at the best odds, and that Tod has a handsome present for his work."

While all this was going on, Kate had wandered over to gaze into the fish pond and discovered it stocked with large goldfish, some in quite striking colors. Standing off to one side, unobserved, she caught the captain's surreptitious wink at Lillie. While she did not understand all that had been said, she felt quite sure that Lillie and the captain had been putting on a performance for the benefit of the jockey, who was so engrossed in himself that he failed to notice how he was being goaded into some sort of action by two people who were far more shrewd than he. In Kate's opinion, Todhunter Sloan might be a brilliant jockey, but he was not a very bright man. And Lillie Langtry was extraordinarily skilled at all sorts of performances.

The men took their leave, the door to the dining room opened, and the ladies went in to luncheon, an elaborate affair that included a julienne soup, salmon cutlets, jellied chicken, a garnished tongue, green peas, almond pudding, and a fruit ice, each served in its turn by Williams the butler and a handsomely liveried footman.

"Now, my dear Beryl," Lillie said confidingly, "while we eat, we shall have a great talk. You can ask me anything you want. There is no need to take notes just now, you can do that later. You are free to use everything I say in your magazine article—although I should like to read it before it is printed." She tossed her head carelessly. "The press is such a useful tool, but one must exert some small control over it, don't you agree?"

Afterward, Kate wondered that Lillie could have managed to eat a single bite, and there was certainly no opportunity for her to ask any questions. The actress talked incessantly, punctuating her conversation with practiced gestures and expressive glances from her smoky eyes, which seemed sometimes blue, sometimes gray. She described at great length the amazing success of her most recent theatrical tour of the United States; the fifty thousand pounds she had realized from the sale of her yacht, *White Lady*, a gift from an admirer named Baird who had died, tragically, before they could enjoy it together; the exploits of her favorite horse, Merman, which she loved above all other things on this earth; her new little house on the Isle of Jersey, which she called Merman Cottage and where Hugo de Bathe often visited her. As she talked, her tone became more confiding and her gestures and expression more intimate, as if she were telling everything about her life. Kate noticed, however, that she failed to mention two other sensational events which the London newspapers had reported extensively: her California divorce, obtained just two years before; and the mysterious death of her former husband, Mr. Edward Langtry.

At the mention of Hugo de Bathe, Lillie paused for a sip of wine and Kate seized the opportunity to speak. "I enjoyed meeting Lord de Bathe," she said, pretending to more warmth than she felt. "He's a charming man. He seems to care for you very much."

"Oh, yes, doesn't he?" Lillie agreed, smiling languidly over the rim of her glass. "Suggie is a dear, dear boy. I expect we shall be married before the end of summer." She laughed dryly. "It won't at all please his father, of course. The old man has threatened to cut Suggie off without a shilling if he marries me." She added, with a cavalier shrug, "But money matters little to true lovers, don't you agree? Love is certainly the most important thing in our lives. As my dear friend Oscar Wilde says, 'They do not sin at all, who sin for love.'"

"But Oscar Wilde has also said," Kate replied thoughtfully, "that 'one should always be in love. That is the reason one should never marry.'"

Lillie looked vexed. "Oscar is nothing if not inconsistent," she said. She pushed away her empty dessert dish and fastened her eyes on her guest's face. Her glance seemed to lay claim to Kate's most precious secrets. "Now that I've told you everything there is to know about me, *dear*

Beryl, you must tell me about yourself. I do so want to be friends."

Kate opened her mouth to speak, but Lillie went on.

"I know that you're an American, that your novels and stories are amazingly popular, and that you and Lord Sheridan don't much like to go about in Society. But I'm sure there's more—much more, hidden away inside your heart."

"I'm afraid that you've already learned all there is to know about me," Kate said with a small smile. "My life is an open book."

Lillie threw back her head and laughed gaily. "An open book!" she exclaimed, much amused. "How very clever! But of course, it is your literary work that I most want to talk about. I can't tell you how excited I am at the prospect of staging *The Duchess*. I know the production will have an enormous dramatic appeal, especially if you agree to the few changes I have in mind. I'm absolutely dying to—"

But at that moment, Williams appeared with a folded note on a silver salver. Lillie read it with a displeased frown and threw it back on the tray, letting out an irritated puff of breath.

"It seems that I have an unexpected caller, Beryl, and after that, I fear I must attend to some business. You and I shall have to continue our conversation at tea." The butler pulled back Lillie's chair as she stood. "Meanwhile, I'm sure you would like to look at the house and grounds so that you can tell your readers all about Regal Lodge in your article. Please do ask Williams if you find yourself in need of anything."

It was some little time later, while Kate was exploring the rose garden within earshot of the drawing-room windows, that she overheard Lillie Langtry's angry interchange with her caller.

11

The Grange House Stable, in Moulton Road

"Newmarket, the home of the Jockey Club, was also home to dozens of racing stables. Each trainer ruled his stable with an iron hand, guarding the horses placed in his yard as if they were the Crown Jewels, for it was their success on the Turf which assured his own success. The trainer might not be so prominent a figure as the jockey, but he and his methods had a far greater and more lasting influence on the individual horse, and on racing itself."

Trainers and Stables
ALBERT J WILLIAM

WHEN CHARLES AND Bradford arrived at the Grange House Stable that morning, they discovered that Bradford's introduction would not be necessary. After a few minutes' conversation, it emerged that Angus Duncan had known the two previous Barons of Somersworth and was willing to be persuaded to undertake the training of the two-year-old colt and the filly that the present Lord Somersworth (obviously a foppish fool of a man with more money than sense) proposed to place in his care.

"They're the last of my brother's stable," Charles lisped, affecting an exaggerated, upper-class tone, "and so I'm anxious to do well by them." He leaned on his gold-headed cane and remarked, "Afraid I'm not a racing man, haven't an ounce of brain when it comes to horses. My brother was quite proud of the line, but my stableman insists that both horses are bone-lazy and ought to be sold." He took out a white silk handkerchief and flicked a speck of dust off the sleeve of his morning coat. "But my brother, bless him, wouldn't've wanted that. I'm anxious to see them well trained and give them a chance to run, if they're fit for it. Of course, I'll pay the tariff, whatever it is," he added expansively.

Bradford, with the demeanor of a cautious adviser, gave him a slight shake of the head. "Your lordship ought to have a look around the stables before making a final decision on the matter. There are, after all, other stables at Newmarket."

"Oh, quite," Charles said, smiling fatuously. He made a fluttering gesture. "Oh, indeed. A look around, to be sure."

Angus Duncan frowned. "Don't like to have owners around horses," he said brusquely. "Don't do horses no good, nor owners neither." He glanced at his lordship, who was stroking his mustache appreciatively, and seemed to conclude that this particular owner was too dim-witted to be dangerous, although the adviser bore watching. "But a quick look shouldn't do harm," he said, relenting. "Pinkie'll take you round."

As Pinkie was being summoned, two other men appeared, one a jaunty waist-coated and bowler-hatted gentleman, the other distinctly not a gentleman, dressed in tweed knickers and rakish tweed cap, a brown-paper cigarette dangling from his lips.

"Reggie, old chap!" Bradford said, and thrust out his hand to the man in the bowler hat. "I say, dear boy, it really was too bad about that horse of yours last week—Gladiator, I mean. Looked like being a winner before that little scrimmage at the Corner." Deferentially, he turned to Charles. "Should like you to meet Lord Charles Somersworth, who is considering stabling a pair of fine horses here." He glanced at Angus Duncan. "*Very* fine horses," he said emphatically.

Reginald Hunt greeted Bradford warmly, acknowledged Charles with a small bow, and introduced his companion, Jesse Clark. Charles recognized the man as the American trainer who, together with Enoch Wishard, was said to have made horse doping into an art. Clark was a small man, in his forties, with a dry, leathery skin and a mocking twist to his mouth.

"So you're Clark," Bradford said genially, giving the American's hand a vigorous shake. "Been hearing about your successes with Mr. Wishard. Quite a string of wins you've had there. Tearing up the Turf, as they say."

Hunt brightened. "Oh, Jesse's a great one, all right. A real wizard, I must say. We weren't having all that much luck with Gladiator—were we, Angus?—until Jesse came along and offered to help get him ready for the Derby. I don't know what he did, but as you saw, he worked a miracle. The horse showed more life than I'd ever seen in him."

Charles saw out of the corner of his eye that Angus Duncan had shifted from one foot to the other.

"Do you have a stable here at Newmarket, Mr. Clark?" Bradford inquired amiably.

Angus Duncan made a noise deep in his throat.

Clark stubbed out his cigarette with the toe of his shoe. "Enoch Wishard and I train a few horses at the Red House

Stable," he said in a broad American drawl. "But mostly I do what you might call consultin'." He hooked his thumbs in his leather belt and grinned at Angus Duncan. "Ain't that right, Angus? Jes' lendin' a hand where it's needed t' bring a lazy horse up to snuff."

Angus Duncan said nothing. His face was dark and his jaw muscle was working.

Charles opened both eyes wide in an expression of surprise and delight. "Well, well, Mr. Clark, this is a lucky meeting. I shall have need of your services, I daresay, for it seems that I have *two* lazy horses." He turned to Angus Duncan. "Mr. Duncan, when the horses arrive, please be so kind as to arrange with Mr. Clark to consult with you about them. I should like him to suggest how they might be"—he stroked his mustache—"brought up to snuff, as it were."

Without replying, Angus Duncan threw a murderous look at Clark and clenched his fists. It was clear that he hated the American and didn't care who knew it. Charles was aware that most trainers were obsessively proprietary when it came to determining how a horse should be handled, and they were careful to keep strangers out of the yard for fear they would steal racing secrets or worse yet, interfere with the horses. If Angus Duncan didn't want Clark hanging about, why did he tolerate it? Why didn't he simply order him off his property, and drop any owner who offered to do business with him?

"That's a topping idea, Somersworth," Reggie Hunt said enthusiastically. "These Americans have some very innovative ideas about training. I daresay our traditional methods are a bit behind the times, at least where some horses are concerned. Gladiator, for instance. If there ever was a lazy horse, it's that one." He screwed up his mouth, vexed. "It's a pity that the jockey wasn't strong enough to keep him running straight at Epsom Downs. We'd've had a winner at 66 to 1. As it is, I've had to deal with a damned objection, which isn't settled yet."

Angus Duncan lost all patience. "'Twa'n't the jockey," he snapped furiously. With a baleful glare at Jesse Clark, he turned on his heel and stalked off.

Bradford looked puzzled. "What was that about?"

Clark gave a dismissive shrug. "The jockey who died was a favorite of his," he said. He turned to Lord Hunt. "Shall we see to those horses now, yer lordship?" He tipped his cap to Charles, and the two men went off together.

Pinkie turned out to be Angus Duncan's nephew and assistant trainer. He was a small, nervous man with a furtive look and a twitchy mouth under a full mustache. Like his uncle, he didn't seem pleased at the idea of showing off the stables and made grumbling noises to himself as they started off—not, Charles thought, an attitude conducive to attracting owners to the stables. Pinkie had the look of a man who would not hesitate to strike out violently against any horse, or any person, who went against him.

The horses were housed in two large U-shaped wooden structures that faced each other across an open yard. Each side of each structure was made up of ten loose boxes, so that there was room for sixty horses. Just then, several lads brought in a short string of horses, and Charles gave them a quick look. Bradford would know better than he, of course, but they appeared to be in good condition.

Pinkie was moving quickly through the yard, as if he didn't want them to linger for a close look at the horses. At the back of the yard, a roofed passageway connected the two U-shaped stables. Quickly, Pinkie opened the doors along the passageway, giving them glimpses of the hay and feed room, which opened at the back so that a wagon could draw up to deliver supplies of fodder and feed grains; the tack room, hung with racks of saddles, bridles, and horse clothing; and a storage room full of other, assorted equipment. Above them, Pinkie indicated with a nod of his head, was the attic dormitory where the stablelads slept.

"How many lads?" Bradford asked.

"Twenty-two, present count," Pinkie said. He added, in sullen defensiveness, "The horses never want for care."

To Charles, Bradford said, "Three horses to a lad is a handful, your lordship. It means that some horses don't get worked every day."

Pinkie thrust out his chin. "Not a bit of it!" he remonstrated belligerently. "Anyway, they doesn't all want workin' ev'ry day, now does they? Some is lame, some is off their feed, others likes light work by their nature." He gestured to a pair of double gates that opened out onto a fenced field, and beyond that, onto Newmarket Heath. "As ye can see, there's lots o' room for gallops. We does two-a-days, fine weather er foul."

They were in the yard again, and Charles looked around. "It's quite an operation. Wouldn't you agree, Marsden?"

"It's large, I'll give it that," Bradford said in an unwilling tone. "But size isn't all your lordship is looking for. You want to know how the horses are trained, how well they've performed."

"To be sure," Charles agreed absently. "But that's your department, I'm afraid." His glance had been caught by a wiry, red-haired lad walking with a springy step along the passageway toward the tack room. He was carrying a saddle.

Charles frowned. That boy—

Bradford and Pinkie had turned away and were walking toward the office. Bradford was saying, "I should like to take a look at the stable's form book on behalf of his lordship," and Pinkie was protesting angrily that this was a great imposition and he was sure his uncle would not consent. Both appeared to be fully occupied with their discussion, so Charles took the opportunity to go in the opposite direction.

In four purposeful strides, he reached the open door of the tack room. The boy was there, reaching up to hang the saddle on one of the dozens of brackets set in the opposite wall. Charles entered the dim room and stood silhouetted against the bright light from the doorway. Sensing another's presence, the boy glanced over his shoulder.

"Hullo, Patrick," Charles said quietly. "It's good to see you again."

The boy turned, his eyes growing large in his freckled face. "Damn!" he breathed.

"I see your language hasn't improved," Charles replied, trying to keep his voice even, so that he betrayed neither surprise nor anger. "What are you doing here, Paddy? Why didn't you stay at Westward Ho!, where you were put?"

Patrick pulled down the corners of his mouth. "Didn't fancy lickin's and bullyin'," he muttered. "Didn't much take to books, neither." He raised his chin defiantly. "I came here to apprentice as a jockey."

"Well," Charles said mildly, "I suppose you could do worse. Do you like it here?"

Patrick chewed on his lower lip. "Yes," he said. He hesitated and then added, with characteristic honesty, "I liked it a lot more, before they did what they did to Gladiator, and Johnny Bell died."

"To Gladiator?" Charles asked in surprise.

"My horse. The horse I do for, that is." He straightened his shoulders proudly. "I'm his traveling lad."

"Amazing," Charles said, more to himself than to Patrick. Finding the boy was a wonderful stroke of luck that he couldn't wait to share with Kate. But finding out that the boy was Gladiator's lad was two wonderful strokes of luck, at a single instant! Now, if he could solicit the boy's help—

Patrick's eyes had filled, and he wiped away the sudden tears with a coarse sleeve. "And Johnny Bell was my good friend. He's the jockey who died at Epsom last week." The words were tumbling out, as if he had held them too long inside himself. "They made the horse drink something out of a bottle. Whatever it was, it made him crazy." He looked up at Charles, his lips trembling. "I'm afraid for Gladiator, sir. If they make him run like that again, it'll *kill* him."

"I see," Charles said. He studied Patrick for a moment, liking what he saw. The boy's hard-won experience of school and life was clearly written on his young face, and the trembling lips and smear of tears on the dirty cheek were testimony to his unhappiness. But he had grown taller and carried himself with a new dignity, and there was a bold thrust to his chin and a spark in his eyes that let Charles know that his fiery spirit had not been quenched.

"As it happens," Charles went on, speaking in a lower voice, "I am here to learn what happened to the horse— although no one but you is to know that. They think I am here only as an owner, to place two new horses."

Patrick's eyes widened and hope flushed in his face. "You can stop them from giving that stuff to Gladiator again?"

"I don't know," Charles said truthfully. "But I would like to persuade the Jockey Club to make 'that stuff,' as you call it, illegal, so that it may not be given to any horse." Thinking he heard a footstep, he glanced over his shoulder. "But it's not a good idea to talk here, where we might be overheard."

"No, sir," Patrick said with emphasis. After a moment,

he added, "I could slip out, sir. After the other lads are asleep." He grinned and his eyes lightened. "It wouldn't be the first time, sir."

"No," Charles said with a little smile, "I'm sure it wouldn't. I am staying with a friend who has temporary lodgings at Hardaway House, on the left side of Wellington Street, just off the High Street. The house has a brick gateway and a green door. Do you think you can find it?"

"O' course, sir." Patrick spoke with a shy confidence. "I think I can manage ten o'clock."

"Ten o'clock it is, then," Charles agreed. He turned to go, then turned back. "Patrick," he said in a softer tone, "I'm very glad to have found you." He held out his hand as if to another man. "I shall look forward with great pleasure to seeing you tonight, and to hearing your adventures since you left school."

A deeper flush spread over Patrick's cheeks. He squared his shoulders and took Charles's hand. "Sir," he said, in a proper schoolboy's voice, "Thank you, sir. Ten o'clock, sir."

12

Regal Lodge

"Mrs. Langtry was dangerously fascinating. She did not for a moment conceal the baseness of the character she represented."

Review of Lady Barter
Dramatic Notes, March 1891
CECIL HOWARD

"Of course, one always has to ask oneself if one is playing the character or merely portraying one's own true nature, or a part of it."

LILLIE LANGTRY

KATE LOVED ROSES beyond all other flowers, and Lillie's were magnificent, blooming extravagantly in shades of pink, red, white, and yellow, filling the entire garden with their scent. The June day was warm, and after a time she found a wrought-iron bench and sat down to enjoy the sweet, heady fragrance, the drowsy harmony of the bees, and the throaty cooing of the doves in a distant dovecote.

But as she sat, enjoying the quiet afternoon, she became

aware that it was not entirely quiet nor harmonious. She looked up. The bench on which she was sitting was placed almost against the house, under an open window. Inside, Lillie Langtry and a man were engaged in discussion.

"Of course I'm grateful to you, Spider," Lillie was saying. She laughed lightly, and Kate could imagine the sweetly flattering smile, the touch of her hand lending endearing emphasis to the affectionate nickname. "You've been of enormous support over the past few years, my dear. I could never forget that you've helped me stage—"

"Helped you?" the man broke in. His voice was clipped, with a cutting edge. "I have financed every one of your plays for the past eight years, and I will certainly never forget them. *As You Like It*—your Rosalind was not well received. *Esther Sandraz*, which the critics hated. *Antony and Cleopatra*—how many thousands of pounds went down the drain with that one? *Lady Barter*, better not spoken of. *Linda Grey*, which closed so quickly that all the props were forfeit. *Gossip*, saved only by your diamond tiara. *The Queen of Manoa*—"

"Please don't be cruel, Spider," Lillie said wearily. "Yes, I acknowledge it. Things have been rather difficult in the past few years, especially here in England." Her voice warmed. "But you've always been an angel. The truest, dearest angel a woman could hope to have."

"And this is how you reward me?" the man demanded roughly. "By announcing that you're to be married? And to that boy of a man, that silly, simpering Suggie, as you call him." His voice suddenly became chilling, and Kate heard the restrained violence in it. "By God, Lillie, I won't stand for it!"

"But I need the security, Spider. The theater is so risky and there's nothing else I can do to support myself. I've passed my fortieth birthday, and I want—"

"Your fortieth! Forty-fifth, shall we say, rather? And of course you want a title." The man laughed, mocking. "Lady de Bathe, eh? Your ticket to respectability, your entrée into Society?" The voice was so sharply scornful that Kate shivered. "Don't go to the trouble, my dear. Society knows who you are and will never accept you as anything else."

Lillie was chill. "I am accepted in the highest Society. The Prince—"

The man laughed. "Of course," he said. "How could I have forgotten the Prince, that fat old fool who's ridden every jade in the kingdom." In the silence, Kate heard the striking of a match and could picture the man lighting a cigar. "Anyway," he went on, "I don't mean you to marry—unless you decide to marry me, of course. You've been free for well over a year now. It's time you agreed."

Lillie sighed. "Please, let's not discuss—"

"I didn't object to your affair with Baird, because it was amusing to watch you play with him and tease him. It was even amusing when he struck back. I thought it was rather clever of you to trade that beating he gave you in Paris for the title to the *White Lady*."

"But my dear, I—"

"He did go too far, though," the man went on. "His treatment of you made me very angry. You were safer with him out of the way." His voice hardened. "And I don't mean you to marry de Bathe, Lillie. I didn't rid you of Ned Langtry to lose you to some fatuous young fool."

"Please, Spider," Lillie said. She sounded genuinely frightened—the first real emotion, Kate thought, that she had heard from the actress. "*Please*, dear, let's not talk about that ugly business. Let's—"

"I think we *do* need to talk about it, Lillie. It's time I reminded you of just how much I have done for you. I've not just been your angel, but your devil as well. The black box full of your jewels that I—"

"No!" Lillie whispered, unmistakable panic in her voice. "We mustn't talk about that! We mustn't! The servants might overhear."

"—sold for you so you could settle your debts," the man continued, as if he had not been interrupted. "That was devilish of me, wasn't it? And it was devilish of me to make sure that drunken fool of a husband wouldn't annoy you any longer." He laughed sardonically. "Oh, you're well taken care of, Lillie. You don't want for a thing, except your soul. You've sold that to the devil, my dear, and he won't give it back."

There was another pause, and when Lillie spoke again, her voice was hard, brittle. "You think you've bought me? Is that it? Well, you can think again. No one controls Lillie Langtry." Her voice was rising now, becoming dramatic. "Many men have had to learn that lesson the hard way. I am my own woman, I tell you! I will not be under any man's rule!"

Kate heard three slow handclaps, as if in a parody of applause, and the man spoke, dryly ironic. "That's an affecting speech, Lillie, but you delivered it much more convincingly in *Agatha Tylden*. Forget that nonsense. If it's money you need, just say so. I can give you enough to—"

"You can't give me respectability," Lillie said. The bravado was gone and only a quiet desperation was left. "I appreciate what you've done for me, and I do care for you. But you must understand that I need a *future*."

By this time, Kate's curiosity was so aroused that she got up, gathered her skirts, and climbed up on the bench, cautiously. But just as she raised her head to peek over the sill, she heard the scrape of a chair and ducked down quickly.

"This is all very touching," the man said, "but I'm afraid you'll have to excuse me. It's a good deal later than I thought, and I agreed to see someone this afternoon. Shall we part with a kiss, dearest?"

Kate heard the rustle of clothing, a stifled cry, and the sound of a slap. Then there was a much louder slap, and Lillie cried out in pain. Kate jumped down from the bench and started down the path as the slam of a door echoed through the somnolent afternoon, followed by the jangling crash of falling china. At the corner of the house she waited for a moment, composing herself, then stepped onto the path, hoping to see the man who would be just leaving.

But she was too late. A male figure was disappearing into a closed carriage, and the next moment, it had driven off.

13

The Devil's Dyke

"I don't say that all those who go racing are rogues and vagabonds, but I do say that all rogues and vagabonds seem to go racing."

SIR ABRAHAM BAILEY

"In his first description of what he took to be 'doped' horses racing in England in about the year 1900, the Honorable George Lambton described 'horses who were notorious rogues running and winning as if they were possessed by the devil, with their eyes staring out of their heads and sweat pouring off them' and one horse, 'after winning a race dashed madly into a stone wall and killed itself.'"

Drugs and the Performance Horse
THOMAS TOBIN

IT WAS NEARLY two by the time Charles and Bradford arrived at the Devil's Dyke, a small out-of-the-way pub on the Exning Road, and Charles feared that Jack Murray might have given them up and departed. But the Jockey Club investigator was smoking his cigar at an inconspicuous table in the dusky rear, and when Charles and Bradford approached, he stood and extended his hand. When they were all three seated, a burly, bearded man in a stained white apron came to the table to ask what they'd have. They ordered a pitcher of ale, with sausages for Charles and Murray, and cottage pie for Bradford.

"We were at the Grange House Stable this morning," Charles said, while Jack Murray poured ale. "The horses will be arriving in a few days."

"Very good, sir," Murray replied.

He was a man of medium stature, well above middle age, with sparse and graying hair, large, sad eyes, and a mournful expression that seemed permanently written across his face. There was a scrape on his chin where he'd cut himself shaving, his tie was crooked, and the sleeves of his tweed coat were too long, reaching nearly to the tips of his spatulate fingers. If he were noticed at all, which was doubtful, Jack Murray might have been taken for one of those invisible men who spend their mornings and evenings on a grimy train and their days in a dreary London office.

But Charles knew otherwise, for he was acquainted with Murray's distinguished thirty-year career at the Yard, and with a few of the difficult cases he had solved. If intelligence, training, and instinct were the necessary qualifications for an investigation into Turf corruption, this retired detective could have easily handled it by himself. Admiral North was right, however; it would be impossible for Murray to carry out an investigation involving gentlemen racehorse owners without attracting attention to himself. He obviously wasn't a gentleman, although he wasn't obviously a policeman, either.

"Did you bring Madame Zahray's report?" Charles inquired.

Murray started, as if he had been recalled from a dream, then reached into his breast pocket and produced an envelope, sealed. "I believe, sir," he said gloomily, "that this is what you're after." His slow, deep voice was flavored with Suffolk.

Charles took the unaddressed envelope, picked up a knife from the table, and slit it. In it was a single sheet of stationery, printed name and address at the top, centered: Lucianna Zahray, 1734 Old Post Road, London. Below this was written, in a spidery hand, the date, and a single sentence: "Regret to report that alkaloids appear present (cocaine most likely possibility) but blood sample insufficient for specific identification." This telegraphic missive was signed L Zahray.

Charles handed the letter back to Murray, who read it without expression, then gave it to Bradford.

"Unfortunate," Bradford said. He raised his eyebrows. "Who the devil is Lucianna Zahray?"

"Madame Zahray," Charles said, "is a respected analytical chemist of Austrian descent who has been of great help in answering previous questions I have put to her. If she cannot positively identify the drug that was used on Gladiator, no one else in England can. This was a long shot, though, and I'm not surprised that she couldn't give us an answer. I expected that the sample would prove insufficient."

Murray spoke in a deeply apologetic tone. "The analytical chemist tested what, exactly, sir? I don't believe I was told."

"Blood that was drawn from Gladiator about ninety minutes after the Derby," Charles said. "Regrettably, it was a small sample, since we obtained it surreptitiously, and the veterinary surgeon was interrupted at his task." He sighed, thinking that had he known Patrick was charged with the horse's care, they might have gotten what they needed a great deal more easily.

"Which leaves us nowhere," Bradford said, over his glass of ale.

"For the moment, at least," Charles replied, "although I haven't given up on the testing just yet. There's more to be learned there." To Murray, he added, "Have you come up with anything, Jack? What about the betting?"

Murray cleared his throat. "The horse ran at very long odds, as you know, sir. Lord Reginald Hunt, the owner, wagered heavily on him. Dick Doyle, and the stable too, all laid on." Murray pulled his thick gray brows together. "When the horse failed to finish, Lord Hunt, for one, had to scramble. It's said that he paid a hasty visit to Henry Radwick, who wasn't kind to him. Took Glenoaks and a horse besides. It's also said that he had a bit on with Alfred Day, off the books, and hasn't yet covered."

"Dick Doyle." Bradford looked thoughtful. "A very astute man, and not a plunger. Doubt he'd lay hard on a whim." He grinned mirthlessly. "Certainly sounds as if something was on, doesn't it?"

Charles thought about what Patrick had told him. "Is it known who was with Gladiator before the race, Jack?"

"Mr. Angus Duncan, of course, and Pinkie Duncan— that's old Angus's nephew—and the traveling lad, a young boy." Murray paused. "Also, a veterinary surgeon who arrived with the farrier."

"The surgeon's name?"

Murray looked rueful. "Sorry, sir. Haven't yet learned it. The farrier isn't saying, and I haven't approached the stable yet." He lowered his voice and leaned forward. "I've had a bit of a talk with Mr. Lambton, though, in confidence, sir. I trust you don't mind."

"That would be George Lambton, the Earl of Derby's trainer," Bradford said in an explanatory tone to Charles. "One of the best in the business."

"Right, sir. Mr. Lambton is deeply concerned about this 'dastardly doping business,' as he calls it, sir. He says it's the Americans who have brought it here, and especially Enoch Wishard and Jesse Clark, the trainers at the Red House Stable in St. Mary's Square. 'Yankee alchemists' is what he calls them." He looked out from under his eyebrows at Charles. "He says if there's anything he can do to help, sir, he's ready."

"I see," Charles remarked thoughtfully. "I don't suppose Mr. Lambton has any evidence to support his opinion that this is a 'dastardly' business. Horses injured, anything like that?"

"One horse killed," Murray said. "Ran into a stone wall after winning a race. Had to be shot." His face settled back into its former gloomy expression, as two plates of greasy sausages and a cottage pie arrived, supplying a diversion. Charles, however, was not finished with his questions.

"The farrier," he said. "What is his name? Where is he to be found?"

"Rickaby, sir," Murray said, around a forkful of sausage. The food did not make him any more cheerful. "Harper's Farm, near Epsom."

"Very well, then," Charles said, "if we are not able to learn the veterinary surgeon's name by other means, we shall travel to Epsom and impose a few questions on Rickaby." He paused. "I should think a talk with Jesse Clark might be profitable, as well."

"Yes, sir," Murray replied. "If he isn't at the stables, he lodges at Chubbs, on Highgate Street, off Fitzroy Street."

Bradford looked at Murray. "I say, old man," he said, bemused, "is there anything at all that you don't know?"

"Oh, I'm sure, sir," Murray replied sadly, and applied himself to his sausages.

14

Regal Lodge

"The Queen of Manoa is based on a fanciful idea that artistically developed might produce a good play, but becomes vulgar clap-trap. Mrs. Langtry's character is that of an utterly heartless creature, and beautiful as she looked as Lady Violet, she never once moved her audience. Her dresses were charming, her diamonds sparkled and her rubies were above price, perhaps, but these do not touch the heart."

Dramatic Notes
8 September, 1892

HER MISTRESS GONE to luncheon, Amelia had taken the back stairs down to the butler's pantry to inquire of Mr. Williams the hours at which tea and dinner would be served, and about the arrangements for breakfast in the mornings, and hot water, and necessary laundry. A few minutes later, the staff of twenty—minus the butler and the footman, who were serving luncheon upstairs—gathered for their own lunch in the servants' hall, and Amelia joined them. With a quick query, she discovered that Mrs. Langtry's personal maid was a stout young woman with cheeks like a cottage loaf. Her name was Margaret Simpson, and Amelia took care to sit beside her.

With so many at table and the butler absent, lunch was a noisy affair, the mutton hash being passed, and potatoes and gravy and stewed cabbage, and bread pudding at the end, with plenty of hot coffee. Amelia was grateful for the clatter, since it gave her an opportunity to talk to Margaret, who welcomed her little confidences and seemed flattered by her attention. Amelia understood why, when it emerged that Margaret was not Mrs. Langtry's personal maid after all, only an upstairs maid who had been temporarily elevated to the position when Mrs. Langtry's own maid, Dominique, fell ill and was left behind in London.

But this substitution proved a boon, as Amelia discovered, for the gossipy Margaret lacked the tight-lipped loyalty that Dominique would undoubtedly have displayed. Margaret had come to work at Regal Lodge shortly before Mrs. Langtry acquired it, and, with just a little urging, seemed eager to show off her knowledge of the household and its workings. After lunch, she offered to show Amelia around, and the two of them fell into an easy, friendly conversation that grew even more confiding as they went through the belowstairs area—the kitchen, the scullery, the pantries, the laundry—then up the narrow linoleum-covered service stairs to the second floor.

"If you don't mind my sayin' so," Amelia remarked as they climbed, "twenty seems a large staff for this 'ouse. Only five bedrooms upstairs, is it?" She already knew the number of bedrooms, for she had counted the doors on her way to lunch, subtracting one for the service door.

"It is big," Margaret agreed without rancor. "Until 'is Nibs comes, or Bertie, as she sometimes calls 'im. She calls all the great men by some silly name er other. A bit cheeky, don't ye think?"

"'Is Nibs?" Amelia asked, blinking, as they entered the second-floor hallway. "You mean—" She stopped.

Some three years before, Amelia had attended Lady Charles—Miss Ardleigh, she was at the time—during a visit to the Countess of Warwick's Easton Lodge, where the Prince of Wales had also been a guest. Amelia had seen and heard the Prince and been much impressed by his stoutness, his guttural voice, and the curious way he rolled his *r*s. The servants there—quite disrespectfully, Amelia thought—called the Prince "'Is Nibs" and "Bertie" because that was what the countess called him.

"O' course that's 'oo I mean," Margaret said. "When 'e comes, the staff ain't big enough by 'alf. 'E brings five er six of 'is own servants, and they takes our quarters, so us maids 'as to crowd all in together." She made a dissatisfied face. "What's worse, we 'as to wait on them, too, as well as 'im and 'er. Makes fer plenty of 'ard work, b'lieve you me."

With a flourish, as if this were her own private secret, she opened the nearest door. "This is where 'e sleeps when 'e comes. Mrs. L too, o' course." She pushed Amelia into the room and closed the door behind them. "We shouldn't be 'ere, so we need t' be quiet."

Amelia murmured an appropriate appreciation and looked around, making careful mental notes in case her mistress might want to know what she'd seen—although these intimate details were definitely not the sort that could be shared with the readers of *The Strand*. Mrs. Langtry's suite was large and ornately decorated, with Oriental rugs laid over the thick gold carpet, gold damask draperies at the windows, and a pair of matching mirrored dressing tables. Three walls were hung with costly looking Oriental tapestries, while against the fourth stood an enormous four-poster bed with a royal-purple and gold bedspread, the letters *HRH* and a crown inscribed on it. On one of the dressing tables lay a pair of gold-backed brushes, also inscribed with the letters *HRH*.

"Oooh..." Amelia breathed a shivery sigh and wrapped her arms around herself. "Oh, to think of it! Right 'ere in this very room!" She gave Margaret an admiring glance. "I'll bet you could tell a few stories, couldn't you, now?"

"She'd 'ave me 'ead if I did," Margaret replied. Her frown was darkly disapproving. "Ye should 'ear 'em in 'ere together, laughin' an' rowdyin' around like a farmer and 'is wife rollin' in the 'ay wiv the cows lookin' on. And 'im with a sweet Princess and a sainted mother at 'ome."

"I 'spose it's 'cause they're Quality," Amelia said, sobered by Margaret's censure.

"'*E* is," Margaret said, with emphasis, "so we can't expect better of 'im. But she's a parson's daughter 'oo was raised to know right. She should niver 'ave gone to actin'. That wuz 'er downfall." She sighed. "While we're 'ere, you'll want to see the bath."

The bathroom was large and bright, its white tile floor and walls sparkling. Like the one in Lady Charles's suite, it was equipped with a water closet and gas hot-water heater. This bathtub, however, was big enough for an elephant, and the taps were gold, while the thick, luxurious towels were emblazoned in gold with the royal insignia. The two women contemplated the splendor, Margaret with a proprietary, albeit censorious, air, Amelia in outright admiration, wishing that she could show it to Lady Charles.

At last, Amelia turned to Margaret. "Wot's she like? Mrs. Langtry, I mean." She put on a starry-eyed look. "I've seen 'er on the stage ever so many times, but never thought to be standin' right 'ere, where she baths." She grasped

Margaret's hand. "Wot's she really like, dear?" she asked in a coaxing tone. "Tell me, please."

"Well," Margaret said hesitantly, then stopped.

"Tell me, Margaret, you must!" Amelia begged. "Is she kind? Is she as soft and lovely in 'er 'eart as she is in 'er person? She must be soft and lovely," she added artlessly, "or the Prince wouldn't love her, now, would 'e?"

Margaret's mouth grew scornful. "Kind? Soft? Why, Mrs. L's 'eart is as 'ard as them diamonds she wears. She niver 'as a pound to 'er name, so she buys everything on the nod, more's the pity for the poor butcher and baker. And she's allus slow to pay our wages, little as they are. Mr. Williams 'as to go and beg fer us, which 'e shouldn't 'ave to do—although she doesn't cheat us, at least not 'ow she cheats 'er bookie."

Now that she had gotten started, Margaret didn't seem to want to stop. She dropped her voice, becoming conspiratorial. "And 'aven't ye 'eard about her daughter, Jeanne-Marie? Mrs. L calls 'erself Aunt Lillie, but she's really the girl's mother, more's the pity fer the child, 'oo everybody knows is a royal bastard. Lives out-of-the-way wiv Mrs. L's mother on Jersey, and sometimes in London wiv Mrs. L."

Amelia was struck with a sudden pity for a young girl growing up in what must be a terribly confusing situation, no father, and a mother who claimed to be her aunt. But she didn't have the opportunity to speak. Margaret was going on.

"Oh, she's a terror, that one," she said darkly. "She murdered 'er poor 'usband, too. 'Ad 'im pushed under the Irish Mail at Chester Station, she did. All because 'e wouldn't give 'er a divorce."

At this sensational revelation, Amelia was moved from pity to something like horror. She drew in her breath. "But

103

I thought she got a divorce. In America, it was. Leastwise, that's what I read in the newspaper."

Margaret made an impatient noise. "That's *America*, ye silly goose. An American divorce ain't worth the paper it's writ on 'ere. If Mr. Langtry wouldn't give 'is wife a proper English divorce, she couldn't marry an Englishman, now, could she? And that would spoil 'er scheme to marry Lord de Bathe, or wotever lord she 'appens to fancy."

"Oh, my," Amelia said helplessly. Perhaps she shouldn't tell any of this to Lady Charles, because it was not the sort of thing her ladyship could write in her article. On the other hand, Lady Charles had said quite explicitly that she wanted to understand Mrs. Langtry's true nature, and—

From downstairs, the sound of a slammed door reverberated in the silence, followed by the crash of falling china. Margaret gathered her skirts.

"That's enough talk fer now," she said. "We'd best get to work." Nervously, she eyed Amelia. "You won't tell wot I said, will ye?"

Amelia gave her a warm smile and a pat on the arm. "Tell? 'Oo would I tell? We're friends, and yer secret is safe with me." She made a little sign over her right breast. "Cross my 'eart."

Back in her suite after another tour of the garden, Kate glanced at the ormolu clock on the mantle and saw that it was nearly four. Amelia came in just then to say that her bath was ready.

"There's oceans of 'ot water, m'lady," she said appreciatively, her arms full of fluffy towels. "And nobody 'ad to carry it up the stairs, neither. It's all owin' to that little gas 'eater beside the bathtub."

"I shall have to mention it to his lordship," Kate said, following Amelia into the bathroom and beginning to undress. Charles was always doing something to modernize Bishop's Keep, but the kitchen and laundry were the only rooms with hot-water heaters. Kate stripped off her chemise and underthings and stepped into the steaming water with a grateful sigh. No matter that the heater was hissing loudly, or that there was a distinct odor of gas in the room.

She leaned back in the tub and closed her eyes. "And what have you been doing with yourself this afternoon, Amelia?" she asked, after a moment's relaxation in the soothing water.

There was a rustle of skirts. "Shall I tell you now, m'lady," Amelia asked, "or would you rather wait until after your bath?"

Kate opened her eyes. Amelia's face wore an expression of excitement and disapproval, oddly mixed.

"Tell me now," Kate replied, thinking there might be something interesting to hear. She wasn't disappointed.

"My goodness," she said, when Amelia had finished her lengthy recital. "Mrs. Langtry's maid told you all of *that*?"

"Margaret's a bit free with 'er tongue," Amelia said, with a disapproving shake of her head that suggested *she* would never tell tales out of school. "Anyway, she isn't really Mrs. Langtry's maid, only temp'rary. She's the upstairs maid, which is a diff'rent thing altogether."

Kate nodded, understanding the distinction in rank and importance—and in loyalty. "Thank you for letting me know what you've heard," she said.

"Well, I don't s'pose it's the kind of thing you can write in your piece fer *The Strand*," Amelia replied doubtfully. "And some of it might not be true. You know 'ow servants love to talk." She gathered up her mistress's clothes. "But where there's smoke there's usually fire, I allus say." And with that sage remark, she left the room, closing the door behind her.

105

Kate soaped a sponge with the lavender soap that lay in a crystal dish beside the tub, thinking about Amelia's report. She was not troubled by the morality of Lillie's relationship with the Prince or even that she had borne a child by him. If one spent one's time and energy passing moral judgments on members of the Marlborough Set, there would be little left for more creative or productive pursuits! It was widely known that the Prince could never bring himself to finally put out the flame of a royal romance, and if there were a daughter (even one passed off as Lillie's niece), the actress might have her own reasons for keeping the embers burning. And Kate couldn't judge Lillie harshly for attempting to run her household on nothing, when most of the gentry were doing exactly the same thing.

No, what concerned Kate was Margaret's more troubling allegation—that her employer had been involved in the murder of her husband. Kate would have dismissed this charge as the wild talk of a malicious servant if she hadn't overheard a reference to the same deed in the bitter exchange between Lillie and her male visitor that afternoon. Was it possible that the charge was true? Was the world-famous actress the kind of woman who could consent to the murder of a troublesome husband who refused to give his wife a British divorce?

But the moment Kate framed the question, she instinctively felt she knew the answer. While she could not say whether the charge was true or false, she knew it was *possible* that Lillie had done this thing, and it was this possibility that was beginning to intrigue her. The more she understood about the woman, the more she realized that her acting career might not be limited to her appearances on the stage. Every moment of her life might be a performance, every gesture carefully theatrical, every encounter a dramatic scene—all of it counterfeit, none of it *real*. In one of her real-life dramas, Lillie might well have played the role of an accomplice to murder, with as little thought to the real-life consequences as she would have given to roles she played on stage. Perhaps she had imagined a reality in which this action was absolutely essential to her life and well-being, and therefore justified. Perhaps she had performed for so long, for so many different admiring audiences, that she had lost all sense of what was true and real.

But while this was an intriguing idea, especially for Beryl Bardwell's novelistic interests, Kate told herself that surely she must be wrong. Surely no one could be onstage every moment. There had to be a real person behind the scenes, some core that was fundamentally and essentially Lillie—not the actress, not the courtesan, but the woman. What was it? Where was it? In what corner of Lillie's life was there one true thing? If Kate could find that reality, that truth, it would be worth writing about!

Kate's thoughts were interrupted by a polite knock at the outer door of the suite. Amelia went to answer it and returned in a moment with an envelope on a silver tray. "A message for you, m'lady. The footman brought it up."

Kate dropped the soapy sponge into the water and reached for a towel. "For me? Open it, Amelia."

Amelia opened the envelope, took out a folded sheet of paper, and handed it to her mistress. The note was from Charles. There were only three short sentences, but they made Kate forget all that she had been pondering:

I've located Patrick, my dear, well and happy, or as happy as boys may be who must work for their living. I'll send a cab for you at ten this evening. If you can get away, you shall see him for yourself.

15

Behind the Great Horse

> "'And what do you think of it all, Watson?' asked
> Sherlock Holmes, leaning back in his chair.
> 'It seems to me a most dark and sinister business.'
> 'Dark enough and sinister enough.'"
>
> *The Adventure of the Speckled Band*
> ARTHUR CONAN DOYLE

PATRICK HAD BEEN so shocked at the sight of Lord Charles
Sheridan standing in the door of the tack room that he
had turned nearly white. But his quite understandable fear
of being tongue-lashed or lashed in earnest for running
away from school—or even worse, that he might be sent
back—had begun to disappear with Lord Charles's first
mild words. This gentleman who treated him with such
grave courtesy was still his friend, however disappointed
he might be at his abysmal failures of discipline and stick-
to-it.

But as Patrick lay on his narrow straw pallet in the airless
loft and waited for the other lads to fall asleep, it occurred
to him that perhaps it was not Lord Charles's expectations

he had failed so miserably to satisfy, but merely his own unrealistic hopes—in which case it didn't matter, for Patrick had already come to terms with his inadequacies. This comforting thought, together with the anticipation of pouring out his fears and his anger—and yes, even his guilt—into his lordship's compassionate ears, lifted his spirits. While he wasn't exactly jubilant, he was on the way to feeling that he was not, after all, entirely alone in the world.

Down in the stable, Patrick heard the soft, snorting whuffle of a horse, and he thought again, uneasily, of Gladiator. Jesse Clark and Lord Hunt had been out on Southfields that day, along with the usual motley crew of bookmakers' touts, to watch the colt. Of course, there had been no repetition of that frightening business with the bottle, but Patrick was unhappily aware that it was only a matter of time before the same thing happened again—probably at the end of the week at Newmarket, where Gladiator was entered in a ten-furlong handicap. But what could he do to prevent it? How could he protect his magnificent horse from such a barbarous and dangerous offense?

Anxiously, he slipped his hand under the pallet and felt the rough lip of the floorboard he had pried up and the sharp splinter of wood he had wedged into it, as notice to himself of any attempt at the discovery of his hiding place. The splinter was still there. His cache was secure, although the question of what to do with it still remained. But Lord Charles had said that he wanted to know about what had happened to Gladiator. Perhaps it could be given to him. The thought brought a little comfort.

When the last lad had started to snore, Patrick climbed noiselessly down the ladder and through the unlatched door at the back of the feed room and then along the

109

footpath that led down Long Hill to Bury Road to Newmarket High Street. The path was familiar and the quarter moon, a ghostly frigate silently adrift on a rippling current of cloud, gave almost enough light for him to see the whole space of open hills and down to the town, where the gas street-lamps were shrouded in an opaque wrapping of low-lying mist.

Patrick was an imaginative boy, and it seemed to him that there was something sinister about the rivulets of mist and fog that twisted and curled like live snakes across Railway Field and along the foot of Long Hill. He drew back, shuddering, when an owl swooped low over his head and he heard the beat of the heavy wings lifting into the dark. Perhaps it wasn't an owl after all, but the sinister ghost of Hawkes, the highwayman who had often ridden the Bury Road, relieving drunken stragglers of the money they'd won at the race meeting. Perhaps—and he cringed at the thought—it was Johnny's ghost, angry at him for failing to warn him about that stuff in the bottle, and what it had done to Gladiator. Or perhaps it was his own guilt, sinister and dark, riding over him like a ghostly winged shadow.

The boy was glad when he reached the first gaslight on the High Street, where the evening revelers were weaving their celebratory way from pub to pub. He knew better than to go along the street, however, for both Pinkie Duncan and the head lad—an older fellow named Grins— frequented the taverns and gambling dens of the Rookery, and he preferred not to be seen. So he slipped down first one dark alleyway and then another, crossed a third, and paused to get his bearings.

The moon had been swallowed by fog, but Patrick knew where he was by the clink of glasses, the rough male laughter, and the smell of sour beer that clung to the damp night air. He was directly behind the Great Horse pub, an old coaching inn which had been made redundant for its original purpose by the railway line and in which every sort of roguery and villainy had been plotted over the years. The Great Horse occupied a long, narrow building with rafters high above and sawdust on the floor, a bar along one wall and scarred deal tables along the other, and a large back room where various belligerent encounters occurred: prizefights, dogfights between vicious red bull terriers, and the cockfights that had been illegal for fifty years but which continued unabated. Staggering sums were wagered in that room— Patrick knew, for he had seen with his own eyes the sums of money that changed hands. Now, there was a vicious flurry of growls and barks and a loud cheer, and Patrick shivered. He was fond of dogs, and he did not like the idea of one dog destroying another.

But Wellington Street was a few paces ahead, and Hardaway House, with its brick gateway, just to the right. More relieved than he cared to admit that he had almost reached his destination, Patrick set off again, hurrying now, for the clock in the tower was striking ten.

He didn't get far. Three or four quick steps, and he was lying flat on his face in the middle of the alley, his nose scraped, the wind knocked out of him. He lay there a moment, stunned and half-bewildered, then sat up, cursing loudly and rubbing his nose. He turned to see what had tripped him up.

A log that someone had carelessly left lying across the alleyway? He put his hand on it.

No, not a log, a roll of canvas, unexpectedly warm to the touch. He frowned, feeling farther along, and then farther still, discovering by degrees that what he had tripped over was neither a log nor a roll of canvas but a *leg*, a man's leg, and that the owner of the leg was lying flat on his back with his toes turned up, dead drunk.

But as Patrick got to his feet, he realized that his hand was wet and slippery and when the moon peered over the fog for her own surreptitious glance at the scene, he saw to his dismay that it was covered with blood. With mounting horror, he turned to look at the man, whose eyes were staring open and whose waistcoat was soaked with blood.

He was not dead drunk after all. He was bloodily and indisputably dead. And he was no stranger.

16

Hardaway House

"Nowadays we have so few mysteries left to us that we cannot afford to part with one of them."

The Critic as Artist
OSCAR WILDE

CHARLES LOOKED UP when he heard steps in the hallway and then the door opened and Kate was in Bradford's drawing room, throwing off her shawl and looking eagerly around.

"Where is he?" she demanded, breathless. "Charles, where's Patrick?"

"Not here yet, my dear," Charles said, folding the *Sporting Times* and putting it aside. "I'm glad you could get away tonight. I was afraid it might not be convenient for you to—"

"He *is* coming, isn't he?" Kate interrupted, almost frantic. "You *said* he would be here, Charles! But it's so late for a child to be out on the streets. Anything might happen to him out there! He might be hurt! He might—"

"Sit down, Kate." Charles stood with a smile and

113

gestured to his wing chair before the fire. "I'll get you a brandy."

Charles watched his wife as she sank into the chair, thinking how lovely she was when she was passionate—and she was certainly passionate about Patrick, who had taken the place in her heart of the child she had lost, of the children she would never have. But Charles knew boys, and he feared that her passion might frighten Patrick and send him hurtling away again.

He cleared his throat. "Patrick is hardly a child," he said quietly. "He's very much a young man. He's working in the stable at the Grange House, apprenticing as a jockey. As it turns out, he was Gladiator's traveling lad at the Derby. He—"

"A jockey!" Kate took the brandy Bradford offered her. "But what about school, for goodness sake?" Her voice rose. "What about our *plans* for him?"

"It would seem that Patrick has made his own plans for himself," Charles said. "He looks fit and in excellent health. But I very much fear," he added, hoping she would understand, "that any pressure on our part to return him to school will be met with resistance."

"But he needs an education!" Kate cried. "He needs—"

"Rather," Charles interrupted firmly, "I propose that we encourage him to make his own choices and stay in touch with him so that we can support him, whatever he chooses to do with his life." He paused. "I hope you can agree to that, my dear. Otherwise, I'm afraid we will lose him again."

"But I did so want—" She turned the brandy snifter in her fingers. "I'm afraid he won't—" After a moment she gave a small sigh. "Perhaps you're right, Charles. Perhaps I'm holding too hard, hoping too much." She studied him for a moment, her head tilted, her hair catching the fire-light. "The problem is that I've never been a boy, so I don't understand all their ways. But I know how often I do just the opposite thing, when someone gives me what sounds like an order." She smiled a little, and her voice took on a tone of light irony. "I shall try not to smother the poor child—the young man—with an overabundance of motherly love."

"Thank you, my dear." Charles sat back, grateful, as he often was, for his wife's intuitive understanding. He had the feeling, too, that when Kate saw Patrick and realized how he had grown in the months since they'd been apart, she would realize that he was right. To stay connected to Patrick, they had to let him go.

The door opened again, and Bradford came in. "Hello, Kate," he said warmly. "I hope that Mrs. Langtry did not think it rude that we took you away this evening."

"Not at all, as it turned out," Kate replied. "At teatime, she received a message from the Prince. It seems that he has come to visit his horses and is staying with Mr. Rothschild at the Palace House. Mrs. Langtry was invited to a late supper, so I was left to my own devices." She leaned forward, her gray eyes intent. "I am so glad I decided to visit Mrs. Langtry. She is utterly fascinating—but frightening, too!"

"Oh?" Bradford asked, amused. "The celebrated Gilded Lily, frightening? What's she done to you, Kate?"

"Well, see what you think," Kate said. Then, speaking slowly and carefully, as if she were trying to recall every detail, she told them what she had overheard in the garden outside Mrs. Langtry's drawing room, and what Amelia had told her afterward.

"Wait a minute," Charles said. "Do I understand that this man claims to have taken her jewels and disposed of them for her? *And* that he got rid of Edward Langtry as well?"

115

"That's the gist of it," Kate replied. "And what is equally interesting, she didn't attempt to dispute him. In fact, she begged him not to speak of it, for fear they might be overheard by the servants."

Bradford frowned. "The jewels—I was out of the country at the time. How was it that they were stolen?"

"It was quite an interesting story," Charles said. "According to the newspaper reports, she kept her jewels—forty thousand pounds' worth—in a black enameled tin box, which was reported to be fireproof. She carried the box with her when she toured with her plays, and when she was in London, left it in the Union Bank, quite close to her home. Several summers ago, '95, I think it was, she went to the Continent for a few weeks, and when she came back to London, sent her butler to the bank for the jewel box. He returned, distraught, with word that the bank had delivered the box to her some three weeks before. He was accompanied by an equally distraught bank officer, who showed Mrs. Langtry the handwritten order for the box. She immediately pointed out that the signature wasn't hers. It was forged from the Pear's Soap advertisement which bears her name."

"But they were her own jewels," Kate pointed out. "If she connived in their theft, she was only stealing from herself."

"But there's more," Charles said. "Shortly after the theft, she sued the bank for negligence, for the full amount of the loss. George Lewis represented her, I think. She settled for something like ten thousand pounds. I remember being surprised that Lewis didn't press for more."

"So it's possible that she had the bank's settlement," Bradford remarked, "and the jewels as well."

"Or the money they fetched," Charles said. "They were probably fenced immediately."

"Not a bad little coup, especially when the value of the publicity is counted into it," Bradford said. "I'm sure that once people learned of the loss, attendance at her plays shot up immediately." He frowned. "But what's this about a conspiracy to get rid of Edward Langtry, Kate? And who the devil was this man she was talking to?"

"Lillie never called him anything but that nickname," Kate said, "and I didn't catch more than a glimpse of him as he left. I cannot say for certain that there was a conspiracy, or how deeply Lillie was involved. She didn't contradict him, though, only pleaded with him not to talk about it for fear of being overheard. Before they parted, they were openly quarreling. They actually traded blows." She shook her head, as if not quite believing what she had heard. "I don't suppose he was injured, but she had to go to supper at the Rothschilds with a badly bruised cheek. She excused it to me by saying that she had run into an open door in the hallway."

"It wouldn't be the first time," Bradford said dryly. "When she was involved with that fellow Baird—the man people called the Squire—she sported black eyes and bruises quite regularly. When someone asked her why she put up with it, she said that for every black eye the Squire gave her, she got five thousand pounds' worth of apology—or so *Punch* claimed."

"An apology?" Charles murmured, "or blackmail?"

"Both, perhaps," Bradford replied in an ironic tone. "She went for a weekend in Paris with Bobby Peel, who had promised to buy her some new Worth gowns. When the Squire caught up with her, he beat the both of them. She was in hospital for a fortnight, and it was said that she suffered a broken nose. But she came out the richer by fifty thousand pounds and the title to his yacht. She called it the *White Lady*. Everybody else called it 'The Black Eye.'"

Kate looked thoughtful. "This man Baird, the Squire—he's dead?"

"He died in New Orleans five or six years ago," Bradford said. "Drank himself to death, according to the newspapers. At the time, it was quite a story—in part because of Mrs. Langtry's disappointment. Baird was worth some three or four million pounds, and she apparently expected to inherit. But he executed a codicil a few days before he departed for America, leaving everything to his mother. The Gilded Lily didn't get a penny."

"I wonder—" Kate began. But she didn't get to finish. There was a loud knocking at the door, and Patrick burst in, wild-eyed. His shirt was torn and dirty, his nose dripped blood, and there was blood smeared on his hand and on his shirt and knickers. He looked utterly panic-stricken.

Charles, taken aback, leapt to his feet with an exclamation of concern. Bradford, too, stood quickly and came forward. But Kate, to her great credit, scarcely batted an eyelash.

"Patrick!" she said warmly, "how very delightful to see you! I was so pleased when his lordship told me that you would be here tonight." She rose and went toward the boy. "My goodness, how tall you've grown, in such a very short time." She bent over and kissed him on both cheeks, then, looking down at his hand, added, with only the slightest concern in her voice, "You seem to have gotten into quite a bit of blood, though. Did you meet with an accident on your way?"

Kate's warm calm seemed to steady the boy. He took in a breath, straightened his shoulders, and turned to Charles. "It's Mr. Day, the bookmaker, sir. He's in the alley, behind the Great Horse." He looked down at his bloody hand and grimaced. "He's dead. Somebody killed him."

"By Jove!" Bradford exclaimed. "Old Badger's dead?"

He started toward the door. "Well, then, let's have a look. Come on, Sheridan. You too, boy. You can show us where you found him."

Kate put out a hand. "I think," she said, "that Patrick might stay here with me."

Charles stood and put his hand on the boy's shoulder, meeting his wife's eyes. "Patrick found the body, Kate, so the constable will want to speak with him. Stay here by the fire, my dear. We'll be back in a little while."

For a moment he thought she might argue to keep the boy with her. Then she reached for her shawl. "I'm coming too," she said firmly.

This time, Charles knew better than to object.

17

A Late Supper

"The first report of doping in racing horses in England occurred at Worksop, where an edict in 1666 banned the use of 'exciting substances...' Since time immemorial horses had been dosed with whiskey before races, but toward the end of the nineteenth century the pace accelerated. Stimulating doping as we know it today was apparently born and bred in the New World and came to the Old World about the year 1900..."

Drugs and the Performance Horse
THOMAS TOBIN, 1981

IT WAS NEARLY an hour later when the group rejoined in Bradford's lodging. The constable had been summoned, Patrick's scanty evidence taken, and the body of Alfred Day, bookmaker, borne off to the surgery of a nearby doctor, who would perform an autopsy the following morning. But as Kate watched the proceedings, she thought that it didn't require a doctor to confirm that the man had died violently. Anyone observing the corpse, even in the flickering light of the constable's lantern, would have remarked on the bloody hole in the front of his brown waistcoat and realized that it was made by a gun, fired at close range.

Bradford went directly to the sideboard. "I think a brandy is in order," he said, and began to pour.

"Patrick and I will have tea," Kate said, with a glance at the boy, whose face was still very white. "And perhaps you might see whether there is any bread and butter in the pantry. While Patrick washes up," she added, with a suggestive smile at the boy. She went to the gas kettle and lit it.

Bradford handed a brandy to Charles. "I think Mrs. Hardaway is still awake. I'll see what she can find for us."

A little later, Kate sat on one end of the sofa, pouring hot tea and passing a plate of bread and butter and slices of cake to Patrick, on the other end of the sofa. To her surprise, he took only one slice of bread and butter and declined the cake, explaining in a serious tone that all apprentice jockeys had to be very careful of their weight, for the lighter they were, the more likely they were to ride. To herself, Kate thought worriedly that Patrick could scarcely be much lighter, but she kept her concern to herself.

By mutual consent, there was little said about the dead man in the alleyway, other than Bradford's remark that Newmarket was a betting town and saw its share of violent quarrels, which usually took place over money or women and often resulted in bloodshed. Kate observed that the crime had nothing to do with them, aside from the unfortunate happenstance of Patrick's stumbling over the body, and changed the subject, drawing Patrick out about his adventures since leaving school and doing her best to show only interest and to hide the deep concern she felt at the thought of the boy tramping alone across half of southern England.

"Lord Charles tells me that you're enjoying your work at the stable," she said, after Patrick had sketched what was no doubt a much-abridged narrative of the months leading up to his coming to Newmarket. She smiled encouragingly. "I'm not surprised. I know how much you have always loved horses. And how very good you are with them."

Patrick nodded. "I do love horses," he said. "Especially Gladiator." There was a pause, and a guarded glance at Bradford, whom he had met for the first time that night. Then, to Charles, a tentative "I was hoping you might help, m'lord."

"Yes," Charles said, tamping his pipe and lighting it, "we must talk about the horse. You said that someone made him drink something out of a bottle. Tell us more, please."

With one more glance at Bradford, Patrick spoke rapidly, as if he were saying something he'd had on his mind for a while. "Well, you see, sir, Gladiator's a lazy horse—at least, on the track. But when he's galloped on Southfields or Across the Flat on the west side of town, he goes like the wind." A small, proud smile ghosted across his mouth. "As he did yesterday, with me up."

"But the horse didn't run like a lazy horse in the Derby," Bradford remarked, from the depths of his overstuffed chair.

"No, sir." Patrick's face darkened. "Before the race, when the farrier was putting on his plates, Mr. Pinkie and a veterinary surgeon came. They gave Gladiator something in a bottle, and it made him..." He gestured with his hands, helplessly, and Kate saw that there were still traces of the dead man's blood under his nails. "Right away, it made him act wild. It was all Johnny could do to get him off to a fair start, and when they got to the Corner, the horse ran against the rail and—" His voice failed him and he dropped his head.

"We know," Charles said sympathetically. "It's too bad."

Patrick's head came up. "It wasn't Johnny's fault," he said, in quick defense of his friend. A look of guilt washed over his face. "I had the chance to warn him and didn't. If I'd told him, maybe he would have ridden differently—or not at all."

"I doubt that's so," Bradford said gently. "When a horse turns savage, there's not much a jockey can do except try to hold on. And your friend couldn't reject a ride he'd agreed to and hope to keep riding—especially in the Derby."

"Gladiator's not a savage horse!" Patrick exclaimed. "At least, not by nature." Kate heard the indignation and outrage in his voice and realized how much he was altered from the boy she had known. "Whatever they made him drink," he said roughly, "that's what made him wild. The ones who poured that stuff down the horse—*they're* the ones who killed Johnny."

Charles took the pipe out of his mouth. "Did either of the two men happen to say what the substance was?"

"No, they didn't." Patrick looked at Charles. "Do you know what it was, sir?"

"Not specifically, no." Charles pulled on his pipe. "It had to have been a stimulant of some sort. Caffeine, perhaps, or cocaine or heroin—or some sort of mixture."

"If you don't mind my asking, sir," Patrick said, "why are you interested in what happened to Gladiator?"

"Because some of the men who monitor racing," Charles replied, "want to make doping illegal. It's unfair, and dangerous, both to the horse and to other horses and riders."

"If you had some of the stuff," Patrick said slowly, "would that help?"

Charles regarded him. "I'm more keen to know who used it, and you've already helped to answer that question." He paused. "Although, from a scientific point of view, I should certainly like to know what it is, so that an attempt can be made to develop a reliable chemical test, using blood or urine, or even the horse's saliva. Without such a test, it will never be possible to say for sure whether or not a horse has been doped." He puffed on his pipe. "Do you know where I might obtain the stuff?"

Patrick looked up, hesitating.

"It's all right, Patrick," Kate said, putting a hand on the boy's arm. "You can tell us. No one will be angry."

"Well, then," he said, "I nicked the bottle."

The corners of Bradford's mouth quirked. "You nicked the bottle?"

Patrick nodded. "When Mr. Angus made me Gladiator's traveling lad, he said I was responsible for anything that happened to the horse, and that I should keep a close eye on him to make sure he wasn't interfered with. I'd never seen the surgeon before, and I don't think much of Mr. Pinkie." He made a face. "He's Mr. Angus's nephew and he's supposed to be the second head trainer, but he's more interested in betting on the races than he is in training the horses and taking good care of them. I couldn't stop them from doing what they were doing, but I thought—" He shook his head, and Kate saw him trying to swallow his anger. "I saw where the surgeon tossed the bottle. After the race, I picked it up and put it with Gladiator's gear. It wasn't quite empty."

"I see," Charles said gravely. "And where is this bottle now?"

"It's under the floorboard in the loft where I sleep," Patrick said. There was an evident note of relief in his voice, and Kate thought that he was glad to be able to share his secret with someone, and perhaps also glad to get rid of the incriminating bottle. "I'll give it to you. Maybe you can find out what's in it." He shuddered. "I don't ever want to see Gladiator like that again—his eyes staring and the sweat pouring off him in buckets, and running as if the devil was after him."

"That bottle," Charles said. "Can you bring it here tomorrow night, without being detected?"

"I think so, sir. The lads work hard all day, and sleep hard, too. We don't bed down the horses until Mr. Angus comes round to feel their legs and tendons and look them over. As soon as he's come and gone, it's supper and bed. Five o'clock in the morning comes awf'lly early. That's when we take the horses out for first exercise."

Kate smiled. "Five o'clock will come early tomorrow, too," she reminded him, and Charles stood.

"Her ladyship is right," he said. "It's late, my boy. But just one or two more questions before you go. When and where is Gladiator racing next?"

"There's a handicap here at Newmarket," Patrick said promptly. "On Friday."

"Thank you," Charles said. "Do you know who'll be riding?"

Kate saw a hopeful look cross Patrick's face, then fade away. She knew he was wishing that he could ride the horse, and knowing at the same time that this was impossible.

"No, sir," he said finally. "Besides Johnny Bell, there are two other jockeys who regularly ride for the stable, Bill Stevens and Dan Watts. It'll be one of them, most like."

And with that, Patrick went out into the night, Kate was driven back to Regal Lodge, and the eventful Monday was concluded.

18

Tuesday, 6 June, 1899

At the Jockey Club

"The Sporting Life of England!
The Charter of the Isle!
Perish the traitor, heart and hand,
That would, with dastard wile,
Sow discord, jealousy, or strife,
Among the gallant band
Who share and shield our Sporting Life,
The Charter of the Land!"

Late 18th-century song in praise of the Jockey Club

As HE HAD previously planned, Bradford took himself off the next morning to spend the day with his fiancée in Cambridge—but not before reminding Charles that they were to have dinner that night at Wolford Lodge, the home of Edith's mother, on the Cambridge Road.

"I'm sure you'll enjoy Edith's stepfather," he said as he left. "Colonel Harry Hogsworth, his name is. He has several horses at the Grange House Stable. He may be able to give us some useful information."

Charles was breakfasting on the omelet and toast that

126

Mrs. Hardaway had brought up for him and reading an article in the *Manchester Guardian* about the annulment of Alfred Dreyfus's sentence and the order for his return from Devil's Island to face a second court-martial at Rennes. It was a case Charles had followed since Dreyfus's first trial in 1894, and he couldn't help but feel both relief and dismay: relief at the hope that the French military tribunal would eventually see reason and clear Captain Dreyfus, who had so obviously been made a scapegoat; and dismay that the man would have to undergo yet another humiliating trial. The fundamental unfairness of this ugly business, this appalling miscarriage of justice, had gnawed at Charles for five long years now, but there was nothing that could be done. Events would simply have to take their course.

These thoughts were interrupted when a young man arrived, bearing a note from Admiral North. With apologies, Charles was summoned to the Club at his earliest convenience, within the hour, if at all possible. Reading the note, Charles raised his eyebrows. He wasn't surprised that Owen North was at Newmarket, for the Jockey Club was officially headquartered here, but he was astonished at such an early-morning summons. He sent the boy back with word that he was on his way, finished his coffee, put on his hat, and set off. Out on the street, he looked up at the lowering gray clouds, turned back, and located a spare black umbrella in the stand in Mrs. Hardaway's front hallway.

It was not quite raining, but the early June air was dense with drizzle and Charles was glad of the umbrella. As he walked, he passed a dress-shop window and noticed a blue wool shawl that made him think of Kate, the thought of her reminding him of what she had said the evening before. He frowned. Was it possible that Mrs. Langtry had connived at the theft of her jewels—and at the death of

127

her husband? And who was this man who cared for her so passionately that he was willing to steal and kill for her?

These thoughts occupied Charles until he reached the Jockey Club, which was located in a collection of buildings that turned its back on the High Street. These headquarters, Charles knew, had begun as a coffee house, first leased by the Club in the 1750s and expanded, with an indifferent attention to architecture, over the years. In the early 1880s, fifty-odd bedrooms had been added to accommodate members coming for the race meetings, and also a suite of apartments for HRH. In addition to the buildings on the High Street, the Club had also acquired large tracts of Newmarket Heath from the private individuals who had originally owned them, and its control extended to Newmarket racecourse as well.

All these physical expansions reflected the Jockey Club's growing authority over the Turf. In the early days and until about twenty-five years before, racing had been clouded by dishonesty, corruption, and outright crime, with crooked jockeys and stable staff manipulating the performance of horses while corrupt handicappers and race officials affected the outcomes at the course. But Lord George Bentinck had used several major scandals to tighten the Club's procedures, Admiral Henry Rous had gone on to clean up handicapping, and by the seventies, the Club had written a set of rules that gave them almost complete control over the Turf: the authority to draw up handicaps; to manage the sums and payment of prize-money; to license officials and racecourses; and to govern conduct and punish misconduct. In fact, the only thing the Club refused to regulate was betting, which the Stewards had delegated to Tattersall's Committee a dozen or so years before, retaining only the right to deal with defaulters.

But while the Club's rules tended toward the autocratic, the Stewards themselves might tend toward the lenient, overlooking infractions when they found it politic to do so. In fact, in yesterday's *Sporting Times*, Charles had read an irreverent remark to the effect that when it came to the American invasion of trainers and jockeys, the current Stewards were "playing Shut-Eye" to such an extent that "they look like the three blind mice." He wondered whether Admiral North had read that criticism, and how he might feel about it.

At the door, Charles pulled a brass bell. A footman took his umbrella and directed him upstairs, where he found Owen North behind a desk in a well-appointed office with a series of paintings of horses on the walls and an enlarged photograph of the Prince of Wales with Persimmon, who won the Derby in '96. To Charles's surprise, the Newmarket chief constable was there as well, perched uneasily on the edge of a chair, turning his bowler hat in his heavy hands. Jack Murray, the Club's investigator, lounged morosely against a wall.

"Ah, Sheridan," Admiral North said, rising and extending his hand. His face was troubled and his voice tense. "I'm sorry to bring you out so early, but we are confronted with an unfortunate bit of business."

"Perfectly all right, Admiral," Charles said, seating himself.

"This," the admiral said, gesturing toward the policeman, "is Chief Constable Watson. He has brought me news of a murder in Newmarket. It seems that one of the local bookmakers, Alfred Day, was shot last night in the alleyway behind the Great Horse."

"As it happens," Charles said, "a boy of my acquaintance stumbled over the body and brought me word of it. I was there when the constable arrived. Bloody business,

I must say." He glanced at Watson, whose expression was unreadable. "One of your men conducted a brief investigation and the body was taken off to the surgeon's." He sat back, crossing his legs, thinking that with the prizefighting, wagering, and general rowdiness in the town, back-alley violence must be a regular occurrence and murders not uncommon. What did this particular death have to do with the Club—or with him?

Rubbing his chin, Owen North at last produced an answer to Charles's unspoken question. "It's possible, indeed, even likely, that there's a connection between the murder of Alfred Day and the business that you and Mr. Murray are currently looking into. At my request, Chief Constable Watson has agreed to take his men off the case and turn the investigation over to you."

Take his men off the case? Charles thought, surprised. *Does the Club wield that kind of power?* "I'm not sure I quite understand," he said, with an interrogatory glance at the policeman, and waited for him to say something.

A red-haired, burly man whose nose was covered with a fine network of tiny broken veins, the chief constable looked as if he'd be much more at his ease in the back room of the Great Horse than in the offices of the Jockey Club. He regarded his hat for a moment.

"Well, sir," he muttered, "as I told the admiral, sir, it seems as it's got more to do with the Club than the town. In which case, sir—"

"Indeed, Watson," the admiral said. "Very well put." He stood and extended his hand. "Thank you for coming, and for assisting in this matter. I think we need not keep you from your duties any longer."

"One moment, please," Jack Murray said, stepping forward. "You've talked to the widow, Constable?"

"One of my men took her the news," the chief constable

said. "That was last night, right after it happened."

"Thank you," Murray said. He stepped back and fell silent again.

When the chief constable had gone, North sat down again. "Sorry for this, Sheridan," he said in a low voice. "Afraid it complicates your task, rather."

Charles regarded this as an understatement. He had hoped, after he'd obtained the bottle from Patrick and had located and spoken with the veterinary surgeon, to make his report and recommendations to the Stewards and be done with the matter. An investigation into a shooting in a dark alleyway, with no suspects ready at hand, was no part of his original commitment—and it was much more than a minor complication. The silence was broken by the wheezy chime of the clock on the wall as it struck the half-hour.

"Why is it that you suspect a connection between Day's death and the doping?" Charles finally asked.

North studied his fingers, straightened the blotter on the desk, and glanced toward the window as though he hoped to find some distraction there. At last he said, reluctantly: "Alfred Day—he was commonly known as Badger—came to me a few days ago, here in this office. He wanted to complain generally about the practice of doping, and specifically as it related to the last running of the Derby. It appears that quite a number of people bet heavily upon Gladiator and have been unable to settle." His smile was crooked. "He said that he felt doping was bad for business."

Jack Murray pushed himself away from the wall. "It is, sir," he said dourly. "For all his other dishonesties, and God knows there were plenty, Badger was an honest bookmaker. He knew horses, and he knew people, and he studied the form book. But doping changes everything,

131

sir. The good bookies hate it, 'cause it makes the outcome less predictable." He waved his hand, speaking more warmly. "O' course, they hear the touts and tips, too, and when they think a horse is doped to win, they're willin' enough to make their own wager, to cover themselves. But they're against it, to a man, Admiral. They'd be glad to see it stopped."

Owen North sat motionless during this speech, his face impassive. He made no answer.

"So it is only Day's complaint that ties him to the doping?" Charles asked. If he had to look into a murder, particularly one in which half the rogues in Newmarket might be implicated, he'd much rather start with some useful information.

North looked away. "He implied," he said, "that he could name names, quite important names. Since the matter obviously involved wagering, I suggested that he approach Tattersall's Committee with his complaint. But he argued that this had to do with the performance of the horse, not the wager, and of course, there is the matter of the objection, which has not yet been settled. He insisted that his complaint was related to the objection, and hence should be heard by the Stewards." The admiral's eyes were expressionless. "I am sure you understand the Stewards' reluctance to hear such a complaint at this time. In the event, I told him that the matter was under investigation and that he would be contacted."

"But he didn't name names," Charles said, watching the other's face. He had thought he knew Owen North well, and could testify to his complete straightforwardness. Now, he wasn't quite sure.

"I'm afraid not." North turned toward the window so that Charles could see only the shadowed half of his face. "Perhaps you're thinking that Day's coming here might have nothing to do with his death, and that the investigation should have been left to the police." He turned back, his jaw set, his eyes narrowed. He spoke with force. "I know these Newmarket constables, Sheridan. They manage to contain the local thuggery, more or less, and they maintain a decent order at the race meetings. But they *cannot* be relied upon to keep matters confidential."

There was a tension in the admiral's face that Charles couldn't quite read. Was it apprehension, or evasion, or was it deceit? Charles gave what might have been seen as an affirming nod, and North appeared to relax.

"Indeed," he said, with a touch of cordiality. "I think you can appreciate why I want you to intervene in this, Charles. The problem is very clear. The Newmarket constabulary simply can't be allowed to intrude into what might very well turn out to be vital Club interests."

"Yes," Charles said. "I see." He didn't, really, though, and he was troubled by that elusive look on Owen North's face. He let the silence lengthen, then sat forward in his chair, engaging the admiral's eyes. He spoke firmly.

"I cannot undertake this aspect of the investigation without your word as a gentleman that the murderer, if and when he is discovered, will be handed over to the authorites and dealt with according to the law." If the Club believed itself above the law, or intended to use him to subvert the law, he would wash his hands of this dirty business forthwith. He would walk out of the room and fetch Kate and they could both go back to Bishop's Keep. He would—

"Oh, very well," North said shortly, "you may have my word—although I cannot think why you should need it. Naturally, the law will be taken into account."

Charles said nothing. It was not the wholehearted assurance he had hoped for. But now he was beginning to feel intrigued. North seemed to know, or suspect, more than he was saying. But perhaps more to the point, if Charles refused to take on the investigation, he felt it quite likely that North would find someone else who would—and who might not be so concerned about the law's jurisdiction.

The admiral, taking silence for consent, smiled with evident relief. "Well, then," he said briskly, "the matter is in your hands. And of course, you shall have Mr. Murray's excellent assistance." He pulled out a gold watch and frowned down at it, then up to the clock on the wall. "Blasted clock is twenty minutes late. I'm afraid I must be off. His Majesty is at the Rothschilds' today and wants to discuss some Club affairs." He stood. "I'm sure he'll be glad to know that you're looking into this matter for us, Charles. He has the greatest confidence in you."

When he had gone, Charles allowed the silence to settle. Finally, he looked at Jack Murray, who was staring out the window. "It appears that there is more to this than we knew, Murray."

"It seems so, sir," Murray said, turning. His face was glum. "But it's just as likely that Badger was done in to avoid the payment of a debt, or because he'd crossed someone he shouldn't." He sighed heavily. "It's happened before, sir."

"I imagine that there is a great deal of risk attached to the profession," Charles agreed. "I don't suppose you'd happen to know precisely where Mr. Day carried out his business."

Murray became more alert. "I do, sir. In St. James Street. Number Twenty-nine."

"And whether he had an assistant?"

"There's a clerk, sir, and a partner. The clerk is called Sobersides. The partner is named Baggs, Edward Baggs. Eddie, they call him."

"Mr. Murray," Charles said, "you are a fount of information." He rose and put on his hat. "I propose that we pay a visit to Number Twenty-Nine and see what we can learn from Sobersides or Mr. Edward Baggs, or both."

19

Regal Lodge

"I love acting. It is so much more real than life."
The Picture of Dorian Gray
OSCAR WILDE

"Try as we may, we cannot get behind things to the reality. And the terrible reason may be that there is no reality in things apart from their appearances."
OSCAR WILDE

KATE WAS AWAKENED at eight-thirty when Amelia brought a tray with tea and a copy of *The Times*, with a front-page story about the International Congress of Women, which would take place later that month at the Church House, Westminster. The Countess of Aberdeen would preside, and delegates from various colonies and foreign countries were expected. Kate noted the date, 26 June, and decided that she would attend. Perhaps there would be an opportunity to speak with interested women about her school.

But important as the Congress might be, it was not

topmost in Kate's mind, for she had a great deal to think about as she sipped her morning tea. Her heart was filled with delight and relief at seeing Patrick. How strong and resourceful he had grown, and how handsome! But although he seemed happy enough, she sensed that he harbored more uneasiness about that horse—and perhaps more guilt over the death of his jockey friend—than he had been willing to show the night before. She hoped Charles would find a way to help the boy.

But while Kate's heart was full of Patrick, her mind was occupied with other things. There was the unhappy event of last night: Patrick's discovery of the murdered man in the alleyway behind the Great Horse. But far more urgently, there was the intense and growing fascination she felt for Lillie Langtry—the Gilded Lily, Bradford had called her. Today she would make a concentrated effort to learn more about the woman—about the private person who must live somewhere within the actress. Under the guise of an interviewer for *The Strand*, she would probe as deeply as she dared, looking for the real Lillie.

Kate dressed and went down for breakfast carrying a small notebook and fountain pen. She was shown to a smaller room adjacent to the dining room, wallpapered in a pale green flock, with green draperies over sheer curtains that softened and dimmed the light from the east-facing windows. French doors opened onto a flower-filled glass conservatory, and the sweet scent of jasmine filled the air.

Lillie Langtry, dressed in an elegant blue shantung silk with chemisette and collar of ecru tucked net, was already at the table, reading a folded newspaper and breakfasting on dry toast and coffee. When Kate entered, she looked up and smiled warmly.

"Ah, Beryl, good morning!" She gestured toward the

sideboard, which was laden with chafing dishes filled with eggs, sausages, kippers, muffins, and toast. "Choose what you like, my dear. If you prefer something else, it can be brought from the kitchen."

"Thank you," Kate replied, and allowed the footman to help her to an egg, a sausage, some fruit, and a muffin. As the footman held her chair, the butler appeared with a silver coffee pot, poured a steaming cup, and both withdrew.

"You're lovely this morning, dear," Lillie said, glancing at Kate. She opened a brocade cigarette pouch and took out a cigarette, fitting it into an elaborately carved ivory holder. "Such a sweet little white dress. I do so like batiste for summer, although I don't wear it myself, as I once did."

Kate smiled slightly as she stirred her coffee. "I trust you enjoyed your dinner with the Prince last evening."

"Oh, I did, very much," Lillie said, "although we made an early evening of it." She lit her cigarette with a match and took several puffs. "I was home and asleep by midnight."

This was strange, Kate thought, since she had heard Lillie's carriage arriving in the gravel drive shortly after three in the morning. Or perhaps it was not Lillie's carriage. Perhaps she had entertained a guest, and he was not arriving, but departing. Glancing up, she saw that the bruise on the actress's cheek, while it was still evident, had been artfully camouflaged, and it crossed her mind that the softly filtered light in the room might be contrived to conceal the facial imperfections of a woman who would be fifty in a few more years. For an instant, Kate felt a fleeting pity for Lillie, whose face and figure were literally her fortune and who lived as a public spectacle. She must fret each moment that someone might take a critical view of the lines on her face, or find fault with the simplicity of her dress, or remark that her figure wasn't what it had once been. But the pity flickered out in an instant, for Kate knew that Lillie Langtry had chosen to live in this way and could choose differently whenever she wished—if she were willing to pay the price.

"And you, my dear Beryl?" Lillie asked, over her coffee cup. Her laugh was light. "I'm so sorry I had to leave you yesterday evening. I expect you were well entertained—although I daresay that it is a rare wife who goes off to a romantic supper with her husband when she is on holiday from home. Most wives of my acquaintance prefer to have supper with their lovers."

"Mine is a rare husband," Kate replied, "whom I much prefer to a lover." She buttered her muffin. "But I'm afraid my evening with Lord Charles was somewhat less than romantic. There was a murder in the alleyway and—"

"A murder!" Lillie exclaimed. She put down her cup and pulled on her cigarette, her eyebrows delicately arched under the hair that was fluffed across her forehead. "Good heavens, how utterly *delicious!* Oh, my dear Beryl, do tell me all about it!"

"There was nothing delicious about it at all," Kate said gravely. "It was quite sordid, I'm afraid. One of the Newmarket bookmakers was shot to death in the alleyway behind the Great Horse."

"But your imagination must have been roused, certainly," Lillie replied, the smoke drifting from her nostrils. "You have written about murders in your stories. As I recall, there's a murder in *The Duchess*. The man who attempts to sell the stolen jewels—he's murdered, isn't he?" She closed her eyes. "I can see it on the stage already, Beryl. It will be a thrilling play, full of drama and high morality." She opened her eyes wide and raised one arm in a sweeping gesture. "The duchess's stolen jewels are redeemed! The villain receives his just punishment! Cecil Howard will love it. He is always looking for the moral in every play he reviews, the nasty man."

Kate thought that very soon she should have to disabuse Mrs. Langtry of her mistaken notion that *The Duchess* was going to be staged—but not quite yet. "The difficulty," she said, "is that fictional murders are quite different from real ones. There was a great deal of blood last night, *real* blood. The ground was soaked with it. And the victim couldn't pick himself up when the curtain came down and go out to take his bows, or hear the applause of the audience, or read the reviews of his performance. He was dead, and his poor wife and children—"

"Oh, pooh," Lillie scoffed, resting her cigarette on a small silver ashtray and picking up her cup. "Bookmakers don't have wives and children. They have mean little men who run after them with black books. That's where they keep the names of the people who owe them money."

"This one had a wife," Kate said. "He wore a wedding ring."

Lillie's laugh tinkled merrily. "How like an author to observe such a thing, Beryl! Who, pray tell, was this poor bookmaker who expired in the alley? Perhaps I know him." She laughed. "Perhaps I even owe him a pound or two." She made a wry face and added, in a different voice. "In fact, I am sure I owe him a pound or two. I doubt there's a bookmaker in town to whom I don't owe something."

"His name is Day, I believe," Kate said, putting down her fork. "He seems to have been called Badger." Suddenly she was not very hungry, thinking of poor Mr. Day's family gathered around a breakfast table where one chair was vacant and would never be filled. Whatever his occupation, he was a human being, who had felt love and anger and fear and—

There was a strangled sound, and a crash of porcelain.

Kate looked up to see that Lillie's face had gone ashen. Her eyes were wide and dark. The cup lay broken on the table, and a splash of coffee stained the bodice of Lillie's blue silk dress.

"Lillie!" Kate exclaimed, putting her hand on the other's arm. "Are you all right? Shall I call someone?" She reached for the small brass bell that sat on the table. "The butler? Or would you prefer your maid?"

"No!" Lillie shook her head violently and sucked in her breath with a small gasping noise. She made a fist and held it to her mouth, coughing. "I'm—I'm fine. A mouthful of coffee just went the wrong way down." She coughed again, and began to fan herself violently with her other hand. "Such a little thing, really. Don't trouble yourself, please."

The momentary lapse into what had seemed to Kate like real emotion was almost under control and the actress had nearly regained command—but not quite. The rouge on Lillie's cheeks showed as bright circles against the pallor of her skin and the hand at her mouth was trembling.

Kate sat back. "I know that sometimes it helps to talk about things that distress us," she said quietly. It was true, or at least it had always been so with her, and she spoke with unfeigned compassion. "I would hold anything you share with me in the utmost confidence, Lillie."

For a brief instant, Lillie's eyes met hers. Her lips trembled and she seemed on the very edge of speaking. But then she stepped back from the brink.

"There's nothing to share, my dear," she said, with an enormous effort at naturalness. She reached for her damask napkin and dropped it onto the small puddle of coffee, which was threatening to drip off the table and onto the floor. "I was... merely startled. You see, I know Mr. Day. Anyone who has ever placed a bet at the racecourse knows him." She forced a careless smile. "He's become rather a Newmarket fixture, and I must say that he's taken a great deal of my money over the past few years." She closed her eyes briefly and opened them again, wide. "But of course winning and losing is part of the game of racing. One doesn't hold his successes against him."

Kate gave Lillie a sympathetic look. "Oh, of course," she said, and added, tactfully, "I'm sure I would be quite startled if one of my acquaintances were to suffer a similar fate. Had you seen him recently?"

Ignoring the question, Lillie glanced down at her stained bodice and pushed back her chair. "My, haven't I made a right royal mess of myself," she said with a shaky laugh. "I'll go and change. And when I come back, you can ask me all the questions you like and write down every answer in that notebook of yours."

Kate watched her make her exit—an impressive one, under the circumstances. But Kate, and Beryl Bardwell, were left to wonder what secret connection had existed between Lillie Langtry and the murdered bookmaker. Her reaction had been so dramatic, yet so *real*. Was it merely surprise, or something more? Was she afraid? Of what? Of whom? Why?

But Kate also knew that while Lillie Langtry might pretend to complete candor, the answers to these questions were not likely to come from her.

20

In St. James Street

"Welshers, bookies who took your money but were nowhere to be found if your horse won, were without question the most hated of all racecourse crooks. If caught, they were usually subjected to a terrible vengeance by an enraged racing crowd. The treatment differed from course to course: at Catterick they were tarred and feathered, while at any course close to a river they were stripped naked and thrown into the water. More than one welsher was done to death."

The Fast Set: The World of Edwardian Racing
GEORGE PLUMPTRE

ST. JAMES PROVED to be a cobbled street only one block long not far from the Jockey Club and the Subscription Rooms, where bookmakers and racehorse owners assembled and called over the racing card on the night before a big race. Number Twenty-nine was a narrow, two-story redbrick building with a small plate-glass window set in the front, hung with heavy green draperies to prevent curious passersby from seeing within. On the outside of the window was painted *Alfred Day, Racing Commissions* in ornate black lettering trimmed and bordered in gold. A folded copy of the *Sporting Times* lay on the stoop where it had been tossed and a CLOSED sign hung crookedly across the front door. Charles pressed his face to the glass and peered into the dark interior, but he could see nothing.

"They ain't in th' office, sir," piped a shrill voice. "They don't gen'rally open up 'fore noon."

Charles turned to see a ragged boy of ten or eleven. The rain that had succeeded the earlier drizzle had ceased, but there was still a fine mist in the air, and the boy's hair and clothing were thoroughly wet. He was pushing a muddy wooden barrow into which a twig cage, bound with leather thongs, had been haphazardly set. The cage contained three twittering ferrets pushing frantically against the bars.

Charles went back down the steps to the street, followed by Jack Murray. "You know Mr. Day, then?" Charles asked.

The boy nodded vigorously, set down his barrow with a thud, and pushed his wet hair off his forehead. "If y'er 'ere to place a bet, sir, yer might go round th' back an' ring. Sobersides 'as a room upstairs. If 'e's in, 'e'll take care o' yer."

Charles reached into his pocket for a coin. "Thank you," he said. "Do you live nearby?"

"Back there, in a room, sir, wiv me mother an' brothers, sir." Pocketing the coin, the boy pointed down a dark passageway between two brick buildings across the street. At the end of the passageway was a dingy courtyard, and yet another building.

"I see," Charles said. He looked down at the ferrets, which were scrambling over one another in their frantic efforts to escape. "I suppose you went out early this morning to tend your ferret traps, did you?" He paused. "I wonder if you saw anyone attempting to enter Mr. Day's office."

The boy gave this question some thought, seemed on the brink of speaking, then hesitated. Charles found another coin and proffered it. The boy took it eagerly.

"I wuz out at three, sir, 'fore the rain. Ferrets is 'ard t' catch in the day. They sleeps then, down in their dens. So they 'as to be got before dawn." He gestured toward the bookmaker's establishment. "When I went out, there wuz two men comin' round from th' back, 'urryin' like. Seemed odd t'me, sir, it bein' the middle of the night, which is why I recollects it."

Jack Murray, standing behind Charles, stepped forward. "What kind of men?" he asked. "Gentlemen?"

"Oh no, sir, not gentl'men, sir," the boy said, "not from the way they talked. But 'twas too dark t'see 'oo they wuz." He picked up the handles of his barrow. "If that's all, sirs, I'll be on me way. Mr. Thatcher 'as promised t'pay well fer th' ferrets, fer th' match tonight."

Charles had never been to a ferret match, but he knew that the little creatures were set against rats, and wagers were laid as to how many they would kill. The caged animals were sleek and beautiful, and the thought that they would be used in bloody sport was utterly repugnant to him.

"How well does Mr. Thatcher pay you to fetch ferrets?" he asked.

"A crown apiece, sir!" the boy said proudly. "It's a great deal more than 'e pays fer rats, which is wot I usu'lly sells 'im. When I kin, I sells ferrets, though they're terr'ble 'ard to catch. Only thing that'll get 'em into the traps is kippers."

Charles squatted down beside the barrow, remembering that he had seen ferrets sold on the London streets for a pound each. Mr. Thatcher was not overgenerous with his ragged young ferret-finder.

"These are very fine ferrets," he said. "Quite fat and amazingly strong-looking. I believe I fancy them myself. Would you take a guinea for the three of them?"

"A guinea!" The boy's eyes grew large. "Oh, yes, sir! 'Deed I would, sir!"

Charles drew out his purse and fished through an assortment of copper, silver, and gold coins. He extracted a gold sovereign and a silver shilling and pressed them into the child's hand. Then he picked up the wooden cage, set it on the street, and released the catch. The trio of ferrets pushed eagerly out, and were gone in an instant.

The boy's face puckered and Charles thought he might cry. "But I thought yer wanted 'em, sir!" he cried, holding onto his fortune as if he feared it might be taken away from him. "An' now they're gone!"

"I wanted to see them run," Charles said mildly, restoring the cage to the barrow. "They're very fast, aren't they?"

The boy looked down at the coins and quickly recovered himself. "Oh, 'deed they are, sir," he said, "an' fierce as kin be wiv rats." Shaking his head at the inexplicable whims and whimsies of gentlemen, he pocketed the coins, picked up his barrow, and turned with alacrity into the passageway on the other side of the street.

"Well, then, Murray," Charles said, dusting his hands, "suppose we go around to the back and see if this man Sobersides will answer our ring."

Jack Murray said not a word about the vanished ferrets. Instead, he went ahead of Charles around the building, past a derelict row of dustbins, to a narrow wooden stoop at the back. A calico cat was sitting on the top step but as the men approached, it jumped down with an annoyed meow and disappeared into the straggly bushes that filled the narrow yard.

Murray climbed the steps. A bell hung beside the door, and he pulled a dirty string, ringing it loudly. After a moment, he rang it again, and then again. From the bushes, the calico cat renewed its complaint.

"It doesn't seem, sir," the investigator said, looking down at Charles, "that there's anybody here."

"Well, then," Charles said reasonably, "I suggest that we try the door. If it's locked—"

It was. But Murray, a man of many talents, took a ring of keys from his pocket and, on the third try, unlocked the door. The hinges creaked when he pushed it open and he hallooed loudly, waited a moment, listening, then hallooed again.

"Doesn't seem to be anyone here, sir," he said, and Charles followed him into the gloomy interior.

They had entered a dark, narrow hallway. There was a closed door on the right, with a sign that said Office, Private and another at the end of the hall, standing open. Charles stepped past Murray, through the open door and into a spacious room, quite elegantly furnished: the Newmarket headquarters of Alfred Day, Bookmaker.

Murray entered behind Charles. "Well," he remarked, "this is a bit of all right, wouldn't you say, sir? Badger's done quite well for himself."

On the way to St. James Street, Murray had told Charles what he had learned about Alfred Day, with whom the investigator had been slightly acquainted before he retired from the Yard. Badger had been variously employed before he transformed himself into a bookmaker, most of his business being conducted on the shady side of the law. Day's father and brother had been Newmarket pawnbrokers, and Badger had started in that business, opening a pawnshop of his own in London. It wasn't long before the enterprising young fellow had branched out into the fencing of stolen goods and occasionally into outright theft. But Badger was also clever, and although he was occasionally picked up for questioning, he managed to keep himself from prosecution. He was adept at gaming, too, and regularly frequented the Hotel Metropole, where the smart and sporting sets gathered in the casino and billiards room. He won and lost a great deal of money there, on the fringes of several substantial frauds.

But after a number of years in London, Badger seemed to have determined on a different course. He returned to Newmarket, married a draper's widow with a bit of money of her own, and set himself up as a bookmaker, catering to the fashionable crowd while making himself available to all sorts. The competition was challenging, since there were already a great many established bookmakers in town, but he had immediately flourished, quickly expanding his business to include a variety of wagering activities. Within three years of leaving London, Alfred Day was accounted one of the three or four leading bookmakers in Newmarket.

When Charles expressed surprise at Mr. Day's speedy success, Murray offered the opinion that it was partly due to his reputation for honesty—that is, he was not known to have welshed on a bet—and partly to his having taken on as his partner a certain Eddie Baggs, from Brighton. Baggs, who apparently knew a very great deal about horses, proved to have a genius for numbers and understood the mechanics of making a book to show a profit. While Badger might have been somewhat less gifted than Baggs in the fine art of making a book, he had proved to be an astute businessman, demonstrating a great skill in manipulating his competitors. The partnership had proved to be a success. Within the first year Badger and Baggs had bought up the businesses of several of their smaller competitors, adding that custom to their own. By the second year, they had established a second office in London—and neither were hole-in-the-corner affairs, either, where fugitive betting was carried out by weasel-faced clerks. These were fashionable offices, located in areas frequented by smart people, where the swells could gather, smoke their cigars, and exchange racing tips and tidbits.

The Newmarket office was of this sort, Charles saw, as he looked around. The room was dark, but enough light filtered through the draperies over the front window to see that it was carpeted and furnished as a gentleman's club, with large sofas and stuffed chairs, elegant mahogany breakfronts and bookcases, tables and chairs for gaming and other tables and chairs for catered meals. The walls were hung with gilt-framed paintings of horses and various landscapes and portraits, the high ceiling sparkled with crystal chandeliers, and the lingering odor of cigar smoke hung on the air. The whole interior spoke of gentlemanly leisure and luxury and good taste. Whatever the actual condition of his financial affairs, Mr. Alfred Day had at least succeeded in making a great show of success.

But the room was empty, and Charles could see there was nothing more to be learned beyond the general impression. Back in the hall, he tapped on the door marked Office. Hearing nothing, he opened it.

This room was far more utilitarian than the club room in the front. There was a large blackboard on one wall, scrawled with hieroglyphics that Charles could not read; the other walls were papered with calendars of sporting events and announcements of various kinds. There was a desk, a wooden cabinet, and a bookcase.

But these things were not what caught and held Charles's

attention. It was the litter of papers on the floor; the desk and cabinet drawers pulled out, and spilled; the books torn and tossed; the two overturned chairs; and the general chaos that had resulted from a violent and haphazard ransacking by someone who was bent on destruction.

Behind Charles, Jack Murray made a low, growling noise.

"Yes," Charles said without turning. "It appears that someone was here before us."

"D'you suppose Sobersides is up there?" Murray asked. He nodded toward a steep, open flight of stairs, almost like a ladder, at the back of the room. "Shall I have a quick look, sir? He might be dead."

"He might be alive," Charles said, "and armed. We'll both go." Carrying his stick, he climbed the stairs. At the top, he put his hat on the stick and lifted it just above the level of the opening in the floor. When nothing happened, he withdrew his hat and climbed up onto the second floor, which proved to be an open loft, with windows at either end.

There was no need for caution, he saw immediately, for the loft room had no human occupant, alive or dead. There was a bed in one corner, the covers flung back, and a square deal table by one window, in the center of which stood an unlit paraffin lamp with a dirty chimney. On the table were the remains of a shepherd's pie and an empty bottle of ale.

Murray went to a wooden dresser and pulled open the drawers, revealing a jumble of shirts and stockings and underclothing, then to a makeshift corner closet, where he jerked aside the hanging sheet to reveal a well-worn black coat and two pairs of black trousers. An empty satchel and a pair of Wellingtons sat beneath.

"Doesn't look like he took his clothes," Murray remarked.

"Either he left in a hurry, or he means to come back."

Back downstairs, Charles poked around in the litter of papers and torn books. There was a small safe in the corner, gaping open. If it had once contained ledger books or the records of betting transactions, they had vanished.

Murray looked around with a frown. "I'd say, sir, that we're left with a question or two. D'you suppose Badger was killed because he failed to pay up on a bet?"

"It's possible," Charles said. "It's equally possible that he was killed because he wanted to collect. But I doubt if we'll find any answers here." He took out his watch. "I'm off to visit the doctor who has possession of Badger's body. Why don't you see what you can learn about Sobersides, and where he might have gone? Baggs, too—we'll certainly want to have a word with him. And anything you might discover about how our victim spent his evening will no doubt be useful. I suppose we shall want to interview the widow."

Murray nodded, agreeing. "I doubt if she knew much about his business, though. Women don't, as a rule."

Charles glanced at his watch. "Shall we say two o'clock, then? At the pub across from the clock tower?"

"Two o'clock," Murray said. He was almost smiling. "Yes, *sir*."

21

Belowstairs at Regal Lodge

"(James Todhunter Sloan) rode throughout the whole of the 1899 season in England, getting home 108 of his 345 mounts... He often stayed the night at Regal Lodge, and it wasn't one of the guest-rooms he slept in. Music-hall star Letty Lind sang a number which became famous as a saucy reference to Sloan's affair with Lillie:

'Click, click, I'm a monkey up a stick,
And you must let me have my way.'

For several years... (Lillie Langtry) operated a betting-swindle, originally imparted to her by Tod Sloan, from Regal Lodge. She systematically received a flash from the course of a winner of a race the moment it passed the post, which enabled her to telegraph a big bet on the horse as if she had been on it before the off."

The Gilded Lily
Ernest Dudley

For Amelia, the occasions when Lady Charles went visiting were almost like a holiday. This morning, for instance, she had only to fetch tea and *The Times* upstairs, assist with her mistress's toilette, and prepare the other outfits to be worn that day—an easy matter, since her ladyship liked to dress in the morning and change only for tea and dinner if necessary—two or at the most three changes of costume, rather than the four or five changes to which other ladies were accustomed. Once these slight chores were finished, Amelia might do as she liked until required to help her mistress bathe and dress.

After the servants' supper the evening before, Amelia had chatted with Margaret until Mrs. Langtry rang and Margaret scurried upstairs to help her mistress dress for dinner at the Rothschilds'. Then Lady Charles left for the evening. With her ladyship's permission, Amelia locked the bedroom door and spent the best part of an hour luxuriating in a hot bath, feeling like the Queen herself, then went off to her own tiny cubicle to read.

Amelia had grown quite proficient at reading in the last several years. Her ladyship encouraged all the servants at Bishop's Keep to read in their spare hours, even providing newspapers and books—and not religious literature, either, as did Lady Kennilworth, Amelia's cousin's employer, who had taught her staff to read so that they could study the gospel tracts she pressed on them. No, the books Lady Charles left on the shelf in the servants' hall were about faraway places and exotic customs, and sometimes even novels, a few of which her ladyship had actually written herself, under the name of Beryl Bardwell. When it was first whispered that Lady Charles indeed *was* Beryl Bardwell, the knowledge had caused a great stir in Dedham, and some concern among the servants who had early on discovered the author's true identity and guarded it carefully. It was now a matter of pride, however, because Beryl Bardwell had actually become quite famous, and Lady Charles was the only authoress that any of them had ever known.

But Amelia had not been reading one of her mistress's fictions last night. She had, instead, shed many tears over the final moving chapters of George Moore's novel, *Esther Waters*. As a young woman, the heroine, Esther, worked in a household entirely given over to racing. Seduced and abandoned, she was forced to go to London to give birth and courageously raised her son alone, eventually marrying the child's father. He had become a bookmaker and was sent to prison when he was convicted of taking wagers in his pub, leaving Esther alone once more. Esther's plight reawakened in Amelia her unhappiness about her husband's betting. For it wasn't just the crown Lawrence had laid and lost on Gladiator at the Derby; he fancied himself a betting man, and Amelia sighed to think of the several lost crowns that might have otherwise gone to pay for Baby's boots.

But this was too fine an occasion to spoil with sighing. The thought of Baby's boots led to thoughts of Baby, safe at home with Amelia's mother, and the thought of her precious daughter sweetly smiling in her sleep chased the more anxious thoughts from Amelia's mind. She extinguished the light and smiled herself to sleep in the quiet darkness, awakening twice: once at her ladyship's return at midnight from her evening with Lord Charles, when she got up to make sure that nothing was wanted; and again later, at the sound of a male voice, definitely not that of the Prince of Wales. Amelia had heard that voice at Easton Lodge, and she knew she would never forget it.

Now it was morning, and after her mistress had gone to breakfast, Amelia went down the back stairs to seek out

Margaret, who was in the laundry, overseeing the ironing of Mrs. Langtry's fresh sheets.

"I've got nothing to do," Amelia said. "I'd be glad to 'elp." She was rewarded with a grateful smile and an armload of fresh towels. Margaret brought the sheets, and the two women went back up the stairs to tidy Mrs. Langtry's bedroom.

As they made the bed, Amelia said, with a little laugh, "It's 'ard not to think 'oo slept 'ere last night." She gave Margaret a significant glance. "I 'eard 'em talkin' in the 'allway."

"Well," Margaret said tartly, "if ye'r thinkin' it wuz 'Is Nibs ye 'eard, ye kin think agin. 'E don't just come an' go when 'e comes—'e comes and *stays*, 'im and 'is flock of servants, all proud as peacocks and just about as useless. So it wuzn't 'im, 'cause none of 'em was 'ere to breakfast."

Taking her place on the opposite side of the bed, Amelia arranged her face in a creditable imitation of bewilderment. "Oh, my," she said. "You don't mean, she 'as *another*—" She stopped, to give Margaret the opportunity to finish her sentence.

Margaret obliged. "That's eggsac'ly wot I mean," she said grimly. "And not just one, but lots. Why, last night at nine o'clock, on 'er way to dinner wiv the Prince, she 'ad a ren-dez-vooz wiv another man, in 'er carriage. Would yer believe it? Three in one night!" She flapped the sheet in Amelia's direction, stern disapproval written in every line of her face.

"Another man?" Amelia asked, widening her eyes in disbelief. She grasped the sheet, clean and sweet-smelling, and straightened it across the bed. "But 'oo? I mean, 'oo's *important* enough to put before the Prince?"

"'Er bookmaker, that's 'oo," Margaret said, tossing her head disdainfully. "The one she cheats." She grasped the end of the sheet and raised one corner of the mattress at the foot of the bed. "Come now, tuck it in."

While Amelia tucked in the sheet on her side of the bed, she frowned, thinking of poor Esther Waters, who had married a bookmaker. "'Ow does she cheat?"

Margaret picked up the heavy gold and purple coverlet and tossed it onto the bed. "She's got one of those newfangled telly-phones in the drawing room. Just when a race is finished, somebody at the course phones 'er with the winner. She gives 'er bet to a boy 'oo rides 'is bicycle straight to the bookie wiv it, like she'd laid it on before the off. Or sometimes she telegraphs 'er bet to London. Either way, it's a cheat."

Pulling the spread even on both sides, the two women tucked it under and over the pillows. "But doesn't the bookmaker get onto 'er?" Amelia asked, straightening up. "Seems like any ninny could figure it out." She turned to the fireplace, where the cinders of last night's fire remained in the grate. "Would you like me to do the fireplace, Marg'ret?"

"That'ud be a 'elp." Margaret picked up the feather duster and went to the dressing tables. "I s'pose she doesn't get found out 'cause she doesn't do it so very often to the same bookie." She flicked the duster lightly over the surface. "I know 'ow it's done," she added, "'cause I 'eard 'er talking on the 'phone, and then to the boy."

Amelia began to shovel cinders and ashes into the ash bucket. "That's clever." She paused. There was a piece of crumpled paper lying loose among the cinders, the edges scorched. It had apparently been saved from burning by virtue of having had wine spilled on it. Quick as thought, Amelia scooped it into the pocket of her apron.

"Clever? Mebbee." Margaret's voice was thick with scorn. "But she wa'n't clever enough to think it up. That

American jockey 'oo sleeps 'ere sometimes—'ee showed 'er 'ow to do it. Americans are smart when it comes to cheatin'." She went to dust the other dressing table.

Amelia cocked her head. "I wonder why she was meeting 'er bookmaker last night. D'ye think she wanted to lay a bet?"

"Don't be a goose," Margaret said, picking up the towels and going into the bathroom. "If ye ask me, she 'ad other business with 'im, and it wa'n't wagers."

Amelia finished cleaning out the fireplace and swept the hearth. She set the bucket outside the door and went into the bathroom, where Margaret was polishing the faucets with a towel. "I just don't see," she said, frowning, "'ow any woman 'ud be daft enough to fancy a bookmaker before the Prince."

"It's true," Margaret said shortly. She gave the faucet one last disgusted swipe and threw the towel on the damp heap on the floor. "She sent 'im a note by Richard, the footman, askin' 'im to meet 'er at nine in St. Mary's Square. I know, 'cause Richard read the note and told me about it." Shaking her head, she hissed through her teeth. "The goin's-on in this 'ouse are enough to make a good Christian girl 'ang 'er 'ead in shame, Amelia. And 'er a parson's daughter, too."

Taking her cue, Amelia patted Margaret's hand. "It's too bad ye 'ave to be privy to such terr'ble things, Margaret," she said piously. "But ye're to be praised fer 'oldin' yerself above it all and stickin' to yer standards. Ye'll 'ave yer reward in 'eaven. The Bible says so."

"Thank ye, Amelia," Margaret said with a smile, her good humor partially restored. She picked up the damp towels. "Rose is doin' yer mistress's room. Let's go down to the kitchen and fix ourselves a spot of tea."

"Won't Cook mind?" Amelia asked doubtfully.

Discipline wasn't overly strict at Bishop's Keep, but the servants took their morning cup in the servant's hall, where they didn't distract the kitchen maids or get in Mrs. Pratt's way.

Margaret shook her head. "Cook likes 'er bit of gossip, same as us. We're safe so long as Mr. Williams don't catch us. Come on."

The kitchen was a large, gloomy room with damp stone walls and a stone-flagged floor, under the old part of the house. Only a little natural light was let in by the windows high up on the walls, at ground level, and gaslights burned around the room. Although it was only midmorning, the room was already quite warm, heated by the monstrous Royale range, a black iron giant that took up almost all of one wall. On the other walls were bins and shelves and cupboards that held dishes and cooking pots, and a solid deal table sat in the middle of the floor, its surface marked by years of vegetable-chopping and bleached white with many scrubbings.

The kettle was already boiling on the back of the range when Amelia and Margaret came into the kitchen. Margaret put tea in a china pot, while Mrs. Redditch, the cook, dropped a lid on the copper kettle on the stove and joined Amelia at the table. She was a large, jolly-looking woman whose good humor seemed to extend to everyone but the kitchen maid, who was sulkily washing up the breakfast dishes in the scullery.

Margaret was pouring tea into three thick china mugs when Mr. Bowchard, the gardener, came in with a bucket of fresh-dug carrots. With a nod to Amelia, who had been introduced to him at lunch the day before, he pulled out a chair and sat down.

"Well, Bowchard," Mrs. Redditch said genially, as Margaret fetched a fourth mug, "ye sart'n'ly look glum enough, and it's not noon yet." She chuckled. "Is the missus makin' life 'ard fer ye agin?" Mrs. Bowchard, as Margaret had told Amelia the day before, was the laundress at Regal Lodge, as well as several other neighboring establishments, and was known to be a harridan.

Mr. Bowchard, who had the gray, bowed-down look of a henpecked husband, blew on his tea to cool it. "I just 'ad a word with the postman," he said in a conspiratorial tone. "Seems as there wuz a killin' in Newmarket last night."

"That's nothin' new." Margaret poured more hot water into the teapot and put on the lid. "Somebody's allus gettin' hisself killed in Newmarket."

"It's the rowdies, ye know," Mrs. Redditch said to Amelia. "They come down from London fer the boxin' matches and cockfights and 'orseracin'. The constables do their best, but they get drunk in the taverns and knock each other over the 'ead."

"Far as I'm concerned," Margaret said darkly, "it's good riddance t' bad rubbish. It's gettin' so Christian folk can't walk down the 'Igh Street without 'earin' some ruffian's crude language. Why, even Pastor Johnson—"

"Wud'n't no ruffian," Mr. Bowchard put in, with the air of a man who knows something important and is having a difficult time containing his knowledge. He put his mug down and leaned forward. "Wuz Badger," he said in a low voice.

"Alfred Day?" Mrs. Redditch asked, surprised. "'E's *dead?*"

"'E's dead," Mr. Bowchard said definitively. He leaned back in his chair. "Somebody shot 'im. Last night."

Margaret let out her breath in a long whoosh. Mrs. Redditch sat staring.

"Badger the *bookmaker?*" Amelia asked in great surprise, remembering how she had met him at the Derby, and how anxious Lawrence had been to drop his bet into Badger's satchel.

"Right," Margaret said grimly. "'E 'appens to be Mrs. L's bookmaker." She narrowed her eyes. "When did 'e get hisself killed, Mr. Bowchard?"

The gardener gave her a meaningful look. "After nine and afore ten. Leastwise, that's wot the postman said. 'E got it from 'is brother Tom, the constable."

"After nine and afore ten?" Mrs. Redditch cried. "But that's when Mrs. L was supposed to meet—" Her hand went to her mouth and her voice trailed off.

"Eggsac'ly, Mrs. Redditch," Mr. Bowchard said grimly. He put down his mug. "My thoughts eggsac'ly."

22

In the Doctor's Office

"In 1835, Henry Goddard caught and convicted a murderer. Goddard was one of the last and most famous of those Bow Street Runners who were the antecedents of the London detective force. Goddard had noticed that one of the bullets in the victim's body had a curious blemish. With this bullet in his pocket, he set out on his hunt for the murderer. In the home of one suspect he found a bullet mold with a flaw, a slight gouge. The ridge on the murder bullet exactly corresponded to this gouge. Confronted with this evidence, the owner of the mold confessed the crime."

The Century of the Detective
JURGEN THORWALD

FOLLOWING JACK MURRAY'S directions, Charles located Dr. Stubbing's consulting room next door to the chemist's shop a few paces off the High Street. Several people were hunched forlornly in chairs in the small room at the front, but when Charles handed his card to the stern-faced woman at the desk by the door, she rose and led him down a hallway. She rapped on a closed door, went inside, and almost immediately reopened the door, motioning to Charles.

The doctor was leaning back in his wooden chair, his feet propped on his desk, reading a newspaper. For a long moment, he didn't stir, even when Charles cleared his throat. Finally, he put the newspaper down and Charles saw a paunchy man with an unruly mane of white hair and bright blue eyes behind gold-rimmed glasses. He regarded Charles with a look of undisguised hostility, not bothering to take his feet off the desk or offer his visitor a chair.

"Chief Constable Watson was here earlier," the doctor said, without preamble or introduction. His voice was raspy, with a slight Scottish burr.

"Was he?" Charles said pleasantly. "Then you know why I've come." Unbidden, he pulled a chair around to the front of the desk and sat down, taking off his hat.

Dr. Stubbing narrowed his eyes. "Watson said that the Jockey Club had some sort of interest in Alfred Day's murder. He said they'd brought some member of the Establishment in to take over the investigation." The doctor's tone clearly implied that he approved neither of the Jockey Club nor of its intervention in what was obviously a matter for the local constabulary.

Briefly, Charles wondered what else the chief constable might have said. He put his hat on the corner of the desk, wishing that he had a better idea of the relationship between the Club and the people of the town. Horseracing might make Newmarket more prosperous, but criminals and crime inevitably accompanied that sort of prosperity. And even if crime were not an issue, there was the constant traffic, the influx of strangers, the noise and the dirt. He could not blame the local citizens if they felt an active hostility toward the Club at the same time that they enjoyed the economic benefits it brought them.

"I wonder," Charles said without inflection, "whether you've finished the autopsy."

Dr. Stubbing folded his paper and tossed it on the floor. "I've finished near as need be," he said, clasping his hands over his belly. He pursed pink lips. "Alfred Day died of a bullet wound in the chest."

"So I presumed, from the entrance wound I observed last night," Charles said gravely. "I also noticed, when the body was placed on a stretcher to be brought here, that there was no exit wound. The bullet must have remained in the body. Did you extract it?"

The doctor swung his feet off the desk, opened a drawer, and took out a cigar case. "Didn't bother," he said flatly. "Somebody shot the poor bastard at close range, and that's what I'll tell the coroner's inquest." He took a cigar out of the case, closed it, and replaced it in the drawer without offering the case to Charles. "Assuming there *is* an inquest," he added. "Or do the gentlemen of the Jockey Club mean to subvert the judicial inquiry as well as the police inquiry?"

Charles did not answer the question. "I'm afraid, Dr. Stubbing, that I must trouble you to extract the bullet. It might be useful in identifying the gun that fired it."

Dr. Stubbing's bushy white eyebrows shot up. "The bullet identify the gun?" He grunted skeptically. "You're joking."

Charles gave an inaudible sigh. "I'm quite serious, sir. A full decade ago, in Lyons, Professor Lacassagne was able to match the marks on the bullet to the rifling of a particular gun barrel. Last year, in Germany, Dr. Paul Jesserich matched a bullet taken from the victim's body with a test bullet fired by a revolver belonging to one of the suspects. The testimony of both of these scientists resulted in guilty verdicts."

"Mumbo jumbo," Dr. Stubbing muttered, lighting his cigar. "Maybe a foreign jury can be taken in by such pseudo-scientific poppycock, but not one of our English juries. They have better sense." He eyed Charles. "There's never been such a case in England, I'll wager."

"There was one, sir," Charles said, "about sixty years ago. But it did not go to the jury. The comparison of the bullet with the mold that formed it persuaded the murderer to plead guilty."

The doctor harrumphed. "Well, you're not going to get a Newmarket jury to swallow such an argument. Unless the Club puts its own men into the jury box, of course. And its own judge on the bench." He pulled on his cigar, his voice rising bitterly. "And don't try to tell me that won't happen, sir. I've seen what money and influence have already bought in this town, and all in the name of sport." He spit the word out. "Who's to say the Club can't buy justice, as well?"

Charles made no reply, because nothing he said would change the other's mind. And at some deeper level, there was a part of him that feared that the doctor might be right, and that he himself had been inveigled by Owen North to participate in something he did not fully understand.

"You see? You yourself can say nothing in the Club's defense!" The doctor slammed his fist on the desk. "The drunkenness, the rioting, the beatings, the assaults on our women—that's what horseracing has brought to this town! And worse, too." He jerked his thumb over his shoulder, his face twisted. "Most of the poor people waiting out there can't afford a doctor, or medicine, or warm clothing and food for the children. They've been seduced into putting their last shilling on the favorite, or on the long shot, or on the dogfight. They'll end up in the almshouse, supported by honest citizens, and all on account of that racecourse out there. Don't talk to me about crime and criminals. The Jockey Club is the greatest criminal of all!"

Outside, the tower clock at the east end of the High Street began to chime. Charles counted as it struck eleven times. When the last note had died away, he said quietly: "Whatever moral judgments you may make on horseracing and the Club, it is of vital importance that the fatal bullet be retrieved from the dead man's body. It is *evidence*, Dr. Stubbing, and the case cannot go forward without it. I should very much dislike to report to the coroner that the autopsy was not completed because the surgeon failed to cooperate fully." He leaned back. "Now, sir. How soon can that bullet be found?"

The doctor regarded the gray tip of his cigar malevolently. "Depends on where it is," he muttered, and applied another match.

"I understand," Charles said. "The body is still here, then?"

"In the next room," the doctor growled, puffing. "The mortician's been summoned to fetch it, but he hasn't arrived yet."

Charles felt some relief. At least he didn't have to go to the mortuary in search of the body—and the bullet. He stood. "While you're completing the autopsy, I should like to examine Mr. Day's personal effects. His clothing, and so forth. It's all here?"

The doctor heaved himself out of his chair. He gestured toward a table in the corner. "Over there. Help yourself." He walked heavily across the room and through a door, slamming it behind him so hard that the windows rattled.

Charles saw that when Alfred Day died, he had been

165

wearing a bowler hat, black shoes, gray jacket and trousers, white shirt, and gray waistcoat. The shirt and waistcoat gave bloody evidence of the shooting: a bullet hole in each and a large, irregular bloodstain; a peppering of black powder burns in a three-inch circle around the hole in the waistcoat. Blood had soaked into the jacket and the front of the trousers as well, suggesting that the man had lived some moments after he was shot.

Apart from the bloodstained clothing, there seemed little else of interest. Charles found some coins, a key on a silver ring, and a penknife in the right front trouser pocket; in the right rear pocket, a few bank notes folded into a leather wallet that also contained several of Day's calling cards; and a stub of a pencil in the jacket's outer breast pocket, but nothing on which to write. It was only when he began to explore the waistcoat pockets that he found something of interest: a piece of delicately scented paper, folded several times and stained along one edge with the dead man's blood.

Charles unfolded the note carefully. It was written in a flowing, expressive hand on cream-colored paper, embossed at the top with the words *Regal Lodge*.

> *Dear Mr. Day,*
> *I don't suppose I need tell you how disturbed I am by your letter. We must meet immediately for a private discussion. I shall be in my carriage in St. Mary's Square at nine this evening. I beg you to be prompt so that the carriage does not attract unnecessary attention.*

The note was signed with two initials, elegantly intertwined: LL.

Charles was staring at the note, considering its implications, when the doctor reentered the room, carrying in his hand a small cardboard box. He tossed it onto the table beside the clothing.

"The bullet," he growled.

"That was quick, I must say," Charles remarked, folding the note. He took out his pocket watch. The doctor had been out of the room for no more than three minutes, clearly not sufficient time to complete the autopsy.

"Take the bloody thing," Dr. Stubbing snarled, "and get the devil out of here."

Without a word, Charles pocketed the small box, the note, and the key, left the clothing lying where he had found it, and walked out of the office. Once on the street, he headed for the livery stable. If he did not want to walk to Regal Lodge, he should have to hire a gig.

23

At Regal Lodge – Kate & Lillie

"In the first place, I shall be seen; and that is no small advantage to a girl who brings her face to market."

Lillie Langtry, playing Kate Hardcastle
in She Stoops to Conquer
Oliver Goldsmith

"(After my first London appearance at Lady Sebright's) the photographers, one and all, besought me to sit. Presently, my portraits were in every shop-window, with trying results, for they made the public so familiar with my features that wherever I went—to theatres, picture-galleries, shops—I was actually mobbed."

The Days I Knew:
The Autobiography of Lillie Langtry
Lillie Langtry

HAVING CHANGED INTO a gray silk dress trimmed with lavender lace, Lillie Langtry, now seeming fully recovered, settled herself on the green velvet sofa in the drawing room.

"Now, Beryl my dear," she said with a gracious smile, "we can talk to our hearts' content. Take out your notebook and your pen and fire away with your questions."

"You're sure you won't mind?" Kate asked tentatively. "I certainly don't want to intrude on your privacy."

"Privacy!" Lillie exclaimed, with a toss of her head. "Whatever is that? Since I attended my first *salon* in London some twenty years ago, I have been a public figure. I have not a moment of privacy. Not one instant."

Kate held her pen poised over the page. "Twenty years!" she exclaimed artlessly. "That can't be!"

"I recall it as though it were yesterday," Lillie replied, and heaved an elaborate sigh. "It was at Lady Sebright's house in Lowndes Square, in May. I was still in mourning for my brother, so I wore a plain black dress—square-necked and terribly unfashionable—made for me by Madame Nicolle, back home on Jersey. So many people were there, all crowding around, and I felt like an *ingénue* suddenly given a grown-up part to play. Jimmy Whistler and Millais both demanded to paint me, and Freddy Leighton wanted to do my head in marble. The great Henry Irving offered me a stage role, and of course Oscar Wilde, poor, dear Oscar, swooned around making a fool of himself—and of me, too, I'm afraid." She gave a little laugh, delicately self-deprecating. "With no effort on my part and *certainly* no design, suddenly I found myself a professional beauty, my picture in all the shops and men tripping over themselves to pay court. Such a whirl it was! Enough to turn a young girl's head. It's a good thing I had both feet planted firmly on the ground!"

Writing rapidly, not looking up, Kate said, "But before you came to London, what? You were married to Mr. Edward Langtry, were you not?"

"Yes," Lillie said shortly. "Two years before, on Jersey.

Ned was a... yachtsman. We spent a great deal of time sailing about, here and there." She became cheerful again. "And then I fell ill with typhoid fever and when I recovered, the doctor prescribed a visit to London to cheer me up. Then there was Lady Sebright's salon, and quite wonderful things began to happen, amazing things, really. His Highness the Prince of Wales asked to be introduced to me at a supper given by Sir Allen Young, the Arctic explorer. Oh, my dear Beryl, can you imagine how I felt?" She laughed a little. "I was utterly panic-stricken. For one bewildered moment I really considered the advisability of climbing the chimney to escape, like a little monkey! But I stood my ground and made my curtsy, and that was the beginning of our friendship. He was kind enough to see that I was presented to the Queen, and there were house parties and race meetings and yachting holidays." Her tone became soft and reminiscent. "Oh, such times, such sweet, wonderful times. It's hard to believe, looking back on it, that so much could have happened in three short years."

"But then things changed?" Kate murmured, prompting.

"Yes, they changed," Lillie replied, almost as if she were not aware of Kate. "Ned became a bankrupt and we were sold up. Bailiffs invaded our little Norfolk Street house and took all our furniture, even my gowns. There was no money, apart from what I was offered by my friends—but who with a brain in her head would depend on others for support? And Ned was worse than useless, of course. Not an ounce of business sense. I knew that somehow I had to provide for myself."

Feeling that much was being omitted here, Kate asked, "Was that when you went on the stage?"

Lillie nodded. "His Highness suggested it. Then Oscar Wilde—we were great friends in those days, before his disgrace—introduced me to Harriet Labouchere. It was she who actually pushed me into it. I wasn't eager for the public exposure, of course, but I really felt I had no alternative. Mrs. Labouchere and I did a two-character play called *The Fair Encounter*—very well received, it was. My first serious role was that of Kate in *She Stoops to Conquer*, for the benefit of the Theatrical Fund at the Haymarket. The Prince favored my performances with his presence, and in no time at all, I was an established actress."

"You make it sound very easy," Kate said quietly.

"Perhaps so, my dear," Lillie said in a confiding tone, "but true success is never easy. Behind the scenes, one must spend a great deal of time working and worrying, and continually searching for funds to support one's efforts. I went on tour in England, and then in America, and then in England again, and so it went for the next ten years or so. Since the early nineties, though, I have more or less settled in England." She grew still, and a reflective look came over her face. "It is enormously exhilarating to be admired, and delightful to find oneself in constant demand. But one tires of the unceasing effort." A small, unconscious sigh escaped her lips, and she seemed to shake herself and become lively once more. "When Suggie and I are married, I think I shall give the theater a rest for a time and simply enjoy being Lady de Bathe. *After* I've produced your play, of course, dear Beryl. We mustn't forget to talk about that."

As Lillie talked, and as she wrote, Kate thought perhaps she had heard several true things: Lillie's remarks about the constant work and worry and the continual search for funds. And of course she had to have tired of the unceasing effort. It must be unspeakably wearying to be always in the public eye, always on stage. How did Lillie restore herself when her energies flagged? And where in her harried, hectic life could she find any peace?

"What about your family?" Kate asked, still scribbling. "Your husband? Your mother? Your niece?" She could feel Lillie's eyes on her, suddenly intent, as if gauging her knowledge. She glanced up, innocently. "Did they travel with you?"

"Travel with me?" Lillie laughed lightly. "Oh, my dear, no! Touring is terribly demanding. Long hours aboard ship and on dirty trains, one hotel upon another, crushing mobs at the railway stations." She sighed theatrically. "It is a purgatory one must not inflict on one's loved ones. Ned pursued his own affairs, of course, up to his death about a year and a half ago. Mother and Jeanne-Marie, my brother's daughter, come to be with me when I'm in London. Jeanne-Marie has grown to be quite a lovely girl, and of course I do all I can for the child." Her smile was indulgent. "Lessons, dresses, whatever she wants that a doting auntie can provide. The Prince has even made it possible for her to be presented at the Queen's Drawing Room next month. And of course I'm anxious to see her make a respectable marriage and lead her own private life." She made a wry face. "I certainly don't want her to live as I do, eternally in the public eye."

The drawing room door opened and the butler entered, carrying a card on a silver tray. "A gentleman to see you, ma'am." There was a slight emphasis on the word *gentleman*.

Lillie frowned severely. "Didn't I say that we weren't to be interrupted on any account, Williams?"

"He insists it is quite urgent, ma'am." The butler was apologetic. "He won't say what it's about, but I fear he won't go away until you have seen him."

"Forgive me, Beryl." Lillie reached for the card. "Let's

see who this insistent fellow is." She read it and glanced quickly up at Kate, her eyebrows arched in a look of great surprise.

"Why, it's Lord Sheridan!"

24

At Regal Lodge – Charles, Kate, & Lillie

"In spite of the many difficult and even dangerous situations in which I have found myself, I have rarely been afraid, because I have usually had the good fortune of having someone at hand to offer protection."

LILLIE LANGTRY

IF CHARLES HAD expected to be overwhelmed by Lillie Langtry's legendary beauty, he would have been disappointed. Beside his auburn-haired wife, whom he genuinely considered the most beautiful woman he had ever seen, Lillie Langtry looked slightly frayed and worldweary. While the actress was still undeniably pretty, the face and figure that had caused such a sensation in the late seventies now carried the marks of two decades of indulgence: there were wrinkles around her mouth and eyes, and one cheek bore the telltale bruise that Kate had described; the waist had thickened; the alabaster arms and throat, still white, had grown noticeably heavy. But there was a firm determination in her mouth and resolution in the set of her jaw, and he could not help but recall Sarah

Bernhardt's retort when told of Mrs. Langtry's plans for a stage career: "She will go far, not with her talent or her beauty, but with her chin."

He bowed over Lillie Langtry's outstretched hand. "Thank you for seeing me," he said, and smiled slightly at his Kate, a pen in her hand, a notebook open on her lap, who was regarding him with undisguised astonishment. "I am sorry to have interrupted your talk."

"Lord Sheridan," the actress said, in a low, velvety voice. "How thoughtful of you to drop in and make sure that your wife is being properly looked after." She patted the sofa beside her invitingly. "Do come and sit beside me, my lord. Will you have coffee or tea? Or perhaps—"

"Thank you, no." Charles took the chair opposite, where he could observe her face. "I'm afraid this is not a social call, Mrs. Langtry. I've come on a rather unpleasant errand."

Kate leaned forward. "Charles, what in the world—" Uneasily, her gray eyes searched his face. "Is Patrick all right? Nothing's happened to—"

"Patrick is quite well, my dear." He looked at Lillie, whose expression was openly inquiring. "Perhaps you would prefer to speak with me in private, Mrs. Langtry. Our conversation may be somewhat... distressing."

"Fie, my lord, fie!" Lillie exclaimed, lifting her chin. She laughed lightly, a teasing laugh. "What distressing thing can you possibly wish to say to me? And what in the world have you to say that your lovely wife might not hear?"

The brittle, half-mocking laugh decided him. This woman was an experienced actress, skilled in imitating a variety of emotions. To obtain anything like an authentic, a genuine response (if that were indeed possible), he would have to shake her, to shock her, and probably Kate as well.

"Mr. Alfred Day has been murdered," he said bluntly.

"He was shot to death last night between the hours of nine and ten. You are suspected of having committed this crime, Mrs. Langtry. Where were you at that time?"

Lillie sat very still, her face suddenly pinched and white, her eyes large and dark. But she did not seem as jarred by his words as she surely should have been: an indication to Charles that she already knew of Day's death and was perhaps even prepared for the accusation. She looked down at her folded hands and after a moment's silence, murmured, "Isn't it curious for a gentleman of your stature in Society to be doing the business of a common policeman?" She managed to make the last word sound obscene.

"I am here at the request of the Prince of Wales," Charles said, in the most autocratic tone he could summon. He saw Kate's eyes widen. "It is His Highness's intention to keep this matter out of the hands of the police as long as possible."

At the mention of the Prince, Mrs. Langtry's head had come up quickly and her eyes had fastened on Charles. Her face was still, the expression in her eyes dark and unreadable. But there was a small tic at one corner of her mouth that she could not control. Charles had rather stretched his commission, but he felt that he had shaken her.

He smiled bleakly and went on. "In the dead man's waistcoat pocket, I discovered a note written on stationery embossed with the words *Regal Lodge*. It was signed with your initials. This message directed Mr. Day to meet you at nine in St. Mary's Square. At what time, Mrs. Langtry, did he join you?"

"You have my note?" Lillie's eyes flashed and her tone was imperious. "You have no right, my lord. I demand that you hand it over to me, this instant!"

176

Charles shook his head. "It is evidence, Mrs. Langtry, in a murder case." He leaned forward, his voice ice-cold. *"At what time did Alfred Day join you in your carriage?"*

Lillie's nostrils flared, her jaw tightened, and she could not conceal the fear that flickered in her eyes. But when she spoke, her voice was clear and without tremor.

"You may tell His Highness that I waited for Mr. Day in St. Mary's Square until nearly nine-thirty. When it became apparent that the man was not coming, I drove on to the Rothschilds', where I arrived at quarter to ten." Her voice was emphatic, even defiant. "And that, sir, is God's very truth. You may confirm it with my coachman. And His Highness will be able to tell you the time of my arrival."

"No doubt he will have checked his pocket watch at the exact moment you made your entrance," Charles said dryly. His look was severe. "Why did you ask Mr. Day to see you? What was the matter you intended to discuss?"

Kate leaned forward, biting her lip. "Charles, I really don't think—"

"Come now, Mrs. Langtry." he said harshly, ignoring his wife. "We'll have no secrets in this matter. What did you mean to discuss?"

Again he saw the undisguisable flicker of fear in the actress's eyes. She bit her lip. "Will you... how much will you tell His Highness?"

"Only as much as absolutely necessary."

She lowered her head. When she spoke, her voice was muffled. "I owed Mr. Day... some money. He had asked me to settle my account in full."

"How much money did you owe him?"

"Ten thousand pounds."

Kate gasped involuntarily, then covered her mouth with her hand. Charles said, "Did you take this money with you?"

Reluctantly, Lillie shook her head. "I... I couldn't. I don't have it. I was going to tell him that I... I needed more time."

"The testimony of coachmen can be bought," Charles said icily. "Can you summon any other evidence that you did not kill Alfred Day?"

Lillie pressed her lips together, to keep them from trembling, Charles thought. After a moment, she shook her head. "I cannot prove a negative." Her voice was low, scarcely above a whisper.

"*I* can, Charles," Kate said urgently. She leaned forward in her chair. Her pen and notebook, forgotten, slid off her lap and onto the floor. "At breakfast this morning. I told Mrs. Langtry that a man had been shot to death, and that I had seen his body. When she heard the name, she was utterly dumbfounded. I thought for a moment she might faint."

Charles kept his voice level and cool. "Mrs. Langtry is an actress, my dear. Astonishment, bewilderment, shock— these are but a few of the many emotions in her repertoire. You cannot say that you were not a perfect audience for a breakfast-table performance that was designed to deflect your suspicion."

Kate flinched at his wintry tone and the formality of his address. "Perhaps," she said. "But I know that no actress, however skilled, could have pretended the shock I saw on her face. It was genuine. I *swear* it, Charles. Until I told her, she did not know that Alfred Day had been murdered."

Lillie turned her head toward Kate, and Charles saw an unfeigned expression of gratitude sweep like a wave of color across her face. Her mouth relaxed. "Thank you," she said quietly.

Charles, too, regarded his wife. Her eyes, meeting his, were clear and intent, her expression open, deeply sincere.

Her voice and her words had been utterly uncontrived, and he could only suppose that she believed what she said.

But was Kate deceived? He could not doubt his wife's honest perception, but he did not dare to accept what she said as the truth. And he could only pray that she would understand and forgive him for his next words, which must seem a terrible betrayal.

"You are too credulous, my dear," he said ruthlessly. "Too readily taken in. You should cultivate skepticism among your many other talents." He turned back to Lillie. "Mrs. Langtry, I require you to surrender your gun to me."

Lillie's eyes widened and she made a half-strangled noise in her throat. "My... gun? How do you know that I own such a thing?"

He had not, of course, but he knew now. If she had not possessed a gun, she would immediately have said so. He regarded her coldly. "Shall we call your servants and ask them?"

She sat for a moment in silence, as if she were deciding whether to test him. At last, she put on a little smile. "Fifteen years ago," she said, "when I was touring in America, I often played in what were called whistle-stop towns. These were primitive places, full of rowdy, drunken men who desired nothing more fervently than to force their romantic attentions on me. I was not unprotected—a dear friend traveled with me. But as an additional precaution, my friend gave me a small, silver-handled derringer so that I might arm myself against unwanted advances. I recall being glad that I was not called upon to use it, for it is such a toy that I doubt it could do a great deal of harm."

She rose from the sofa and went to a small table that stood in front of a window. "I have no great need of the gun here, for England is a civilized country." Her smile was almost saucy. "When a gentleman wishes to kiss me, he asks permission first. My dear little gun is a souvenir of a time past and a reminder of a kindhearted friend, but if you insist, Lord Charles, you may take it."

Having delivered this almost playful speech, she pulled open the table drawer with a dramatic flourish and reached inside. But within the instant, her face changed. She bent over to search the drawer, frantically pushing papers and other things about. After a moment she straightened, grave and very pale. Her mouth was trembling.

"Let me guess," Charles said ironically, as if this were a game of charades. "Your dear little derringer is missing."

"It was here yesterday morning—I saw it!" she cried. "One of the servants must have made off with it!"

"No doubt," Charles said. He stood and bowed to Kate. "Your ladyship," he murmured. "I am glad to see you well." To Lillie, he said, "I must ask you not to leave this vicinity until after the coroner's inquest."

Lillie seemed to shudder. "But you can't mean..." Her voice sharpened. "You said that the police weren't to be involved!"

"I said that the matter will be kept out of their hands as long as possible," Charles replied. He looked gravely at Lillie. "In the end, however, justice must be served." He bowed again. "Ladies, I thank you. Good day."

25

In Newmarket

"George Lambton remarked to an American that he supposed there were a good many rogues and thieves racing in America. 'There is not one,' was the reply. 'They have all come over here.'"

Neck or Nothing:
The Extraordinary Life and Times of Bob Sievier
JOHN WELCOME

THE MORNING'S DRIZZLING rain had given way to a gray mist by the time Charles drove back to Newmarket and found Jack Murray waiting beneath the tower clock, a brown-paper package under his arm. Charles pulled on the reins, stopping the hired gig, and Murray climbed up onto the seat.

"'Afternoon, sir," he said. The mist was beaded on his wool cap and the shoulders of his tweed coat. "Lovely weather, eh? Trust you had good hunting."

"Better than I expected," Charles said, lifting the reins and chirruping to the horse. "Which way are we headed?"

"North, toward Snailwell. But let's stop under those

trees up ahead, sir." Murray put the package on the seat and took two bottles of beer out of his coat pockets. "In case you missed lunch, sir. Hot fish and chips."

"Good man, Jack." Charles grinned and pulled the horse under a large beech tree. While they ate, he sketched his conversations with Dr. Stubbings and Mrs. Langtry.

Murray wiped his mouth with the back of his hand. "Stubbings, he's a deep one. Doesn't like the Club and abhors racing. And Mrs. Langtry?" Both gray eyebrows went up. "Now, there's a shocker for you. Cert'nly sounds as if she had a motive. D'you think *she* shot Badger?"

Before he answered, Charles thought back to what Kate had said. His wife had an intuitive understanding of what motivated people to act and what actions they might be capable of, and he had always before trusted her judgment. But Lillie Langtry was skilled at impersonations. She had carved out a place for herself in the world because she knew how to deceive—and not just on the stage, either. Thinking back on what he knew of her relationship with the Prince and others, it was clear that deception must be habitual for her. Recognizing this, did he dare to rely on Kate's belief that Lillie Langtry was innocent of the murder? He wished that he could, but feared he could not.

"I think Mrs. Langtry is capable of killing Day," Charles said cautiously. "But unless we recover the gun—"

He shook his head. Even if Mrs. Langtry's derringer were found and proved to have fired the fatal bullet, it could not be conclusively proved that she had fired it. Dr. Stubbings was right. The circumstantial evidence offered by a ballistics expert would not sway an English jury, nor would fingerprint evidence, even if they were fortunate enough to secure it. In a case like this, a jury would convict only upon the testimony of an eyewitness, or a confession. And at this point, neither seemed likely.

He sighed. "What did you learn, Jack?"

Murray delivered his report succinctly, between swigs of beer and mouthfuls of fish and greasy chips. When he and Charles parted company that morning, he had gone to the Great Horse, where the owner, a burly fellow named Harold, had just flung open the doors and was airing out the place. Murray had purchased a glass of ale and led Harold into a narration of the events of the previous night. Harold had plenty to tell, and a decided opinion as to the identity of Badger's killer.

Badger had come into the pub at his usual time, around eight-thirty, an hour prior to the evening's scheduled entertainment—a rat-killing dog and a boxing match—which Harold described at some length. The dog was Billy Sturgeon's celebrated terrier bitch Queenie, who set a local record by dispatching seventy rats in five minutes. Following Queenie's triumph, the rat-pit had been quickly converted to a boxing ring and Red Roy and the Manchester Strong Man had gone twenty-two rounds. The Strong Man prevailed. Harold said that both Queenie and the Strong Man—"fair champions in a fair fight"—were toasted long and loud before the evening came to an end, while Queenie herself, regally enthroned on the bar, lapped up her customary dish of ale.

Prior to these festivities, Badger had seated himself at his usual table in the far corner and conducted a little business. All was calm until a quarter to nine, when Eddie Baggs, Badger's partner, had entered, in the company of Mr. Pinkie Duncan, the assistant trainer at the Grange House Stable, and Jesse Clark, one of the American trainers at the Red House Stable. Clark, Harold said contemptuously, was a filthy horse-doper, and Pinkie bid fair to follow in his footsteps. Harold himself did not like Clark, he confided, because the man, as he put it, was in the "pockets of them

183

American rogues and scoundrels 'oo've come over 'ere with no other purpose than to steal honest folks' money."

The sight of Baggs in the company of this entreprenurial pair had angered Badger. ("Couldn't blame 'im, meself," Harold confided. "'Twas like 'is bloody partner 'ad gone over to the enemy.") The four of them fell into a loud argument about the merits of horse-doping, Badger asserting that it ruined the horse and altered the odds in unpredictable ways, and the other two retorting that all was fair in love and horseracing.

This disagreement had gone on for some time, getting louder and angrier, when Badger suddenly pounded on the table for silence. When he had the crowd's attention, he stood and announced a radical plan to organize the Newmarket and London bookmakers into a coalition against Jesse and his cronies. Since the Jockey Club's Stewards refused to outlaw the disgraceful and unsportsmanlike practice of horse-doping, the coalition would take the matter into its own hands. Members would refuse to accept wagers on horses that had run doped in the past or were owned by individuals or a stable that had run doped horses. Badger intended to see that every reputable bookmaker became a member. At this, most of the crowd gave a loud cheer, for they were sick to death of watching their money end up in the Americans' pockets. Not all, though. The dopers had their backers too, and there was a sharp division among the onlookers.

Charles whistled under his breath. "Would such a coalition have any effect?"

"Cert'nly," Murray replied. "There's plenty of sharp feeling among bookmakers on the subject, and Badger could prob'ly recruit enough to make their influence felt. But whether it worked or not, the newspapers would grab the story and use it to raise a public hue and cry, which the

Stewards do not want. They might find it politic to take some sort of action that would shut Badger up and halt the scandal."

Or find a surer and more direct way to shut Badger up, Charles thought to himself, remembering the odd look on Owen North's face that morning. But he didn't voice the thought, for Jack Murray, likable though he might be, was the Club's man. He would have his own talk with Harold, and ask him whether any members of the Jockey Club had been in the pub the night before.

Charles brought his attention back to Murray's last remark. "So one way or the other," he said, "Badger would win. I suppose," he added, "this likelihood was not lost on Pinkie and Clark. And Baggs too, I'll warrant. Strange that he was with them," he added. "Do you suppose he was planning to leave the partnership?"

"I wondered that too, sir," Murray said, taking another pull on his beer. "According to Harold, Pinkie was furious at Badger, as was Clark, and Baggs too. Harold thought Badger seemed pleased with himself, gloating, actually. Maybe he thought that the more trouble he caused, the quicker the Stewards would hear of it. He might have been planning to go around to some of the other pubs and make the same announcement."

"What time did Badger leave?"

"Something after nine, Harold says. P'rhaps ten past."

"He must have been on his way to meet Mrs. Langtry," Charles mused. Hearing all this, he was now more inclined to agree with Kate that Lillie was innocent.

Murray nodded. "Some of the men who were arguing followed Badger out the door. Some came back in a few minutes, others didn't. Harold noticed, because he thought that several were very angry. He remembers wondering whether Badger knew how to take care of himself."

"Who didn't come back?" Charles asked sharply.

"Pinkie Duncan, Jesse Clark, and Eddie Baggs." Murray swigged the last of his beer. "Of course, they might have gone on to another pub."

"Or they might have followed Badger into the alley and shot him," Charles said.

"That's what Harold thinks." Murray rolled the greasy paper into a bundle and thrust it and the empty bottles under the seat. "He says his money is on Clark, because he and Enoch Wishard, the other American trainer, had the most to lose if Badger succeeded in organizing the bookies, or forcing the Jockey Club to outlaw doping."

"We should talk to Baggs," Charles said.

Murray nodded. "I went to his lodging, but the landlady said he'd left. Took his clothes with him." He gave Charles a significant look. "We're not the only ones looking for him, either. She said that another gentleman had been around, asking for him."

"She couldn't say who, I don't suppose."

"No," Murray said regretfully. "She couldn't. But whoever he was, the fact that he'd missed Baggs made him angry."

Charles wiped his hands on his handkerchief and picked up the reins. "How about Sobersides? Was he at the Great Horse with the others?"

"Not then. Harold said he came in earlier in the evening. He had left by the time Badger arrived."

"Did you discover where we might find him?"

Murray nodded. "His brother Thomas has a small farm the other side of Snailwell. Harold says he may've gone there, or to another brother, in Edinburgh. His real name, by the way, is Oliver Moore. He's called Sobersides because he never smiles."

"Maybe he doesn't have anything to smile about,"

Charles said, and urged the horse back onto the road. "Let us hope that Oliver Moore stayed close. I have no great wish to track him to Edinburgh."

26

At Regal Lodge – Kate, Lillie, & Jeanne

"It was for me that (Oscar Wilde) wrote *Lady Windermere's Fan*. Why he ever supposed that it would have been at the time a suitable play for me, I cannot imagine. (The character had a twenty-year-old daughter, who had never been acknowledged.) 'My dear Oscar,' I remonstrated, 'am I old enough to have a grown-up daughter?'"

The Days I Knew:
The Autobiography of Lillie Langtry
LILLIE LANGTRY

"'How on earth could I pose as a mother with a grown-up daughter? I have never admitted that I am more than twenty-nine, or thirty at the most. Twenty-nine when there are pink shades, thirty when there are not.'"

Mrs. Erlynne in Lady Windermere's Fan
OSCAR WILDE

WHEN CHARLES HAD gone, Kate sat very still, trying to collect her thoughts. The man who had been in this room—stern-faced, so severe as to be almost abusive—was not her husband, but some other person, a stranger she had never seen before and hoped never to see again.

But at the same time that her heart felt wounded by the harshness of his words and the coldness of his expression, her mind understood that he had been playing a part, and that he had done so in an effort to force Lillie Langtry to tell the truth. Kate knew, too, that he had left Regal Lodge unconvinced of Lillie's innocence, and for that she was sorry. For she herself was sure that Lillie had told the truth, about the murder, at least, and also about the gun. The actress might well be hiding something else—indeed, Kate knew that she almost certainly *was*—but she had not been aware of the bookmaker's death until that morning at breakfast, and she had fully expected to find her gun when she opened that drawer.

When at last Lillie spoke, her voice was ironic. "Beryl, I must say you are right on one count. Lord Sheridan is certainly a 'rare' man—although not, I think, in the way you meant."

"I'm sorry," Kate said sincerely. "He was unpardonably rude. But he was only trying—"

Lillie began to pace across the room. "I know what he was trying to do," she said bitterly. "He was trying to wring the truth out of me—or at least, the truth he wanted to hear." She turned and held out her hands with a look of pure appeal. "I *swear* to you, Beryl. I learned of Alfred Day's death from you, this morning. And I had no idea that the gun was gone. Everything I said to Lord Charles was the truth."

"I know," Kate said simply. Whatever the reasons Charles had for coming here, she trusted that they must

189

be important. Perhaps she could help him by finding out what he could not. Perhaps she could persuade Lillie to tell her—

"Well, thank God for that," Lillie exclaimed, casting her eyes upward. "But you must convince your husband, Beryl. You *must*! Imagine the scandal if I am accused in court of murdering a bookmaker, on top of all my other sins!" She closed her eyes and clasped her hands to her breast. "Even if I were acquitted, the Prince could never again be able to give me any notice. And if it came out that—" She stopped. "I would be ruined," she said, almost in a whisper. "Utterly and eternally ruined."

"If I am to convince Charles of your innocence," Kate said in a practical tone, "I must know *all* the truth. For instance, I must know who might have taken your gun— besides the servants, that is."

"It was a servant," Lillie snapped. "I've never trusted them, *none* of them. They steal and gossip and—" She threw up her hands. "Why, the person who is serving as my temporary lady's maid here cannot even dress hair! One is such a victim of one's servants."

"You saw the gun yesterday, you said. Who besides the servants has been in this room since yesterday morning?"

"Well…" Lillie frowned. "You, of course. And Dick Doyle and Tod Sloan, whom you met here. But I can't think why either of them would want to take my little pistol. It makes no sense."

Kate thought about the enormously fat man and the slender young jockey. Both of them were involved with racing, and Alfred Day had been a bookmaker. Surely they had known the dead man, and might have had a more sinister connection with him. But there was something else.

"I was in the garden yesterday afternoon," she said,

"and saw a gentleman leaving the house. Was he in this room alone? Would he have had an opportunity to take the gun?"

The change in Lillie's face was so subtle that if Kate hadn't been watching closely, she would have missed the tension in the mouth, the almost imperceptible narrowing of the eyes. But when Lillie spoke, her voice was light and easy.

"Oh, that was just Spider," she said, with a careless toss of her head. "And he wasn't in this room at all—we met and talked in the library."

For the moment, Kate did not challenge Lillie's lie. She remarked, instead: "Spider—an odd nickname."

"I give nicknames to all my male friends," Lillie replied. She frowned. "It had to be one of the servants, I'm sure of it. It wouldn't be the first thing they've stolen. Jewelry, silver, pieces of valuable lace. One never knows what will go missing next." She returned to the sofa and sat down, an irritated look on her face. But there was something else, too. Was it apprehension? Fear? Had Lillie realized that her afternoon visitor had taken the gun?

"Well, then," Kate said, "let's try a different angle. You've known Mr. Day for some time, I think you said. Do you have any idea who might have wanted to kill him?"

"Who *didn't* want to kill the man?" Lillie retorted, arranging her skirts around her. "He had enemies everywhere, not just in Newmarket." She became scornful. "In London, he was nothing more than a common thief, dealing in stolen goods."

"A fence, you mean?" Kate asked, wondering how Lillie had come by this information about Mr. Day, and whether Charles knew it as well. "Like Harold Knight in *The Duchess's Dilemma*?"

Lillie sat suddenly very still, pinching a fold of silk

between her fingers. "Yes," she said slowly, "now that you mention it. He was a fence, like Harold Knight." She lifted her chin, regarding Kate with a guarded expression. "In fact, I must confess that when I read your story, Beryl, I was sure that you had known someone like Alfred Day, perhaps even Day himself. After all, the names Knight and Day—" She shrugged expressively.

Kate gazed at her, and suddenly into her mind came the tale of Lillie's missing jewels and the similarity she had already noted between that story and *The Duchess's Dilemma*. Did Lillie Langtry fear that she might have some secret knowledge about those gems? Had the actress invited her to Regal Lodge, not to discuss the staging of her story, but rather to determine how much she knew about the theft of Lillie's own jewels?

She gave an uncomfortable laugh. "I do assure you, Lillie, Harold Knight is *not* a real person. I'm afraid that my acquaintance is rather limited when it comes to criminals. I made him up."

"But the two are so much alike," Lillie persisted, an odd tension in her voice. She eyed Kate narrowly. "Even the manner of their deaths is similar. Don't you see?"

The hair on the back of Kate's neck prickled. She hadn't thought of it until this moment, but what Lillie said was true. In the play, the man who had sold the duchess's jewels had been shot to death when he and one of the other thieves had fallen out—a just reward for his many evil deeds.

She smiled a little. "Art and life frequently mirror each other. The events may be similar, but Harold Knight is an entirely fictitious character. I assure you, Lillie—there is no connection between him and Alfred Day. None at all."

Lillie's eyes held hers. "And the duchess? Did you make her up, too?"

"Not exactly," Kate said, and saw the involuntary flare of Lillie's nostrils, the pulling-in of her breath. She leaned forward. "The duchess is modeled after one of my neighbors, you see, and the theft in the story was based on a real event that occurred several years ago. The lady's emeralds were taken and pawned by her son to buy some worthless stock, and were only thought to have been stolen. In real life, they were eventually redeemed and returned to their owner." What she didn't say was that the neighbor was Bradford Marsden's mother, Lady Marsden, and that Charles had written a check for five thousand pounds to redeem the pawned emeralds and keep Lady Marsden from learning what her son had done.[1]

"I see," Lillie said, relaxing almost imperceptibly. "So there *was* a real event behind your story, after all. Perhaps that's what gave it the ring of truth."

"Yes," Kate said, with a rueful sigh. "In fact, I've often regretted having drawn the duchess so near to life. While it is tempting to take real people as the models for one's characters, it may be dangerous to blur the line between fiction and reality. Someone who knows the facts might be misled by the fiction, or a reader of the fiction might be deceived by taking invention for the truth." She took a deep breath. This discussion gave her the opportunity to make her intention clear—and an understandable excuse. "That is why I must tell you that I cannot allow you to stage the story," Kate added. "If the owner of the emeralds were to see it or hear of it, she might feel betrayed."

If she were disappointed, Lillie hid it rather well. In fact, she was clearly relieved.

"Now that you've put the matter in those terms," she said brightly, "I understand completely. When one's

---

1 The story of the missing Marsden emeralds is told in its entirety in *Death at Gallows Green*.

artistic work is important to one, one does not want it misinterpreted."

"Thank you," Kate said. "Now, might we go back to my question? Do you know of anyone who might have wanted to kill Mr. Day?"

Lillie pulled her brows together. "I really do not think—"

The drawing room door opened and the butler reluctantly stepped in. "Mrs. Langtry—"

Lillie turned, suddenly angry. "Oh, what *now*, Williams?" she cried. She seized a velvet cushion and fired it at him as hard as she could. "Can't you leave us alone for an instant?"

Williams raised his arm to deflect the cushion that would otherwise have struck him squarely in the face. "Miss Jeanne-Marie is here, ma'am," he said, with infinite dignity.

He stepped back, opening the door wide. A brown-haired girl of seventeen or so, her face blotchy with tears, blouse rumpled, straw sailor askew, pushed past him. Hands on hips, she planted herself in front of Lillie and stared down at her.

"Jeanne!" Lillie gave a little gasp. "I thought you were staying with Lady Ragsdale." She peered around the girl. "Have you run on ahead? Where is she?" She stopped and looked up at the girl. "And why are you crying?"

"I came down by myself," the girl said, in a voice so low that Kate had to strain to hear. "On the train."

"On the train?" Lillie exclaimed. "Alone? Has something happened, Jeanne?"

"I know the truth at last," the girl said. "That's what has happened. After all the years of make-believe, I finally know what's real."

"*Ma petite chérie*," Lillie said, taking the girl's small white hand. "Whatever are you talking about?"

Kate half-rose from her chair, thinking that she should not intrude on this private scene, but realized that Lillie had entirely forgotten her and that the girl, Jeanne-Marie, had never even noticed that she was there. She sat back as the girl took out a pocket handkerchief and mopped her streaming eyes.

"Lady Ragsdale says that you're not my aunt, after all, Aunt Lillie. You're my *mother!*"

Lillie stared at her for a moment in unfeigned consternation, her lips trembling, tears starting in her eyes. Then she pulled the girl onto the sofa beside her, took the handkerchief, and began tenderly to wipe away her tears.

"For once in her life, sweetheart," she murmured, "Emily Ragsdale has told the truth. My darling Jeanne, I *am* your mother. And I love you more than life."

At this confession, the girl pulled away and began to weep again, even more stormily. Lillie held her tightly, trying to calm her without success. "Hush, Jeanne!" she commanded at last. "Do you want the servants to hear? You know how they talk."

This admonition seemed to produce the desired result. When Jeanne was calm enough to speak, she managed to choke out, "If you loved me, why did you pretend? Why did I have to spend all those dreadful years with Gram on that hateful little island? Why couldn't I have been with *you?*"

Lillie took her hand. "I had hoped to put off this discussion until you were older, my dear, but now that you know part of the story, you might as well know the whole. You were born after your father and I agreed to live separately and I was forced to make my own way in the world. I decided to become an actress. But the theater is no place for a child, and I knew that if I were to be successful,

I should have to be away a great deal, traveling. Your grandmother and I felt it would be best for you to live with her on Jersey, where you could have friends and lessons and a stable life."

Jeanne's face twisted and she jerked her hand away. "But to tell me that my parents were dead—"

"I'm so sorry for that, darling Jeanne," Lillie said. She leaned forward and pushed the disheveled hair off the girl's forehead. "I know it seems cruel, but we all thought it was for the best. All through your life, you have had powerful friends and protectors. The Prince of Wales—"

"But what about my *real* father?" Jeanne demanded, her voice shaking. She pushed her mother's hand away. "Uncle Ned was my father, wasn't he?"

Lillie stiffened. "Of course he was your father. What makes you ask a question like that?"

"Because Lady Ragsdale said that the Prince of Wales—"

Lillie laughed merrily. "Oh, what utter nonsense! Do you think for a moment that if the Prince were your father he would openly sponsor you at court? Think of the scandal!"

Jeanne pouted. "Well, then, what about Uncle Ned? If he was my father, why couldn't I have lived with him?"

Lillie pulled herself up and said, in a calm, chill voice, "Edward Langtry was not the kind of father a daughter deserves, Jeanne. Marrying him was a terrible mistake. I could not compound my folly by imposing it upon you." Her voice softened. "Anyway, he was totally incapable of supporting himself, let alone a daughter. And he drank a very great deal. I could not even let him know that you were his daughter, for fear that he might insist on involving himself in your life."

"But I should like to have been able to love him as my father," Jeanne said fiercely. "And now he's dead, and I shall never—" She looked up and caught a glimpse of

Kate. Quickly, she turned back to Lillie. "Who is *she*?"

Color flared across Lillie's face as she realized that there had been a witness to this intimate scene. "This is Lady Charles Sheridan, Jeanne. She is my houseguest. Lady Charles, may I present my... Jeanne-Marie."

"I'm very glad to know you, Jeanne," Kate said gravely. There was nothing more she could say.

The girl rose from the sofa and bobbed a little curtsy. "Yes, my lady," she said, very low.

The mood had been broken and Lillie was once more in command. "Jeanne, dear, I suggest that you go to your room and wash. We have not yet had our luncheon, and I should like you to join us. You can tell us all about Lady Ragsdale's plans for your presentation at court. Has your dress arrived? You must be very excited."

The girl dropped her head. All the fire seemed to have gone out of her. "Yes, Aunt—" She looked up. "What should I call you?"

Lillie gave her a narrow smile. "Under the circumstances, my darling, I think it is best if you simply continue to call me Aunt Lillie. This will remain our little secret until you've been presented at court, and perhaps for a few months after. We don't want to confuse our friends, do we?"

Jeanne gave her mother a long, dull look in which Kate read all her heartache. "Yes, Aunt," she replied, and left the room.

There was a silence. At last, Lillie said, in a low voice, "Now you know my deepest, most closely held secret."

Do I? Kate wondered. But she only inclined her head and said, "I'm sure you did what you thought was best for her. It must have been difficult."

"There were rumors, of course, and endless sly innuendoes. That's why Jeanne had to live on Jersey."

Lillie's voice became acid. "If she had been with me, the newspapers would have made such a game of it, counting my age against hers and forever speculating about the identity of her father. Once she is safely married, perhaps I can tell her who—"

A strange, haunted look crossed her face and she stopped, clearly feeling that she was giving too much away. Kate, though, could complete the sentence: once Jeanne-Marie was safely married and living somewhere out of the public eye, Lillie could tell her who her real father was. Not Edward Langtry, obviously. Was it the Prince of Wales, or someone else? Who was Lillie protecting, besides herself?

"How difficult for the child," Kate said quietly. "And for you."

Lillie gave an elaborate sigh. "I must confess that I feel a little relieved that she has found it out at last. At least I will no longer have to pretend to her." She slanted a glance at Kate, and her tone was cautionary. "I hope, however, that I may rely on you to keep my secret. You won't include any of this in your article for *The Strand?*"

"Of course not," Kate said without hesitation.

"Thank you," Lillie replied, and added, reflectively, "I should not want your readers to know that I am old enough to have a daughter who is soon to be presented at court." She sighed heavily. "And I simply cannot tell Suggie that he would be step-papa to a grown daughter, only a half-dozen years younger than he!"

27

Near Snailwell

"What splendid lies shall be found among the cheeses?
What disappointed hopes, what epic deeds?"

Elegies
THOMAS PUDDING

THOMAS MOORE RESIDED on a small dairy farm a half-mile to the east of the hamlet of Snailwell. With Jack Murray beside him, Charles drove the rented gig down a narrow lane. On one side, a stone fence opened onto a wide view of the heath and a river valley; on the other, an ancient hedge enclosed a parcel of rocky hillside and a picturesque herd of black-and-white cows, grazing on the June grass. The hedge was interwoven with wild roses and honeysuckle and blackberry in blossom, and patches of yellow flag, bright as new gold coins, bloomed in the ditch.

At length, passing through a wooden gate, they came upon a prosperous-looking farm. Before them was a large two-up, two-down stone cottage with a chimney at either gabled end, the roof thatched with straw and netted to keep birds away. The central door, painted green, was bowered with a pink China rose and a purple clematis, and fragrant rosemary clothed the whole foot of the walls on either side. The gray mist had risen, the sun was gleaming through the silvery clouds, and the casement windows with their red-checked curtains had been flung open to catch the warming breeze. From indoors, Charles could hear the melodic voice of a girl, singing a lullaby. The song stopped when they pulled up in front, and a moment later the girl appeared at the door, a tow-headed child on her hip. She was plump and red-cheeked, with long brown braids and a white apron over a plain gray dress. She dropped a curtsy when Charles got down from the gig.

"We're looking for a Mr. Oliver Moore," Charles said. "Is he here, miss?"

The girl pulled her brows together in a pretty frown, as if wondering how she should reply. "I'll ask, sir," she said, and disappeared indoors. In a moment she was out again, without the child, who could be heard wailing disconsolately within. She picked up her skirts and ran around the front corner of the cottage. With a nod to Jack to accompany him, Charles set out after her.

The girl was darting up a path that lay between a large vegetable garden filled with lettuce and rhubarb and potatoes and peas climbing a lattice of hazel twigs, and a stoutly fenced pigsty containing two pink porkers. An arrogant rooster rose up threateningly in her way, but she flapped her apron at him and he scuttled under the railing to join his hens looking for bugs around the bee hive.

At the end of the path, the girl ducked into a low stone building, with netted windows equipped with shutters in the front. Following close behind, Charles saw through the windows that it was a cheese-house, built for the drying of large cheeses, no doubt produced from the milk of the black-and-white cows on the hillside. The stone floor was raised up several feet above the ground to protect the cheeses from damp, and wide wooden shelves had been hung round the walls. These shelves were lined with cut nettles, over which had been laid large rounds of yellow cheese, as bright as the yellow flags in the ditch. These were being turned by a slight, rusty-haired man, his shirt-sleeves rolled to his elbows.

"Ollie," Charles heard the girl say in a low voice, "there's a pair o' gentl'men lookin' fer ye. Wot'll I tell 'em?"

"Yer s'posed t' keep it quiet that I'm 'ere," Moore hissed.

"I din't say," the girl protested, and turned with a start as Charles's shadow fell across the threshhold. She dropped a frightened curtsy and fled back down the path.

"Good afternoon, Mr. Moore," Charles said quietly. "I am Charles Sheridan, and this is Mr. Murray. We've come to talk with you about the murder of Mr. Alfred Day."

"Don't know nuffin 'bout it," Moore growled with a show of belligerence. "Nuffin a'tall. If ye don't b'lieve me, ask me brother Thomas. I bin 'ere fer three 'ole days. 'E'll swear to it."

"No, sir," Murray contradicted him firmly. "You were in the Great Horse in Newmarket High Street yesterday evening, before eight. The proprietor testifies to that, and others will, too."

Furtively, Moore glanced from one to the other. He wore thick-soled boots, stiff brown trousers tied at the waist with a length of dirty rope, and his shirt was home-spun—the usual farmer's garb. But he was clean shaven, his hair was neatly cut and pomaded, and his hands and nails were clean. He did not have the look of a country man.

"Are ye from the p'lice?" he asked nervously.

"No, Mr. Moore," Charles said. "We are conducting a private investigation."

This seemed to make Moore feel easier. His shoulders relaxed, and he became more confident. He glanced from Charles to Murray. "Wot'cher want from me, then?"

"We want you to tell us what you know about your employer's murder," Charles said. "Everything you know about it, please, sir."

"Don't know *nuffin*," Moore repeated, with emphasis. "I wuz at the Great 'Orse, true. But then I went up to the Owl and stayed an hour or so. You can ask Mrs. Thorpe. 'Fore I left, I bought one of 'er shepherd's pies. She wrapped it fer me to take 'ome."

"To St. James Street?" Charles asked, thinking of the remains of the pie on the table in the loft.

"Where else?" Moore countered. "I went 'ome, ate me pie leisure-like, and went t' bed. I wuz woke in the middle o' the night by men movin' round in the office below. Thieves, they wuz. Bangin' drawers, pullin' out papers, talkin'—"

"What time was this?" Murray asked.

"I din't strike no light, now, did I?" Moore was truculent. "They din't know I wuz there. I wuzn't goin' to call their attention to me, now, wuz I?"

Charles pictured the situation, the clerk cowering in his bed with the covers pulled over his head, afraid that the men would come up the stairs and discover him. "You say you heard them talking," he remarked. "What were they talking about?"

Moore chewed on his lip. "One of them said as how Badger wuz dead. Shot in th' alley b'hind the Great 'Orse. I reckoned when they 'eard 'e wuz dead, they come lookin' fer money." He shook his head as if with disgust. "Prob'ly figgered t' find a satchel full o' gold sovereigns."

"But they didn't?" Charles asked.

"Badger wuz a careful man," Moore said. "'E never kept no money in the office. 'E 'ad a safe at 'ome."

"I see," Charles said. Perhaps it would be a good idea to interview the widow after all. The safe might contain some sort of clue to the killer's identity. "You didn't recognize the voices, I suppose." And might not readily tell them if he had.

Moore shook his head.

Charles narrowed his eyes. "Why did you come here?" he asked abruptly. "Why are you hiding out? What do you know?"

Again the furtive glance, and a silence.

Murray stepped closer, crowding Moore against the shelves. "Don't be a fool, man," he snarled. "Your employer's been murdered and you've run away to hide. Who's to say there was no money in that office? Who's to say that you didn't kill Badger, ransack the office, and make off with that satchel of sovereigns? I promise you, the chief constable won't be so tender, nor the judge at the assize. Answer the question!"

Moore seemed to deflate in front of their eyes. His shoulders slumped as if his backbone could no longer support them, and his head dropped. "I'm 'iding out from Baggs," he muttered.

"Baggs?" Charles frowned. "Why?"

"'Cause 'e's 'oo killed Badger."

"How do you know?"

Moore chewed on his lower lip. "'Im and Badger 'ad sharp words about 'orse doping, more'n once. Badger din't like doping, ye see. It interfered wiv the book. Badger said it's the bookie 'oo gets 'urt when there's doping—the bookie and the ord'n'ry bettor. Badger went through 'ard times in 'is life. 'E 'ad a warm place in 'is 'eart fer the ord'n'ry bettor, 'oo saves up 'is pence to 'ave a go on a good 'orse."

"And Baggs?" Murray asked. "What was his view on the subject?"

Moore's face darkened. "Baggs 'ad got in wiv the American dopers and saw a chance to make some big money, like they're doing. When Badger told 'im that 'e'd been to talk wiv the Stewards, Baggs wuz fierce wiv 'im. And when 'e said 'e intended to organize the bookies, Baggs wuz fiercer. Said 'e wudn't stand still and watch 'im meddle in wot din't concern 'im." He hunched his shoulders and added darkly. "Baggs is the one 'oo killed Badger."

"Do you have any certain knowledge of that?" Murray demanded.

"I 'eard 'im say 'e would, din't I?" Moore replied. "They wuz arguing, and Baggs told Badger that if 'e tried to organize the bookies to stop the dopers, 'e'd kill 'im dead. Right in front of me, 'e said it. Loud and nasty-like. 'I'll kill ye dead wiv me own two 'ands,' 'e said, just like that."

"When did he say that?" Charles asked.

"Recent. A couple of days ago. When I 'eard the men sayin' how Badger was shot to death in the alley, I figgered it wuz Baggs as done it. Since 'e knew I wuz there when 'e threatened Badger, I feared 'e might come after me. To keep me from telling. So I come 'ere, to me brother's 'ouse. And 'ere is where I'm staying." He held out his hands and added, fervently. "That's the truth, sirs, the 'ole truth and nuffin but the truth, so 'elp me God."

On the whole, Charles rather thought that it was—the truth, at least, as Sobersides saw it.

28

At Regal Lodge

"No man but a blockhead ever wrote, except for money."

SAMUEL JOHNSON

"Do right to all men, and don't write to any woman."

LILLIE LANGTRY

WHEN AMELIA LEFT the kitchen after her conversation with Margaret, Mrs. Redditch the cook, and Bowchard the gardener, she went straight up to her mistress's room in the hopes of finding Lady Charles. Bowchard's news about Alfred Day's murder had surprised Amelia to no end, and the servants' veiled accusation of Mrs. Langtry had not been lost on her. Of course, she understood that none of the servants liked their mistress; in fact, most of them seemed to actively dislike her, some from a narrowminded (and probably hypocritical) distaste for Mrs. Langtry's low morals; and some from a general unhappiness with her slow payment of wages.

But even taking these hostile feelings into account, Amelia

knew that something unusual was afoot here. Mrs. Langtry's bookmaker had been shot to death at about the same time that he was to rendezvous with her. And what was more, Mrs. Langtry's silver-handled derringer was missing from a drawer in the drawing room, where it was always kept.

Amelia and Margaret had learned this intriguing intelligence from Pru, the parlormaid, whom they encountered in the passageway outside the kitchen on their way back upstairs. Pru was tall and angular, and the absence of brows (scorched off by an exploding gas lamp) gave her a look of perpetual dismay. She was entrusted with dusting and straightening the dining, breakfast, and drawing rooms, a duty which permitted her to sew a lace edging on her apron to distinguish her from the other maids. Parlormaids were not supposed to snoop in drawers, of course, but Pru had seen the gun on more than one occasion when she had opened the drawer to put something away. She had thought then that it was a careless sort of place to keep a dangerous weapon, and now she was sure of it. For this morning when she opened the drawer, the gun was gone.

"Mrs. L took it and shot poor Mr. Day to death," Margaret said, with great satisfaction. "I'm sart'n of it!"

Pru, who did not seem to share Margaret's deep animosity toward their employer, disagreed. "Might not've been Mrs. L wot took it," she said. She dropped her voice to a sinister whisper. "'Er friend Spider was in the drawing room yestiddy afternoon, see, waiting fer 'er. When I comes in wiv a vase of roses, 'e's standing by the table, 'is hand in the drawer. When 'e sees me, 'e shuts it quick like. 'E could've took it."

"Spider?" Amelia asked with a shudder. "Wot a name fer a man! 'Oo is 'e?"

"Spider is all she ever calls 'im," Pru said with a shrug.

206

"A friend of Mrs. L's, up from London. 'E comes every so often. Sometimes 'e stays for a day er two."

"'E gives 'er money to put on 'er plays," Margaret explained to Amelia. "It's the on'y reason she puts up wiv 'im. 'E don't have a title or nothin'. Just money."

"Just money, huh?" Pru giggled. "Well, ye won't see me turnin' me nose up at money. 'Oo cares about a musty ol' title? Ye can't trade a title for beef at the butcher's."

There was a heavy footstep behind them and Amelia started nervously. "What do you girls think you're doing, gossiping in the hallway?" Mr. Williams demanded in a stern voice. "Margaret and Pru, get on with your duties. Miss Amelia, I should think her ladyship might wish you to find something more profitable than gossip to occupy your time."

The three of them had scattered guiltily, Margaret and Pru to their respective tasks and Amelia to her mistress's room in the hope of sharing what she had just learned. But her ladyship was apparently detained in the drawing room downstairs, and the servants' lunch bell sounded before she returned.

At lunch in the servants' hall, Mr. Williams was once more absent, serving luncheon upstairs, and the gossip flowed freely. To her surprise, Amelia learned that Lord Charles had called that morning and that Mrs. L had been much perturbed by his lordship's visit. Shortly after his departure, Miss Jeanne-Marie had arrived unexpectedly from London, unescorted and visibly distressed, and loud weeping had been heard through the drawing room door. There was a good deal of whispering about her visit, as well as about Mrs. L's planned rendezvous with the murdered bookmaker and the silver-handled derringer that had gone missing from the drawer in the drawing room.

After lunch, Amelia volunteered to help Rose, the

other upstairs maid, iron the freshly laundered sheets and pillowcases for Miss Jeanne-Marie's bed, which had not yet been freshly made up. As they worked over their ironing tables with irons heated on the kitchen range, Amelia turned the conversation to the girl.

"Is she as pretty as 'er auntie?" she asked, deliberately innocent.

"Auntie!" Rose snorted. "Don't be a goose. Mrs. L is 'er *mother*. Lady Ragsdale told 'er the truth so Mrs. L 'ad to admit it at last. The girl's upstairs just this minute, cryin' 'er eyes out. Refused to come down fer luncheon, though she was sent fer twice."

"Oh, the poor thing!" Amelia exclaimed in genuine sympathy.

Rose, a flat-faced, sallow-cheeked girl with a worldly air about her, seemed to share Margaret's judgmental view of her employer. "Pore thing is right," she said sharply, spitting on a flatiron to test the heat. "I'd cry too, if I'd jest found out I wuz Mrs. L's daughter. Nobody respect'ble will marry 'er now, only one o' them turrible rogues and wastrels 'oo 'ang 'round 'er mother."

"Really?" Amelia asked. She hadn't considered Jeanne's dilemma from the perspective of her opportunities for marriage.

"Really," Rose said, mocking. She pushed the iron over a pilllowcase with swift, hard strokes. "If ye wuz a mother er father with a good fam'ly name to pertect, would ye let yer son marry Lillie Langtry's daughter—even if she was a royal bastard?"

"Well, I—"

"'Course ye wouldn't. Like mother, like daughter, is wot ye'd say." Rose folded the pillowcase neatly and pushed the iron across it again, setting a crease. "She can be persented in court a dozen times and it won't do 'er a shillin's worth of good. Mark my words, that girl'll end up jest like 'er mother, on the stage er worse." She folded the pillowcase once more and whacked it again with the iron. "Worse, most likely."

And that had to settle it, for the ironing was finished, Rose sailed off upstairs with the linens, and there was no more opportunity to talk.

But the conversation had given Amelia even more to think about, and she was still thinking when she went back upstairs to lay out her ladyship's tea gown. In fact, she was so deeply engrossed in her thoughts that when she put her hand into her apron pocket and her fingers touched the rough edges of a crumpled paper, she did not at first remember what it was. It wasn't until she drew out the small, wine-stained ball of paper that she recalled retrieving it from the fireplace in Mrs. Langtry's bedroom, where it had obviously been intended to burn. When Amelia smoothed it out and read it, she understood why:

Monday, 5 June

My dear Mrs. Langtry,
I write because I find myself in a difficult financial situation and no longer able to carry large overdue accounts. According to my records, you owe me some ten thousand pounds. If you are disinclined to find this money, I must remind you of what I know about the theft of your jewels and about Mr. Langtry's death. I expect payment in full as soon as possible. If I do not receive it, I shall be forced to go to the elder Lord de Bathe and tell him what I know. I'm sure he will be most interested in the information.

I shall look forward to hearing when you will honor your obligation.

Yrs faithfully,
Alfred S Day

Amelia had scarcely finished reading this revealing missive when the door opened and Lady Charles entered, carrying her notebook and pen.

"Oh, Amelia," she said breathlessly, "I'm glad you're here, my dear. I must write a note to Lord Charles, and I shall want you to carry it to him as quickly as possible. I do hope you won't mind walking into Newmarket. I particularly don't want Mrs. Langtry to know that I've written to his lordship." She stopped, seeing the note Amelia was holding out to her. "What is this?"

"I found it in the grate in Mrs. Langtry's bedroom," Amelia said, very seriously. "I think ye should read it, m'lady. And I've learned some things belowstairs that ye'll likely want to 'ear."

Lady Charles scanned the wine-stained, slightly charred note, pulling in her breath sharply. Then she went back to the beginning and read it again, more slowly, her lips silently forming the words.

"I think I'm beginning to see," she whispered, as if she were speaking only to herself. "Is it sufficient proof? I doubt it. But of course Charles must decide. And he may have found out more that will help him." Then she looked up, starting, as if she had forgotten Amelia's presence. "You have something else to tell me, Amelia?"

Carefully, trying to recall exactly what had been said, Amelia sketched out what she had learned from Margaret, Mr. Bowchard, Rose, and Pru. Lady Charles listened carefully, seeming most interested in Pru's report.

"You say the parlormaid saw this man, Spider, take the gun out of the drawer?"

"Not 'xactly, ma'am." Amelia shook her head. "She said 'e *might've* took it, 'cause she saw 'im standing at the table with his 'and in the drawer."

"That fits with what I know," her ladyship murmured.

"But I wonder why Lillie lied to protect him." She looked up. "None of the servants know this man's real name?"

"They don't seem to, ma'am. Just that 'e's from London, and 'e comes 'ere ev'ry so often."

Lady Charles glanced down at the paper in her hand. After a moment's hesitation, she went to the small writing desk that stood beside the window. She took out a piece of paper and her pen and sat down to write, giving careful thought to some of the sentences, as though she were telling a complicated story. Once, apparently having forgotten some detail, she went back to insert a phrase in the margin. Then she folded the note Amelia had given her into the paper she herself had written, and thrust both into an envelope. On the desk was a candle, with a stick of red sealing wax and a metal embosser beside it. She lit the candle and melted a blob of wax onto the envelope, embossing it carefully. She gave it to Amelia.

"Lord Charles is staying at Hardaway House, on the left side of Wellington Street, just off the High Street. The house has a green door, behind a brick gateway. Go there, and give this envelope to his lordship. If he isn't in, you must wait for him." She frowned. "No, it might be very late when he comes, and your return here would attract attention. Best to give the note to Mrs. Hardaway, the landlady, and ask her to keep it for Lord Charles. On no account should she give it to anyone else. Do you understand?"

"Oh, yes, m'lady," Amelia said eagerly, pleased to be entrusted with this important mission.

Lady Charles stood, went to her purse, and took out a coin which she pressed into Amelia's hand. "Give Mrs. Hardaway this to ensure that she does as you say." She found another coin. "And use this to hire a hansom to bring you back. If you are asked where you've been, say that I sent you to the chemist for lavender water." She added a third coin. "You may keep the lavender water for yourself, for your trouble."

"Oh *yes*, m'lady!" Amelia exclaimed, now struck almost breathless by the prospect of being involved in such fascinating intrigue, and by the anticipation of the lavender water.

"Very well, then," her ladyship said. "Put on your hat and go. And do *hurry*, my dear! His lordship must have that envelope as soon as possible."

29

On Newmarket Heath

"It was customary for boys to go into racing stables at the age of ten or eleven, some of them before they reached that age. They were often spotted by men who saw them going well to hounds, or riding ponies at some village sports. One well-known owner when asked where he found the light-weights who rode his horses so well, replied: 'I breed 'em on the estate.' The earlier boys begin their tuition and ride against other jockeys, the more likely they are to succeed."

Paddock Personalities
J FAIRFAX-BLAKEBOROUGH, 1936

WHEN PATRICK WOKE at five on Tuesday morning, he was tired and still shaken by his adventure of the previous night. But he got through morning stables in good order, none of the other lads having noticed that he had been absent from his bed until past midnight. And when Pinkie Duncan told them at breakfast that Badger the bookmaker had been murdered, Patrick looked down at his plate and pretended to know nothing at all about it. He noticed, however, that despite Pinkie's efforts to conceal his true feelings, his satisfaction showed on his face. Clearly, the dead man had not been one of Pinkie's friends, although Patrick could not guess why. Patrick did not like Pinkie any the more for this secret gloating. It was not that he had cared very much for the bookmaker, whom he knew only from seeing at the racecourse. But it did not seem right that one man should gloat over another man's death, however unpleasant their association might have been.

Gladiator was exercised with the afternoon string, so Patrick readied his other horse, a two-year-old filly named Starling. The morning sky was lightening in the east when he took her out with the other lads. They walked their horses around the paddock's cinder path under the watchful eye of Mr. Angus Duncan, who was making the daily exercise assignments: the more experienced lads to the more difficult or valuable horses, the less experienced to the horses least likely to give trouble. The inexperienced were left behind in the yard to walk the unfit horses.

Patrick was extraordinarily pleased when he was put up on Constant, a promising seventeen-hand bay with a great deal of sparkle, for the match suggested that Mr. Angus might be testing his abilities, as well as those of the horse. Constant was a stable favorite, usually exercised by Arch Adams, another apprentice jockey who had already ridden in several races at Newmarket. Arch and his friend Jim gave Patrick a disgruntled look as he shortened the stirrup leathers (Patrick rode short, in the style of the American Tod Sloan) and when he went into the saddle, Jim muttered something derogatory under his breath. But Patrick did his best to ignore them and concentrated on settling onto the horse, which danced and fidgeted under him.

When all the lads were mounted, the string departed for

the gallops on the west side of Newmarket at Southfields, not far from the racecourse. They crossed the Bury Road and went behind the other stables and right through the town, taking the High Street. This was the regular route to the Heath taken by all the stables, and often they encountered other strings on their way to exercise. But they were early this morning, and when Southfields came into view, it was empty.

It was full light now, but cloudy and gray, with a slight drizzle. The air was cool, the ground soft but not slippery, the breeze quiet—the very best sort of morning to exercise horses. Mr. Angus began immediately with the canters, watching carefully to make an assessment of the individual horse's capabilities. As always, the touts and tipsters had arrived early, too. They watched from their distant stations up the hill and along the road, peering through their field glasses, collecting tidbits of information on the health and performance of one horse or another to pass along to the bookmakers and racing papers. There was nothing that could be done about this peering and prying, and the stables had learned how to turn it to best advantage by showcasing some horses and concealing others, thereby influencing the odds.

Canters completed, the string rode back through the town to the stable, where Patrick unsaddled Constant, rubbed him down, washed the dirt out of his hooves, rugged him up, and carried water and oats to his box. Then it was time for more chores, lunch, and then the afternoon string—and here it was that the gray day became suddenly much brighter, for while Mr. Angus was making assignments, his nephew Pinkie came out to join him. There was a hurried conference, Mr. Angus shaking his head and Pinkie gesturing emphatically, and Patrick was put up on Gladiator.

Then, while the head lad marshaled the string and headed off to Southfields, Patrick rode Gladiator behind Mr. Angus and Mr. Pinkie to the trial ground beyond the Limekilns, accompanied by Arch Adams on a four-year-old colt named Rag who had won well the previous year, and Jim on Cannon, a promising, eager chestnut, another stable favorite. No one said a word, but Patrick knew that they were going to run a full-scale trial to see how well Rag would do against Cannon, and whether Cannon had as much promise as he seemed to have. He leaned over and patted Gladiator's neck, hoping that the horse would run well. He thought briefly of Johnny's fair, bright face and smiling optimism, and felt a stab of sadness. But he had to put that out of his mind, for Johnny was gone now. And if he felt any fear that Gladiator might suddenly turn savage, as he had at the Derby, Patrick put it away too. What had happened in that race happened because of the doping, and today Gladiator was as calm as could be, and perhaps even a little lethargic.

The mist was clearing and the sun breaking through the silver clouds when the group reached the trial ground. Three men on horseback were watching from the brow of the hill through field glasses as Mr. Angus rode on to the end of the course and reined in where he could observe. After a few moments, the watchers were joined by several more. Mr. Pinkie stayed with the three runners, giving them brief instructions.

"Don't ride 'em into the ground," he said. "We don't want any injuries. If there's faltering, ease off." He looked at Arch Adams. "But let 'im run 'ard if 'e wants," he said.

The riders nodded, the horses danced eagerly, and Mr. Pinkie dropped a red handkerchief to signal the start. They were off quicker and faster than Patrick expected, accelerating in a hard run, Rag opening up a strong lead,

Cannon running second. Loping lazily, Gladiator did not seem compelled to keep up until Patrick, seeing the distance to Cannon open to ten lengths, loosened the rein, crouched forward on the horse's withers, and whispered urgently, "For Johnny, boy, go! *Go!*"

At this, Gladiator pricked his ears, gathered his strength, and shot forward, making up length on length against Cannon and then pulling past, working up close behind Rag, and then flying past him too, and passing Mr. Angus in a strong finish, neck stretched out. The other two horses slowed to a canter immediately, but Gladiator continued to run as if he were enjoying the pleasure of it, until Patrick gradually pulled him up and circled back to the others.

"Well," Mr. Angus said, as if he were surprised. Frowning, he looked at Patrick, then at Gladiator, who was prancing and shaking his head, exactly as if he were proud of his win. "Decided to try at last, did he?"

"Yes, sir," Patrick said. "The start was faster than I expected and I had a tight rein, so I might have held him up some, just from not knowing. But he moved up fast when he was asked." He wanted to add, proudly, *He's the best horse in the world*, but he held his tongue and contented himself with a pat on Gladiator's sweat-flecked neck.

While Patrick and the other riders let their horses cool, Mr. Pinkie rode up, frowning, as if he were not entirely pleased with the outcome of the trial. He and Mr. Angus pulled off to one side for a brief discussion, Mr. Pinkie speaking with unusual animation. Mr. Angus looked irritated at first, then angry, but finally gave a vexed shrug and seemed to give in, though his look was dark. Mr. Pinkie then turned to the watchers on the hill, who'd had their glasses trained on the entire event, and made some sort of signal. Mr. Angus rode back to the group.

"That's it for the afternoon, lads," he said gruffly, not

looking at Patrick. "Let's take 'em back to the stable."

As they started off, Pinkie motioned to Patrick to ride behind with him.

"That was Lord Hunt up on the hill, watching the trial," he said. "He wants you up on Gladiator for the ten-furlong handicap on Friday."

Patrick stared at him, almost uncomprehending. It was what he'd been longing to hear, yet couldn't quite believe. His first ride as a jockey—not in a trial, but in a real race, and on Gladiator, the best horse in the world!

"Thank you," he managed at last. "I'll do my best to win, Mr. Pinkie. And Gladiator will too, I know it." He thought briefly of the Derby, and swallowed hard. They wouldn't try to dope the horse again, would they? But now that they'd seen how fast Gladiator could run if he were asked, they had to know that the dope wouldn't be needed. He could run just as fast, and with a lot more control, without it. And he would watch Gladiator like a hawk before the race. No one would put anything into his horse. If they tried, they would have to contend with *him*.

But there was an expression on Pinkie's leathery face that Patrick couldn't quite decipher. They rode in silence for a moment; then the man said, "There's a condition to yer riding, boy. Ye're to promise to ride exactly as yer told on the day of the race. Ye *will* follow instructions— or ye'll not ride again, for this stable or any other. Is that understood?"

"A condition?" Patrick stared at him, at the steely eyes, the hard mouth. He began to comprehend what was being asked of him.

"We don't need to go into the details now," Pinkie said roughly. "Let's just have yer promise, shall we?"

"I don't—" Patrick swallowed. He could stop worrying about Gladiator being doped, for he understood all too well what his instructions for the race would be: to stop Gladiator from doing his best, to hold him back so that another horse might win. Those men on the hill with Lord Hunt must have been tipsters. They'd seen the horse run well, and they'd carry the message back to the bookies. Gladiator would be short odds. Lord Hunt would bet against him, and would win by losing.

"Speak up, boy," Pinkie snapped. His eyes were narrowed and dark. "Say it now, or 'is lordship'll give the ride to Arch Adams. Arch does as 'e's told."

Patrick took a deep breath. "I… promise," he said numbly. He had to. If he didn't, he'd lose any chance he might have to keep Gladiator safe.

Pinkie grinned and leaned over to clap him hard on the shoulder. "Well, then, buck up, lad! It ain't every day that an apprentice jockey goes up on a 'orse that nearly won the Derby, is it?"

Patrick nodded. That much, at least, was true.

30

At Wolford Lodge

"British racing fans bitterly resented the intrusion of American jockeys, trainers, and owners into what had been their own private preserve, just as the British aristocracy complained when peers began marrying wealthy American heiresses and installing them in their hereditary castles."

Trainers and Stables
ALBERT J WILLIAM

IT WAS WELL past teatime and growing dark when Charles returned to Newmarket that evening and dropped Jack Murray off at the Stag Hotel. If they had returned an hour earlier, he would have gone back to Hardaway House to change, and hence would have discovered and read Kate's urgent note. But the hour was late and he was expected for dinner at the home of Bradford's fiancée's parents, so he drove straight on to Wolford Lodge.

Edith Hill's mother and stepfather lived in a small, newly built Tudor-style plaster-and-timber house, behind an iron fence some distance off the Cambridge Road.

Charles gave his hired horse into the care of a ragged boy who came out to greet him. Edith herself answered his knock and led him into the sitting room, where Edith's mother and stepfather were chatting with Bradford. A fire blazed cheerfully beneath a mantel ornately draped with a tassled red-velvet flounce, and after the cool out-of-doors, the room seemed stifling. It seemed small, as well, because it was crowded with large pots of green foliage and a dozen oddly shaped tables decorated with exotic-looking souvenirs, many carved of ivory. On the walls were displayed foreign-looking tapestries and hangings, as well as several large paintings of elephants and peacocks and a gilt-framed photograph of the Taj Mahal. A tiger-skin rug was artfully draped over a large bamboo chair with an arched back, beside which stood a trunk inlaid with many colorful woods. It appeared that the Hogsworths had spent some time in India.

"So sorry to be late," Charles said apologetically, when Edith had introduced him to Colonel and Mrs. Harry Hogsworth, who was a small woman with gray hair, dressed in a stiff purple poplin and old-fashioned beaded dolman. "I drove out to Snailwell this afternoon, and the errand took longer than I expected. I didn't take time to dress, I fear. Please forgive me."

"No matter about the dress," Colonel Hogsworth boomed. "We're quite informal here." He was a large, loud-voiced man with gray side-whiskers, heavy jowls, and an air of outspoken jovialty better suited to the Guards' noisy clubroom than his wife's small parlor. "Snailwell, eh? Not to be forward, but what was your lordship doing out there? Nothing but sheep and cattle and miserable little cottages overrun with dirty children."

"Edith," murmured her mother, "do be a good girl and fetch his lordship a brandy." To Charles, she explained

221

delicately: "After so long a stay in Bombay, I fear that we find English butlers arrogant and clumsy. The colonel has promised to turn up an Indian for us. Until then, we have vowed to do without, even if it means answering our own door."

Charles bowed to Mrs. Hogsworth as Edith, lovely in a pale yellow gown, poured for him. She handed him the snifter with a glance of mute apology, and Charles smiled at her.

Bradford remarked, "I suppose you were looking after that business for the Jockey Club, Sheridan. Did you manage to locate the veterinary who did the doping?"

Taking his brandy, Charles glanced at Bradford in some surprise, then remembered that the two of them had not spoken since breakfast that morning—before Owen North had asked him to take on the investigation into Alfred Day's murder. A great deal had happened in a relatively few hours, and Bradford knew none of it. He was trying to decide what sort of answer he should make when the colonel, in his emphatic way, broke in.

"Horse doping." He gave a disgusted grunt and went to stand before the fire, blocking most of its heat. "Nasty business. Worst disgrace ever visited on British racing. All the doing of those bloody Americans. Don't understand why the Stewards don't put their foot down. No stomach, I suppose."

"Now, Colonel," his wife said in a cautionary tone.

"Don't 'now, Colonel' me, Clarice," Colonel Hogsworth said angrily. "I mean what I say. Appalling disgrace. Damn those Americans."

With a little sigh, Mrs. Hogsworth leaned toward Charles and confided, "I'm afraid that my husband is rather vehement on the subject of people who come from the States, Lord Charles." She lowered her voice to a whisper. "He doesn't like them. Particularly those from Brazil. Something to do with coffee, I believe."

"Mama," Edith said quietly, "Brazil is in South America."

"Of course, dear," Mrs. Hogsworth replied. "It's near Texas, I understand." She shivered a little. "One hears so many strange stories about Texas. It must truly be a wild place."

"No true horse lover likes the Americans!" the colonel exclaimed, rising to his toes, his jowls reddening. "No care for the horses. Buy 'em, dope 'em, run 'em, and shoot 'em when they've run their hearts out. In it for the money, that's all. And now they're corrupting honest English stables."

Mrs. Hogsworth made yet another attempt to retrieve the conversation. "Well, then, Lord Charles!" she exclaimed, smiling brightly. "Pray tell me what you think of our Edith's engagement to Lord Bradford. We're quite pleased, of course." She bestowed a kindly glance on Bradford. "Edith and his lordship seem to have so many common interests. Edith occasionally helps her godfather, Cecil Rhodes, by writing a letter or two for him. Not a position, of course, just an occasional offer of help. It was at his office that they met." She tilted her head to one side, like a bird. "Your lordship has heard of Mr. Rhodes, I'm sure. He's going to put a stop to that ridiculous Boer business down there in Argentina. The idea of those savages, daring to rise against their Queen!"

Charles was saved the embarrassment of answering this preposterous remark by the colonel, who turned round to say to Bradford: "Don't suppose you've heard the latest news, since you and Edith were traipsing round Cambridge all day. One of the local bookmakers, rather clever chap by the name of Alfred Day, was murdered last night—by an American trainer, I understand. Jesse Clark. Shot him dead with a revolver as big as a cannon. Aimed to keep Day from organizing the bookmakers against doping."

"Really, Colonel," Mrs. Hogsworth said in a plaintive tone, "Shooting isn't a fit subject for—"

"Actually, Mama," Edith said cheerfully, "Bradford has told me all about the murder. He and Lord Charles saw the poor man's dead body, terribly bloody and quite shot full of holes, in the alley behind the Great Horse. In fact, they were the ones who summoned the constable."

With a little gasp, Mrs. Hogsworth raised her hand to her mouth. "Goodness gracious!" she exclaimed weakly. "But I do so wish we would not speak of—"

"Did you now?" Colonel Hogsworth said, pulling his furry eyebrows together. "Capital, what? Did y'see Clark there too? Did the police nab him? Cert'nly hope so. Americans can't be allowed to go around shooting civilized folk as if Newmarket were the Wild West."

"I don't think it's been definitely established that Mr. Day was killed by Mr. Clark," Charles said mildly.

"Well, if it's not, it soon will be," the colonel said in a settled tone, rising once again to his toes. "The Newmarket police may be slow, but they're thorough. Always get their man." He shook his head, glowering. "It's not just the trainers and their doping, y'know. It's the whole damned American invasion—don't try to stop me, Clarice, it's true. That pesky little jockey Sloan, for one. Outrageous! Hit a waiter in the face with a champagne bottle at the last Ascot. And those American gamblers, a whole string of 'em, coming over with their pockets full of gold. Heavy plungers, and all's well if they win. But if they lose, they simply abscond."

"You mean," Mrs. Hogsworth said with a look of incredulity, "that the Americans don't pay their lawful debts?"

"Hard to believe, but that's the case, m'dear. When our English chaps lose, they lose honorably. They pay up, even if it takes the family's last shilling. Take Lord Hunt, f'r instance, handing over Glenoaks to Henry Radwick so he could settle fair and square. That's the way to lose, by Jove!" He punched the air. "You may be bloody and sore, but stand up and take your losses like a man—that's a sportsman for you. Not the Americans, though. Not an ounce of honor, not a shred. That sniveling little fellow John Bass, for instance. Took the boat back to New York owing Alfred Day sixty thousand pounds on the Derby."

"Sixty thousand pounds?" Charles murmured in some amazement, thinking back to his conversation with Badger's clerk. That was an enormous loss for a bookmaker, even one as successful as Day. Why hadn't Oliver Moore mentioned it? But then, perhaps he hadn't known about it. Perhaps it had been a private wager, off the books. He frowned, wondering who the devil John Bass was, and whether the loss might have had anything to do with Alfred Day's murder.

"Sixty thousand pounds," the colonel repeated emphatically, with some satisfaction. "I heard Lord Hunt talking about it at the stable this afternoon, when I went over to have a look at one of my horses."

"Colonel Hogsworth is speaking of the Grange House Stable," Bradford said in a meaningful tone, with a glance at Charles. To Hogsworth, he remarked, "Sheridan is planning to have a couple of horses trained at the Grange. We were there yesterday, as a matter of fact, to have a look around. Old Angus Duncan used to train for my father at Marsden Manor, you know. He's quite an impressive fellow."

The colonel pursed his lips. "I'd think twice about putting my horses there if I were you, Lord Charles," he said judiciously. "I'm pulling out as soon as I find another stable. Old Angus is fine, as you say, but I don't like the idea of that nephew of his taking over. Pinkie, his name is."

"Oh?" Charles asked, raising his eyebrows. "Pinkie is assuming responsibility for the stable? Nothing was said of that." Out of the corner of his eye, he saw a stout lady in a stained apron open the door and signal to her mistress that dinner was ready.

"Well, it's so," the colonel said. "I shouldn't wonder if the stable goes right downhill when Angus is gone. Afraid Pinkie does not have his uncle's upstanding character. Been involved in several rather shady—"

"Dinner has been announced," Mrs. Hogsworth said, standing. "Tonight is the serving maid's night out, so we shall be served by our cook." She stood and took Charles's arm. "And might I suggest that we find some other subject for our dinner discussion than horses and murders?" She smiled sweetly at Bradford, who was taking Edith in. "Perhaps you and Edith could tell us, Lord Marsden, what you did in Cambridge today. And after we've eaten, dear Edith has agreed to honor us with a few songs."

And with that, they all went in to dinner.

31

At Hardaway House

"If, of all words of tongue and pen,
The saddest are 'It might have been,'
More sad are these we daily see:
'It is, but hadn't ought to be!'"

Mrs. Judge Jenkins
BRET HARTE

As CHARLES AND Bradford drove back from Wolford Lodge to the livery stable, Charles gave Bradford a sketch of the long day's doings, beginning with the conversation at the Jockey Club and ending with the talk he and Jack Murray had had with Sobersides, at the farmhouse near Snailwell.

"So Mrs. Langtry may be involved in Day's murder," Bradford said, in some amazement, having heard of her note to Day that Charles had found in the dead man's pocket, and her missing gun.

"Kate doesn't think she shot him," Charles said, getting down to turn the horse and gig over to the sleepy stable-boy. "And on the whole, I'm inclined to agree. It's clear that

227

Mrs. Langtry meant to meet Badger in St. Mary's Square to tell him that she could not repay the money she owed him, but I doubt that the man actually made it that far. The evidence suggests that he was murdered shortly after leaving the Great Horse."

Bradford alighted from the gig. "But her gun is missing," he said, frowning. "And ten thousand pounds is a great deal of motive. Doesn't it strike you as highly coincidental?"

"We have no idea whether it was her gun that killed him," Charles reminded him as they walked off.

There was a silence. "Well, then, what do you think of Colonel Hogsworth's theory? Jesse Clark certainly had a strong motive, as well as opportunity. If Badger were successful in organizing the Newmarket and London bookmakers, they could put an end to doping."

"To some of it, perhaps," Charles said. "Although I'm not as certain as you and Jack Murray that a coalition of bookmakers could stop the practice. More likely, they'd just stir up a scandal in the newspapers—which the Stewards certainly don't want." He thought again of Owen North, and the strange undercurrents in their morning interview. "The Stewards had as much reason as Clark to stop Badger from doing what he threatened to do."

Bradford slanted him a questioning glance. "Are you suggesting that the Club might have arranged Badger's murder?" His tone implied that it was an incredible suggestion.

They turned off the High Street and onto Wellington Street. A horse and rider passed them, hooves clip-clopping on the cobbles, but otherwise the street was silent and deserted, and dark shadows filled the intervals between the gas lamps. "I think we ought to entertain the possibility," Charles said reluctantly. "You know how strongly the Marlborough Set feel about public scandal, especially where wagering is concerned. The last time they were dragged into court, in the Tranby Croft affair, it was a complete fiasco. In the eyes of the country, they looked like fools and dilettantes, with nothing on earth to do but play cards and hurl petty accusations of cheating at one another. If the press made a scandal out of horse doping—"

"But murder!" Bradford exclaimed. "Do you really think the Club would stoop to it?"

"The Stewards have a motive," Charles said firmly. "I can't overlook it. But I want to interview Eddie Baggs. According to Badger's clerk, he threatened to kill Badger. Murray is getting a line on him. I hope to be able to see him tomorrow or the next day."

"What of the clerk himself?" Bradford asked. "Might Sobersides have done it? You say he fled and is hiding out."

"He's afraid of Baggs," Charles said. "After talking with the fellow, I doubt he'd have the courage to fire a gun, even in self-defense." He paused. "But there's no shortage of other suspects. I wonder what we should make of this business of Day's being cheated of sixty thousand pounds by John Bass. Seems like a great amount of money." Frowning, he added, "I suppose I ought to have a look in the safe at Alfred Day's home and see what can be found there."

Still talking, Charles and Bradford turned through the gate and up the path to Hardaway House. As they mounted the stoop, a figure slipped out of the shadows and stepped forward. Charles was startled, until he saw that it was Patrick.

"I've brought the bottle, Lord Charles," he said, holding out a brown-paper package. "It's got a label on it."

For a moment, Charles had to ransack his memory. Then

he exclaimed: "The dope bottle! A label, you say?"

"With the veterinary's name on it," Patrick said. "I hadn't noticed it before, but it's there."

"Very good, boy," Bradford said. He held open the door. "Come in. Let's go upstairs where there's light and see what you've brought."

Now, in the best of all possible worlds, events would have fallen out exactly as Kate had described in her instructions to Amelia that afternoon. Charles would have been mounting the dark stairs behind Bradford and Patrick when the door to Mrs. Hardaway's apartment opened and that lady appeared in the hallway, wearing a lace nightcap and a flowered wrapper and holding an envelope in her hand, sealed with a blob of red sealing wax. Waving the envelope, she would have called up the stairs after him. Charles would have turned, surprised, then gone back downstairs for the envelope. In Bradford's rooms, he would have stood next to the lamp and taken out the two notes folded together, the one in Kate's neat, careful script, the other in a strange hand. He would have read Kate's first, with growing surprise, and then unfolded the other and read it, too—and some, at least, of the mystery would have been revealed to him, and his detective work substantially shortened.

But this is not the best of all possible worlds. Mrs. Hardaway, a poor widow who had to rely upon her own strenuous efforts for all her support, had spent a long and trying morning dealing with the hired roofing-men who were supposed to stop up the leaks over the kitchen. She had been so distressed by the poor quality of their work that she had lost her temper with them, and afterwards with the butcher and the greengrocer. These disagreements had taken a severe toll on her limited energies, so that, while she fully intended to sit up with Lady Sheridan's envelope until Lord Sheridan returned, she had fallen asleep in her chair beside the gas grate.

Thus, since the lady was still sleeping soundly when Charles followed Bradford and Patrick up the stairs, no apartment door opened, no Mrs. Hardaway appeared, no envelope was handed over, no message from Kate was read. And Charles—who could not know that his wife had written urgently to him and was even at that moment lying wide awake, staring into the dark and thinking over all her suspicions—had no idea what might have been.

Consequently, when he reached Bradford's apartment, he turned directly to Patrick, while Bradford went to the grate and lit the small fire that was laid there. "Well, Patrick," he said heartily, "let's have a look at this bottle you've brought. It's the one you nicked after the doping at the Derby, I take it?"

"Yes, sir," Patrick said, unwrapping the brown paper to produce a bottle that, according to the colorfully printed label, had once contained Dr. March's Licorice Cough Syrup, Guaranteed to Cure Coughs in Man or Beast. He reversed the bottle and pointed with a grubby finger. "And that's the veterinary's label, sir, with his address on it."

Charles held it up to the light. "Doctor Septimus Polter, Exning," he read aloud. "Well done, Patrick! Well done, indeed. We shall certainly have a visit with Doctor Polter tomorrow. He should be able to tell us what he used to dope Gladiator, and by whose orders."

"It don't matter now," the boy said, and dropped his head.

"It doesn't matter?" Charles put his hand on Patrick's shoulder, noticing for the first time the boy's evident dejection. "Come, come, Paddy. This isn't like you. Your information will help us get to the bottom of the doping. Why doesn't it matter?"

Patrick looked up, blinking away tears. In a low voice, he said, "I'm to ride Gladiator in the ten-furlong handicap on Friday."

"Hey, now!" Bradford put a lump of coal on the struggling fire and straightened up. "Why so glum, boy? Your first ride as a jockey—it's a time for celebrating! If you were a little older, we'd pop a cork and have some bubbly." He looked around the room. "If we had any bubbly, that is. We seem to be fresh out."

Patrick shook his head. "No celebrating for me," he said. "We rode trials this afternoon, and Pinkie said that Lord Hunt wants me up. But only if I promise to follow instructions."

"I don't see anything wrong in that," Charles said.

"I do," the boy said fiercely. "I know what they'll be. I'll be told to stop the horse. Gladiator could win that race, I know it! But he isn't supposed to win. He's supposed to *lose*."

"Ah," said Bradford, comprehending. "So that's their game."

"The game?" Charles asked, looking from one to the other. "I'm not sure I understand. Would someone explain it to me, please?"

"There's no great mystery to it," Bradford said, putting his hands in his pockets and backing up to the fire. "It's a classic method of cheating, one that's practiced all the time. The owner or the stable picks a horse and consistently runs him to lose, usually by telling the jockey to pull him, sometimes by doping him with some sedative. After running slow in a half-dozen races, the horse is low in the handicap and unbacked. Then he's put up to win at long odds against horses he ought to be able to beat—in the case of Gladiator, by boosting him with a dose of dope. He wins, his backers clean up, and they haul their earnings home in a handcart."

"But Gladiator didn't win in the Derby," Charles objected.

"No, but he might have," Bradford responded. "If it hadn't been for the melee at Tattenham Corner, he'd likely have beaten Flying Fox, or perhaps have finished second. You watch the postings in that ten-furlong handicap on Friday, Charles. Gladiator will be a short-odds favorite, especially with a light rider up." He squinted at Patrick, measuring him. "What are you, Paddy? Seven stone?"

"Six stone ten," Patrick said with a sad sort of pride. "Pinkie's been telling me to keep myself light."

"Right. Carrying that weight, the horse will go short odds and the stable will bet heavily against him. If Patrick does as he's told, Gladiator will finish out of the money, and they'll clean up again."

"At least," Patrick said bitterly, "I don't have to worry that they'll dope him to win—at least not for this race."

"You might keep an eye out still, though," Bradford said in a cautionary tone. "If they don't trust you, they may dope him to lose."

Patrick groaned.

"But don't the Stewards keep a strict control over this sort of thing?" Charles asked, with an eye on Patrick. If he was set on becoming a jockey, the lad ought to know the rules of the game—especially those that were not in any handbook or manual. "Isn't it the Club's job to make sure that the horses are run fairly?"

Bradford shrugged. "That's the beauty of putting up an inexperienced jockey. If the owner or the stable is called to account, they blame the boy. They say that he didn't ride as he was told, or that he just didn't know enough to get the best from the horse. They may be faulted for giving the ride to an inexperienced jockey, but they can't be warned off for generosity." At the look on Patrick's face, he shrugged. "Sorry, Paddy, but that's the way it is."

"Maybe," Patrick said quietly. "But it's not the way it *ought* to be. Maybe I don't want to be a jockey after all. I want to ride, but even more, I want the horse to do as well as he can. For the horse's sake, though, not the owner or the stable. And I want the races to be fair!"

Charles put his hand on the boy's shoulder, loving his youthful idealism, regretting that he was inevitably to be disappointed by a world in which very little happened the way it ought. "You don't have to go back to the stable, you know," he said softly. "You can come back with Lady Sheridan and me to Bishop's Keep."

Patrick looked up at him. "I'd like to, but I can't," he said stoutly. "I have to see that Gladiator's safe." He glanced at Bradford. "I thought I didn't have to worry about doping. Now I see that I do. So I have to convince them that I'll ride the race as I'm told." He was silent for a moment, then broke into a sudden grin. "But you should have seen him run in the trial today, Lord Charles! He beat both Rag and Cannon, and he *loved* it." The grin faded. "I wish he could win on Friday," he said wistfully. "He would love it so."

Charles looked at him, wishing that he could give the boy what he wanted, but knowing that he could not.

32

Wednesday, 7 June, 1899

In Oxford Street

"The widow who considers with seriousness whether she will best express her sense of loss by a Marie Stuart cap or an Alsatian Bow of tarlatan, is already half consoled, and will return in a month for another which will express 'mitigated' grief by various lightsome pleatings. The black dress will soon require a dainty frilled fichu of tulle to make it endurable. She will, ere long, bestring herself with jet beads that will take the place of the tears that have ceased to flow, and the day when grey, and violet, are permissible, is one characterized by a sober but genuine joy."

The Gentlewoman's Book of Dress, 1890
Mrs. F Douglas

LEAVING A NOTE to let Mrs. Hardaway know that they would not require breakfast (and thereby once again thwarting the delivery of Kate's letter), Charles and Bradford left Hardaway House well before seven on Wednesday morning, to have breakfast at the Stag Hotel with Jack Murray. Over poached eggs, broiled sheep's kidneys, mutton chops, toast and marmalade, fresh strawberries, and coffee, they discussed the plan for the day's investigations.

Jack Murray had not yet got a lead to Eddie Baggs, so he would continue working in that direction by questioning some of Baggs's known associates, including both of the men in whose company he had been seen at the Great Horse on Monday night: Pinkie Duncan and Jesse Clark. Charles was not anxious to intrude on the grief of the widowed Mrs. Day, but felt it necessary to discover whether there might be anything helpful in Alfred Day's safe. He also thought it would be useful to have a conversation with Owen North. Bradford, meanwhile, would drive to Exning for a visit with Dr. Septimus Polter. If possible, they would meet back at the Stag sometime around one o'clock and decide what directions should be pursued next.

The Alfred Day family resided at Number 32 Oxford Street, in one of a row of dignified two-story brick houses set close to the street, behind a low iron fence and a pocket garden with an ornate multi-tiered fountain in the center. The house was obviously in mourning, for straw had been laid on the street so that the family's grief should not be disturbed by passing carts and the brass door knocker was muffled by a black wrapping and adorned with a large crape bow.

The door was opened by a shy parlor maid in a black dress and black apron, who took Charles's hat and his card and ushered him into the sitting room. Like that in the Hogsworth home, it was crowded with furnishings, but Mrs. Day's taste in decor ran more to family snapshots, African violets, and lace curtains than to red velvet, tiger-skin rugs, and exotic Indian souvenirs. A state photograph of the long-dead Prince Consort hung on one wall, on another two gold-rimmed plates bearing the images of the Prince and Princess of Wales, and opposite, a large photograph of the Queen in an oval frame, taken on her Jubilee. The photographs and plates were dressed in swags and bows of black crape, as were the lampshades, the potted plants, the chair backs, and the fireplace mantel. Centered on the mantel, between two black candles in gold candlesticks, stood the black-draped photograph of a prosperous-looking man, slightly above middle age, posed in front of Number 29 St. James Street, the words "Alfred Day, Racing Commissions" visible on the plate-glass window of the building behind him. He wore a gray frock coat with a pale gray top hat and an unsuitably mirthful smile on his round face. The deceased Alfred Day looked like a man who was proud of his accomplishments.

Charles was studying the photograph when he heard the rustle of skirts and turned, bowing to the woman who had just entered the room. She was petite and slender, with an attractive face and pale blond hair, and seemed considerably younger than her husband. She was dressed entirely in black, with a full skirt banded in crape, a pleated bodice, and a tulle fichu at her throat, also of black. On her gleaming hair, she wore a becoming Marie Stuart cap with black lace veil behind, and jet earrings on her ears. She carried a black lace handkerchief in one hand and Charles's card in the other.

"Mrs. Day," Charles murmured, with another bow. "Please accept my deepest condolences upon the death of your husband. I am sure it is a very great loss."

"Thank you, Lord Sheridan," the widow sighed, sinking into a black-dressed chair. "You were an acquaintance of my dearest Alfred?" Her glance went from Charles's card to the photograph on the mantel. Her pretty blue eyes brimmed with tears.

"I fear I had not the honor of knowing him," Charles said regretfully. On the way to Oxford Street, he had considered various pretexts and ruses, but none seemed to quite fit the sad circumstances. In default of a plausible lie, he had determined upon the truth, although he hoped to tell as little of it as possible. "I am deeply sorry to intrude upon your grief at this time, Mrs. Day, but I fear it is necessary. I have been asked to undertake a private investigation of your husband's death. I understand that he kept a safe here, and hoped..." He paused, knowing that what he was asking must seem unforgivably presumptuous to the grief-stricken widow. He took a breath and plunged on. "I hoped you might permit me to take a look into it, to see if I might find anything there that could lead me to his killer."

The widow regarded him thoughtfully, and an expression of something very like shrewdness came into her eyes. She did not ask upon whose authority he had come or precisely what he was seeking—questions she should certainly have felt entitled to ask. Instead, she said, in a low, calm voice: "I should not object to your looking into the safe, Lord Charles, but I very much regret that it is impossible. I myself have desired to do so. Unfortunately, I do not have a key." She produced the black handkerchief and touched it to one eye. "My darling Alfred kept it always with him, but it was not with his effects when they were returned to me. I very much fear that his assailant took it from him."

"Ah," Charles said, reaching into his pocket and pulling out the key he had found in Alfred Day's trousers. "I wonder if this might be what you have been looking for." He held it out, adding apologetically, "I examined your husband's belongings yesterday in the surgeon's office. I felt the key might be material to the investigation, so I retained it."

The widow leaned forward and snatched the key from

him. "Yes!" she exclaimed, with evident relief. "This is the very key! Lord Sheridan, I do thank you!"

"You are most welcome." Charles bowed deferentially. "Would you mind—That is, do you think—?"

The widow did not wait to hear his request repeated. She stood with alacrity. "Come with me to the library, your lordship," she commanded, sweeping purposefully out of the room, Charles following in some surprise. He had not expected quite so eager a compliance with a request that he considered rude and peremptory.

The library was devoid of books, containing only a desk, a leather sofa, and two wooden chairs. One of the chairs was placed in front of a window. On it sat an elderly manservant holding an ancient percussion cap shotgun across his knees.

"Thank you, Fisher," the widow said. "You may end your watch now. I have the key."

"Very good, ma'am," the old man mumbled, and shuffled out of the room, carrying the gun.

Mrs. Day apparently felt that some explanation was necessary. "I feared," she remarked, "that if my husband's assailant had taken the key, he might attempt to enter this room and open the safe. I asked Fisher to station himself here as a guard."

"Very prudent, I'm sure," Charles murmured.

Mrs. Day went to the opposite wall, took down a gilt-framed print of a Constable landscape, and exposed a metal safe concealed in the wall. Charles watched as she deftly inserted the key into the lock and swung open the door. Swiftly, before he could move, she had reached inside and seized a large packet of bank notes, thrusting it into the recesses of her full-skirted dress. Leaving the safe door open, she retrieved the key from the lock and turned with great dignity.

"Thank you, my lord," she said, inclining her head. "It was a great kindness to bring me the key to my dearest Alfred's safe. I am sure that I shall be forever grateful."

And with that, she turned and swept from the room, leaving a bemused Charles to explore the remaining contents of the safe at his leisure.

33

In Exning

"I believe that I was the first jockey in England to ride a doped horse over fences at a race meeting. The animal was Sporran, and he was doped by that well-known veterinary surgeon, Captain JG Deans. Captain Deans wrote: 'As the first veterinary surgeon in England to attempt the hypodermic injection of a stimulant into a racehorse before running, I confidently assert that it is possible to treat a horse by this method, not once but many times, without any detrimental effect, either immediately or in future.'"

Paddock Personalities
J FAIRFAX-BLAKEBOROUGH

THE VILLAGE OF Exning was about two miles to the north and west of Newmarket. Bradford, glad to have something useful to do while Edith and her mother were negotiating agreements of great significance with the dressmaker, made inquiries at the postal office in the rear of the greengrocer's shop. The grocer's daughter, who was also the village postmistress, was a charming young

241

woman with nut-brown hair tied with a pink ribbon. She gave him a flirtatious smile and directions to Dr. Septimus Polter's animal surgery, at Hill House. She glanced up at the clock.

"If ye want t'find the doctor in this mornin', sir, best ye 'urry," she said, with an enchanting flash of dimples. "'E's off t' Ipswich today on business. 'Is 'ousekeeper, Mrs. Flagg, said 'e was takin' the noon train from Newmarket."

"Thank you," Bradford said. He tipped his tweed cap smartly and turned to go, thinking that if a detective wished to learn something about a villager, the best place to begin was with the village postmistress. And if they were all as pretty as this one, detecting would be a fine business. He had forgotten, for the moment, about Edith.

"Oh, wait, sir," the woman called, and Bradford turned back. "Since ye're goin' to 'Ill 'Ouse, mebbee ye wouldn't mind—" She took a shoebox-sized package from a shelf and pushed it across the counter. "Would ye be so good as to deliver this to the doctor? The letter carrier was meant t'take it, but she left it be'ind." The postmistress gave her pretty head an irritated shake, as if to comment on the careless ways of letter carriers, and watched Bradford out the door.

Following directions, Bradford turned his hired hack off the village road at a painted sign bearing the words DOCTOR SEPTIMUS POLTNER, VETERINARY SURGEON. At the end of the shrubbery-lined lane stood Hill House, and behind it the surgery, in a separate frame building with two windows in the front and a Dutch door. Behind this was an ancient timber-and-stone barn, open on one side to a fenced paddock. Within, Bradford could see several horses. A ragged boy was carrying a bucket of oats into the barn, followed by a motley flock of chickens looking for their share.

The top half of the surgery door stood open. Bradford opened the lower door and went inside, carrying both the package from the postmistress and Patrick's bottle, wrapped in brown paper. There was a waiting room just large enough for two empty chairs, with a door in the opposite wall, standing open. Bradford went to it and put his head through.

"Dr. Polter?" he asked.

A stooped, gray-haired man was sitting at a cluttered table with a soot black cat draped across his shoulders like a fur piece, peering at the pages of a large book through a magnifying glass. The room in which he sat was cluttered as well, heaped around with piles of books, papers, medicine bottles, surgical implements, and baskets of oddments, everything strewn here and there in no apparent order. Several large colored drawings of the anatomy of horses and cows were pinned to the walls, and on a hook by the door hung a lantern, a waterproof cape, a large waterproof hat, and a pair of waterproof fishing trousers. Beneath them stood an umbrella and a pair of Wellingtons.

The man had taken no notice of him. "Dr. Polter?" Bradford said again, raising his voice, and then, when the man still did not respond, shouted "Dr. Polter?"

"Eh?" The man looked up and Bradford saw that he was getting on in years, in his seventies, perhaps. "What d'you say? Are you looking for me?"

"Dr. Polter," Bradford said, loudly and distinctly, "I've brought you this." He handed over the package the postmistress had entrusted to him. "From the post office in Exning."

The cat jumped down from the doctor's shoulders and sat on the book he had been reading, licking a paw. "You're the new letter carrier, then?" Dr. Polter asked, in the overly loud voice of the hard-of-hearing. He set the package on the table beside him, and squinted at Bradford. "Bit old for the job, aren't you? Must be new here, too. Don't remember seeing you around the village."

"I'm not the mail carrier," Bradford said loudly.

"Not the mail carrier? Then why are you carrying the mail?" The cat yawned, flicked its tail, and began to sniff delicately at the package.

"I've come to ask you some questions, Dr. Polter," Bradford said, louder still. "About horse doping." On the way to Exning, he had given careful thought to the approach he would take with the doctor and had decided to be direct and straightforward, thinking that he might thereby catch his informant off guard and startle him into revealing what he knew. But he had not counted on the doctor's being deaf.

"Questions about what, did you say?" the doctor asked. He reached under his chair and picked up a large green-painted ear trumpet, putting it to his ear. "Speak up, or I won't hear you, young man."

"Horse doping," Bradford said loudly into the bell of the trumpet, then repeated the words, feeling foolish. It was one thing to put questions to a man in a normal tone of voice, quite another to shout them at him in simplified form, as if they were both idiots.

"Ah." The cat abandoned the package and lay down on the doctor's book, purring. "Horse doping, eh? What sort of horse is it you want to dope? Where is it running?" The doctor eyed Bradford's dark green tweed jacket, green cloth breeches, ivory waistcoat and tie, and added, with raised brows, "Not a trainer, I'll warrant. Owner, I s'pose." He held the trumpet in Bradford's direction. "What sort of horse, eh? What sort of horse?"

Bradford leaned forward. This was not the tack he had planned to take, but under the circumstances, it would have to do. "I own a three-year-old colt," he said distinctly. "I want to run him to win in the ten-furlong handicap at Newmarket on Friday."

"Friday, eh?" Dr. Polter stroked the cat, frowning. "Don't know why you've come to me directly, Mr.—what did you say your name was?"

"Murray," Bradford said, deciding of a sudden that he would rather not give his real name. "Jack Murray, sir."

"Well, Mr. Murphy, weren't you told that I usually work through trainers? Prefer not to deal with owners—they get in the way." He scowled. "If you want to race a doped horse, take it to Clark and Wishard, at the Red House Stable, in Newmarket. They're experts in that game."

"Yes, I know about Wishard and Clark," Bradford said. "But I..." He smiled rather foolishly, then put his mouth to the trumpet and said, in an approximation of a whisper: "I'm alone in this, don't you know. Just my own little secret. Not particularly keen on anyone else knowing about it. Particularly the Americans."

Dr. Polter thought about this for a moment, still stroking the cat. "I see," he said finally. "Well, I s'pose it can't hurt. Run your colt to lose, you say?"

"No," Bradford said emphatically. "I want to run him to win." He leaned into the trumpet. "To win, sir!"

"Ah. Well, then, you'll want some speedy balls." He pushed his chair back.

"Speedy balls?" Bradford put on a confused look. "No, I don't think so. Actually, a friend gave me this." He pulled Patrick's bottle out of its wrapping and put it on the table in front of Dr. Polter. "You used it on his horse recently, and he was quite pleased with the outcome. Wonder if you'd be so good as to sell me a dose, and to give me some idea what's in it. I'll pay your price, of course," he added quickly. "Whatever you ask."

At the mention of money, a crafty look crossed the doctor's face, and he picked up the bottle, turning it in his hands. "Hmmm," he said thoughtfully. "Yes, I remember. Galahad, owned by Lord Bunt. In the last Derby."

"Gladiator," Bradford said loudly, for the doctor had put down his trumpet. "Lord Hunt."

Scowling, Dr. Polter replied, "That's what I said, Mr. Murphy. You don't need to shout."

"Yes, sir," Bradford said contritely. "It was Lord Bunt who gave me that bottle and suggested I talk to you. He said to be sure that you gave me the same substance you used on Galahad." He paused, and asked, enuciating carefully, "What sort of dope was in that bottle?"

"What sort?" the doctor said. "Why, cocaine, to be sure. Much more effective than caffeine or opium. What size?"

"Size?" Bradford frowned. "I don't know. What sizes does it come in?"

The doctor gave him a look of disgust. "What size *horse*, Murphy? How high does he stand?"

"Oh," Bradford said, feeling foolish. "Sixteen hands." He paused. "I suppose that matters."

"Of course it matters," the doctor said sharply, reaching for the package Bradford had brought him. The cat, dislodged from the book, jumped onto the floor and stalked off, tail in the air. "Too much will kill him. Not enough, or administered too long before the start, it won't do the job. You ought to let Wishard or Clark give you a hand with it." He took out a pen knife and slit the wrapping. "They know how to do it, you see. They're scientific, those Americans. They gallop the horse before the race to find out exactly how much dope will push it along. Very scientific."

Bradford watched as the doctor unwrapped the box and opened it. Inside was another, smaller box. When the lid was opened, Bradford saw that it was filled with a white powder.

"Good thing you brought this with you," the doctor said, putting a quantity of the powder into a small envelope and sealing it. "Or you would have been out of luck." He gave the envelope to Bradford. "Pour this into that cough syrup bottle. Fill it with water and shake it until it dissolves. No more than ten minutes before the start, put it down the horse's throat. Then stand back."

Bradford looked doubtfully at the envelopes. "Until Lord Bunt told me that you doped with the bottle, I was expecting there'd be some sort of injection."

"What?" the doctor shouted, and picked up his ear trumpet. "Don't mumble, Murphy. Speak up!"

Bradford repeated what he had said.

"If it's an injection you want, you'll have to see Captain Bean," the doctor said shortly. "He's injecting jumpers, I understand. But that's not something you can do for yourself. If you want to do the administering, use what I've given you." He frowned. "But mind you put up a strong, experienced rider, Murphy. A doped horse wants to run. I told Lord Bunt not to ride that lightweight boy on Galahad, but he didn't listen." He gave his head a sad shake. "Hear there's been an objection."

"Yes," Bradford said.

"Don't like that," the doctor said darkly. "No need to call attention to doping, don't you agree? Stewards wouldn't like that."

"The Stewards?" Bradford asked innocently.

The doctor laughed. "Are you as green as that, young man?" His voice turned bitter. "The Stewards know who's profiting from the American invasion, especially from that boy Sloan. They don't want to do anything that might upset the applecart."

"Tod Sloan, the jockey? He's connected with Wishard and Clark?"

"You *are* green," the doctor replied with a sniff. "Lord William Beresford brought Sloan over here, and Sloan brought Wishard and the others. Lord William has arranged with the Prince for Sloan to ride in the royal colors next season. Who knows? Maybe Wishard will be moving over to Egerton House to show what he can do."

"But that's the royal racing-stables!" Bradford exclaimed. "HRH wouldn't be associated with something as unsportsmanlike as—" He stopped, recollecting himself just in time, and pocketed the envelope. "Your fee?" He leaned closer and shouted. "How much?"

"A tenner ought to do it," the doctor said.

"Greedy old buzzard," Bradford muttered, reaching into his pocket.

"What's that you say, Murphy?" the doctor asked sharply.

"Cheap at twice the price," Bradford replied.

34

At the Jockey Club

> "Here in her hair the Painter plays the Spider and hath woven a golden mesh t'entrap the hearts of men."
>
> *The Merchant of Venice*
> WILLIAM SHAKESPEARE

ADMIRAL NORTH LOOKED up from the papers on his desk. "Ah, Sheridan," he said, and stood with a broad smile, extending his hand. "I was just thinking of you, and wondering how you and Murray were getting on with things." He gestured courteously. "Please, sit down."

"I thought it was time to let you know what progress we have made," Charles said, seating himself in one of the leather chairs. "Although I fear that what we have learned is of precious little practical use." He added, "I was hoping that perhaps you might have learned something you would be willing to share with me."

"Only a bit of gossip here and there," the admiral said. "Nothing very material, I'm afraid." He opened the desk drawer, took out a box of cigars, and pushed them toward

Charles. "Help yourself, Sheridan. The finest Cuban. A present from HRH."

"Thank you, no," Charles said. He was not fond of the Prince's cigars, costly though they might be. He took out his pipe and while he filled it, tamped it, and lit it, sketched out what he and Murray had pieced together from their inspection of the St. James Street premises; from the proprietor of the Great Horse; and from their questioning of Day's clerk, the man called Sobersides.

"No progress?" North asked, raising one tufted eyebrow. "On the contrary, Charles, you seem to have made quite a lot of it. You've certainly narrowed the field of suspects to a great degree. It sounds to me as if Day was playing a dangerous game that was bound to make him a very unpopular man in several circles." He clipped off the end of a cigar and lit it. "Organizing the bookmakers against certain stables—that's a risky business, however one looks at it. I should have thought Badger had been playing the game long enough to know better."

"He was doing what he thought had to be done," Charles said, watching North's face. "Since he hadn't been able to persuade the Club to rule doping illegal—"

North slammed his fist on his desk so hard that the lamp chimney rattled. "We can't rule it illegal, damn it!" he exploded angrily. "To do so would be to invite gossip, even scandal. It would suggest that unsportsmanlike behavior has already taken place, that the Club has not properly controlled—" He stopped, recollecting himself, and wiped a drop of spittle from his gray beard. "It would stir up a great deal of Turf controversy and focus undue attention on Turf practices," he said carefully. "And you know how HRH feels about that. How we all feel about it."

"Yes, I know," Charles agreed, "although I must say that from what I have seen, doping injures horses and plays havoc with ordinary betting. And it would seem to encourage a certain criminal element and invite the commission of crime—as Day's murder suggests."

"It is not at all clear that Day was killed because of the doping," North said flatly. "In fact, all the evidence goes in the other direction. He was obviously murdered by that partner of his—what did you say his name was?"

Charles sighed. "Baggs, Edward Baggs."

"Yes, well. If the clerk—Sobersides, or Moore, or whatever he's called—will testify that he heard Baggs threaten Badger, that should be enough to convince the coroner's jury. I know Coroner Drummond. I'll speak to him about the matter so that he's aware of our interest, and to the chief constable, as well. Meanwhile, I suggest that you have Murray concentrate on locating Baggs. The very fact that the man has left town so precipitously ought to make his guilt plain. And don't bother interrogating him—we can turn that little job over to the police."

"There are one or two other possibilities," Charles said. "The American trainer, Jesse Clark, was in the Great Horse just before the murder, engaged in argument with Day. As was Pinkie Duncan. Their motives seem to me to be at least equal to that of Baggs."

North frowned. "I shouldn't like—" He paused, as if he were thinking how to frame his sentence. "The partner made a clear threat in the presence of a witness. I should focus on that fellow Baggs, if I were you."

Charles drew on his pipe, reflecting that North seemed inordinately eager to view the murder as a falling-out between business associates. If Baggs were indicted, no other motives would be explored in the coroner's inquest and the question of doping would be separated from that of the murder—an outcome that North obviously desired. But it was not as easy as that.

"There is one other thing you should know," Charles said quietly. "Mrs. Langtry is involved in this business, exactly how and to what extent, I have yet to determine."

Owen North seemed, Charles thought, to turn pale. "Mrs. Langtry?" he asked. He coughed. "I must say, that seems rather... far-fetched. However, people *will* gossip. I'm sure you haven't found any evidence of her involvement." He placed an unmistakable emphasis on the word *evidence*.

"As a matter of fact, I have," Charles said, and thought that North seemed even paler. "When I went through Day's effects, I found a note from the lady in his pocket, instructing him to meet her at nine on Monday night, at St. Mary's Square."

"But she was at the Rothschilds' on Monday night!" North exclaimed in an agitated tone. "We talked there! She could not have—Why, it's impossible! She was as cool and lovely as always. She—" He pressed his lips together for a moment, then said again, "It's impossible."

"She says she arrived at something close to ten," Charles said. "There would have been ample time for her to have met Day and shot the man. And as far as coolness is concerned, Mrs. Langtry is an actress. She is perfectly capable of masking her real feelings." *If she has any*, Charles added to himself.

North took out his handkerchief and blotted his forehead. "I'm sure it was much earlier than that when she came in. In fact, I'd swear to it. At least nine, I believe, perhaps before that. Yes, surely before that. Ponsonby was there. He saw her arrive. He'll swear, too."

Fritz Ponsonby was one of HRH's closest confidants. He would swear to anything to protect the royal person. "Mrs. Langtry herself told me that it was three-quarters past," Charles said without inflection.

North's eyes opened wide. "You've already spoken to

her about this?" There was a note of panic in his voice.

"She denies knowing anything about Day's death." Charles blew out a cloud of pipe smoke, wondering whether he should mention Mrs. Langtry's missing gun. On balance, he thought not. "I don't think she killed him," he added, "if that's what concerns you, Owen."

For the second time in their brief meeting, North became passionate. "Concerns me!" he cried, his voice trembling. "Concerns me! Why, man, of course it concerns me! I have been friends with the lady for some time. I—" He stopped, biting his lip as if to control his outburst. When he spoke again, his voice was taut but disciplined, and he had chosen a different tack: "As you know, the Prince is at present deeply involved with Mrs. Keppel. However, he still visits Mrs. Langtry on occasion and he looks out for her always, financially and otherwise. If His Highness thought for a moment that—" North shook his head. "You know how protective he is toward those of his friends who are in trouble. Foolishly so, at times."

Charles remembered the royal reaction when the Countess of Warwick, whose place in the royal heart had been taken by Mrs. Keppel, had come dangerously close to being accused of murder. "I take it, then, that you're suggesting—"

"I'm suggesting that, whatever else you do, you absolutely *must* keep Mrs. Langtry's name out of this," North said fiercely. "His Highness will not thank you if she is dragged into the matter." Then, apparently recollecting that he was speaking to a peer of the realm, he pulled in a deep breath, softening his tone. "Of course, Charles, I know that you won't do anything that might attract attention to the lady's role in this unfortunate business. As you have said, she is innocent of any wrongdoing, so I'm sure you will guard her reputation." He seemed to find no irony in this last remark.

Charles was tempted to point out that he had said nothing of Mrs. Langtry's innocence, only that he did not believe she had shot Alfred Day. But instead, he smoked in silence for a moment, listening to the ticking of the clock on the wall. "By the way," he said at last, "we've located the veterinary surgeon who doped Reggie Hunt's horse. A fellow named Polter. Septimus Polter, at Exning."

"Well, that was a bit of fine detective work," North said in a heartier tone, clearly relieved to leave the subject of Mrs. Langtry. "How did you get onto him? Have you talked to him yet?"

"I have not," Charles said, failing to mention that Bradford Marsden was probably doing exactly that, even as they spoke.

North reached for a pen and a sheet of paper. "Polter, did you say? Septimus? At Exning?" He dipped the pen into an inkwell set in the desk and wrote rapidly. "No need for you to go further with this particular line of inquiry, Charles. I believe that you've gotten to the heart of the matter. I'll see to the rest of it myself."

"As you wish," Charles said.

There was another long silence. At last, North pulled open a drawer. "I have a photograph here you really must see," he said, in an obvious effort to change the subject. "A friend sent it to me from New Zealand, to add to my collection. Given your interest in scientific photography, I think you will find it fascinating." He took out a photograph and laid it on the desk.

Charles regarded it, frowning.

"What is it, exactly?" he asked. "I don't believe I recognize the creature."

"Stumped you at last, have I?" North exclaimed. "It is a rare species that lives along the coast of New Zealand. Found only in the sand dunes, I'm told, hiding under driftwood and the like. Katipo, its name is."

Charles was looking at a photograph, much enlarged, of a spider.

"Ah," he said. "Katipo. The New Zealand spider." He looked at North. "Surely I should have guessed." He pushed himself out of the chair. "Thank you, Owen, for showing it to me. I fear I must be going."

North laid the photograph aside and summoned a smile. "Right. Don't forget, then. Instruct Murray to concentrate on locating Baggs. When the man has been found, let me know immediately and I shall alert the chief constable to pick him up for interrogation. That will resolve the matter, and you can get back to your own affairs—with my enduring gratitude," he added warmly.

Out in the street, Charles drew a deep breath, glad to be out of the Club office. For the moment, he did not want to think about all of the implications that had been raised by his conversation with Admiral North. He took out his watch. It was nearly time to set out for the Devil's Dyke, where he was to lunch with Bradford and Jack Murray and learn what they had discovered that morning.

Charles was striding quickly along the next block of shops when he ran into a woman coming out of a butcher's shop, carrying a shopping bag full of packages.

"Oh, Lord Sheridan!" the woman cried delightedly. "Oh, how *fortunate* to encounter you in this fashion! I'm afraid I missed you this morning at breakfast and—"

Charles raised his hat. "Yes, indeed, Mrs. Hardaway," he said with a slight smile. "But I fear I am rather in a hurry. If you will excuse me—"

"No!" Mrs. Hardaway laid hold of his arm. "I am sorry, my lord, but you must accompany me home immediately. I have something in my keeping that you must have without delay."

"Well, then," Charles said, seeing nothing for it but to go with the lady, "you will let me carry your parcels, I hope."

"Oh, so kind," Mrs. Hardaway murmured, taking the arm he offered, and they proceeded together down the street.

35

The Grange House Stable

"Wishard perfected his doping into an art and his success rate was phenomenal. Time and time again mediocre or bad horses won totally unexpectedly, and the Americans raked in their winnings."

The Fast Set: The World of Edwardian Racing
GEORGE PLUMPTRE

"(Wishard and his cronies) took approximately two million pounds out of the ring (i.e. from the bookmakers) between 1897 and 1901... This period was known as the era of the 'Yankee alchemists.'... The dope that Wishard was using was the newly introduced cocaine."

Drugs and the Performance Horse
THOMAS TOBIN

CONTRARY TO JACK Murray's expectation, he did not find Jesse Clark when he called at the Red House Stable that morning. Mr. Clark, he was told by the head lad, had gone with Mr. Wishard to Brighton to have a look at a filly that was for sale. They would not return for some time, for they were traveling on to the Continent to examine some horses at a racing stable near Paris.

Murray frowned, wishing he'd had the foresight to come looking for Clark before the man departed. "When did they leave?" he asked.

"Yesterday, on the early train," the head lad replied, and added that it had been an unscheduled trip. "They wuz plannin' to be 'ere fer the ten-furlong 'andicap on Friday, but 'eard about this good filly and din't want to miss the chance o' gettin' 'er."

Of course, Murray thought sardonically. Long years at Scotland Yard had taught him that when people left town immediately after a crime in which they were involved, they usually had a very good reason—and not an innocent one, either. He left the stable, reflecting that both Clark and Baggs were currently unavailable, and that Oliver Moore had done his best to disappear. Of those who had argued with the unfortunate Badger in the Great Horse just prior to his murder, there remained only Pinkie Duncan to be questioned. With any luck at all, Murray would find him at the Grange House Stable. He set off determinedly in that direction.

But Murray was destined to be disappointed in this, as well. For when he reached the Grange House, he was informed by the housekeeper that Mr. Pinkie Duncan had gone to London on business for the day, to return the next. She eyed his green-checked tweed suit and bowler approvingly and added that Mr. Angus Duncan was in the office at the stable, if the gentleman would care to step around.

Murray went into the stableyard and, after an inquiry, located the office. He opened the door, announcing himself. With a frown, Angus Duncan looked up from some race entry forms on which he was working, a mug of tea at his elbow and a pipe curling smoke around his head. Behind him on the wall was a telephone. Murray was not surprised. Most of the stables were finding it to their advantage to be connected by telephone with the various racecourses in order to obtain the latest word on the running of their horses—and sometimes to lay a very late bet or two. Between the newfangled race ticker and the telephone (new at least in the provincial towns), the bookies were sometimes hard pressed to know whether a lastminute bettor was honest or a cheat.

"Wot name did ye say?" Duncan asked, his leathery face creased in a frown.

"Jack Murray, sir," Murray repeated humbly. "I'm assisting the investigation into the death of Alfred Day."

Duncan's pale eyes narrowed. "Investigation? What investigation? Are ye from the police?"

"No, sir." Murray spoke in a deferential tone. "This is a private investigation. I fear I'm not at liberty to tell you who has sponsored it. It is, however, being carried out in cooperation with the police." He nodded at the telephone on the wall. "I'm sure Chief Constable Watson would be glad to vouch for me."

Duncan considered this for a moment, then shook his head. "No need fer me t'call 'im, since I've nothin' t' tell. I'm sorry fer Badger," he added. "'E'd 'ad some rough years, but 'e was honest, as bookies go. Which ain't sayin' much, o' course."

"The proprietor of the Great Horse believes that Jesse Clark may have had something to do with his murder," Murray said in a tentative tone, watching Duncan's face. The morning was gloomy and the gas lamp had been lit, throwing a shadow that exaggerated the old man's expression. "I don't suppose you would care to venture an opinion on the subject."

Duncan's mouth tightened. "Clark, eh?" He cast his pencil onto the table with a grunt, perhaps of satisfaction. "Can't say I'm much surprised."

"And why is that, Mr. Duncan?" Murray asked respectfully.

"Because of wot Badger was up to." The old man leaned back in his chair, picked up his mug of tea, and drank.

"I'm sorry, sir." Murray frowned. "I'm afraid I must have missed something. What was he up to?"

Duncan wiped his mouth on the back of his hand, smiling contemptuously. "Ye're an investigator and ye 'aven't found out wot Badger wuz plannin'? Why, everybody in Newmarket knows 'ow 'e meant t' wreck the Americans' game." He took a long pull on his pipe, removed it from his mouth, and glared at it.

Murray looked quizzical. "Their game? I'm afraid I don't—".

"Do I 'ave to spell it out fer ye, man?" Duncan demanded sourly. "Their dopin' game, that's wot! They've been runnin' 'orses doped t' win and takin' a fortune out of the Ring. If they're not stopped, every bookie in Britain will 'ave 'is pockets pulled inside-out. Badger's tried more'n once t' get the Stewards to put an end t'it. Then 'e gave up on them and figured t' do it 'imself, by organizing the Ring. 'E was goin' t' let the newspapers in on it, too."

"Organizing the Ring, eh?" Murray asked. He put on a skeptical look. "I'd say that would be a hard thing to do."

"Oh, ye would, would ye?" With a short laugh, Duncan leaned forward and tapped his pipe into a china ashtray already full to overflowing with pipe ash. "Well, I'd say ye didn't know much about Badger, then, or the Ring, neither. Badger knew the bettin' business, and 'e knew bookies. Wot's more, the bookies knew Badger, big and lit'le. If anybody could pull 'em together, 'e was the one." He opened the desk drawer and pulled out a tin of tobacco. "Reckon that's why 'e wuz killed. That, and the newspapers." In a tone of scornful rebuke, he added, "Reckon ye should 'ave figgered that out fer yerself, if ye wuz any kind of investigator."

"I'm sure I should have," Murray said apologetically. He cleared his throat. "I wonder, sir, while we're on the subject, what you might think of Eddie Baggs as a possible killer. He was with Jesse Clark at the Great Horse and went out with him shortly after Mr. Day left. The proprietor seems to think—"

"Baggs?" Duncan frowned. "Eddie Baggs wuz with Clark? Ye're sure ye din't get that wrong?"

"Well, I might have." Murray gave him an uncertain look. "You don't think they'd have been together?"

"I doubt it," Duncan said firmly, tapping tobacco into his pipe. "Maybe it was 'appenstance, them comin' in together. More like, Baggs wuz 'elping Badger organize the bookies. They been partners fer sev'ral years."

"I've been trying to locate Mr. Baggs to clear up this point," Murray said, "but his landlady says he's left Newmarket. Unfortunately, I haven't been able to find anyone with a notion as to where he might have gone. I don't suppose you could help me?"

Duncan hesitated, pushing his lips in and out as if he were deciding whether or not to speak. At last, he said, "Well, ye might try 'is sister. She lives over Newnham way, in Cambridge. She'd know where 'e's gone."

"Thank you," Murray said gratefully. He paused. "I'm sure it's a great deal of trouble, but would you happen to know his sister's name and where she might be found? I wouldn't ask, but no one else seems to—"

"Thompson," Duncan said. "Sally Thompson. She's cook

fer the Darwins, at Newnham Grange. She wuz married to my cousin, b'fore 'e died."

"I'm very grateful, Mr. Duncan." Murray half turned to go, then turned back. "Oh, there's one thing more, if you wouldn't mind. I wonder if there's anything you can tell me about the connection between your nephew Pinkie Duncan and Mr. Clark."

"Wot connection?" Duncan's seamy face darkened.

"I'm afraid I haven't been able to discover that yet, Mr. Duncan," Murray said contritely. "It seems that he was at the Great Horse with Mr. Clark and Mr. Baggs on Monday night, and that there was some sort of argument—a rather violent argument, or so it's reported. He is said to have gone out with Clark and Baggs after Mr. Day left. There is some thought that he is connected with—"

"'E's connected with nothin'," the old man snapped. "'E's a fool of a boy 'oo's got 'isself into something 'e don't understand." He pressed his lips together, obviously having said more than he intended.

"I suppose you mean," Murray said in a speculative tone, "that he's fallen in with bad companions—the Americans, I assume. Of course, I wouldn't know the truth of it," he added, "but there's talk that Pinkie will take over the stables here, upon your retirement. It is supposed that he would then adopt the Americans' method of—"

"Rot!" the old man shouted, jumping to his feet. "If ye 'ear that kind of talk, Mr. Murray, ye can bloody well tell 'em to shove it up their arse. There's going to be no American methods 'ere, not so long as I'm alive and kickin'! English way's best. Allus 'as been, allus will be."

"Admirable, sir, admirable!" Murray exclaimed. He added, humbly, "Then I suppose it must be true, as others have told me, that Pinkie will be moving to the Red House Stables and training with Clark and Wishard."

The old man looked at him, struck silent. He sank back down in his chair. "It's them damned Americans," he whispered. "They're the devil incarnate, and they've tempted Pinkie past 'is limits." He dropped his face in his hands. "But it's only dopin', that's all," he whispered. "Not murder, not Pinkie. I swear it. Just dopin'."

For the old man's sake, Murray wished he could believe that.

36

The Devil's Dyke

"A well-known peer who, having lost a great deal of money racing, thought he saw an easy way to settle his debts. He mustered the family diamonds and carried them off to one of the most respectable Bond Street jewellers, (asking) the man to take out the diamonds and replace them with paste.

'I need the money,' he said, 'and her ladyship will never know.'

The jeweler's eyes twinkled. 'I am very sorry, my lord, but I have already done so at her ladyship's request.'"

"The jewels stolen from me comprised the following pieces: a large tiara; a riviere of immense sapphires and diamonds in a Tiffany setting; a tiara, necklace, and bracelets, en suite, of rubies and diamonds; a parure of large emeralds and diamonds, which had formed part of the Empress Eugénie's collection..."

both selections from
The Days I Knew: The Autobiography of Lillie Langtry
LILLIE LANGTRY, 1925

AFTER HE LEFT Mrs. Hardaway's house with Kate's note in his pocket, Charles had even more to think about and yet another stop to make. On his way at last, and very late, to the Devil's Dyke, he decided to proceed exactly as if he had not had that conversation with Owen North earlier in the morning—in fact, he would not even mention it. For one thing, he did not intend to turn the investigation over to the chief constable without some further assurance that the principle of due process would be respected. For another, he now had to consider whether Owen North himself—a man who collected photographs of spiders— might be the pseudonymous friend of Lillie Langtry. It was an unwelcome and unpleasant consideration, for he had known North for some time and had rather liked the man. But justice demanded that he entertain it.

The men gathered around a table in a dark and quiet corner of the half-deserted pub. Over their food, Bradford and Murray reported on their various morning's activities.

"Well, gentlemen," Charles said, sitting back from his empty plate, "it would seem that the three of us have had a most productive few hours." He nodded at Bradford. "Marsden has learned from Dr. Polter what kind of dope was used on Gladiator, and has even fetched us a sample."

"I'm not sure what good it does to know what it is," Bradford muttered, pushing the last of his steak-and-kidney pudding around on his plate. "These people are going to keep using it just the same, all the while swearing that it does no harm. And winning pots of money thereby," he added darkly.

"Perhaps his lordship intends," Jack Murray said in a respectful tone, "to suggest to the Stewards the development of a scientific test that will make it impossible to use the stuff without detection." He finished his boiled beef and dumplings and sat back with a sigh of satisfaction.

"That's the hope, Jack," Charles agreed, "although I'm afraid the test may be a long time coming." He did not offer his opinion that, judging from Owen North's response that morning, the Stewards had no interest in any sort of test, nor in pursuing the matter of the doping either, no matter how much evidence might be summoned.

Bradford refilled his mug from the pitcher of ale in the middle of the table. "But it seems to me that Murray's discoveries are far more to the point of the murder investigation." He took a cigar out of his pocket. "He's found a possible lead to Eddie Baggs."

"As well as confirming the threat that Alfred Day posed to the Americans," Charles said. "And when Pinkie gets back from his visit to London, I suspect he'll find his uncle in a less yielding mood when it comes to doping. You might have done some good there, Jack."

Jack Murray chewed reflectively. "I'm only sorry that Jesse Clark got away before we could question him," he said. "When I was at the Yard, we were continually frustrated by people leaving for the Continent, or for points unknown, just as we were ready to nab them."

"I suspect that Clark will be back," Charles said. "And certainly Pinkie intends to return. But wherever they are, both Clark and Pinkie are still on our suspect list, as is Baggs." He said this firmly. Owen North might wish to limit the investigation and to conclude it as quickly as possible, but Charles refused to allow North to tie his hands. As long as he had any say in the matter, justice would be served here, regardless of who was involved or what their social connections might be.

Bradford took out a cigarette and lit it. "I wish I could go with the two of you to run Baggs to earth," he remarked, leaning back in his chair. "Perhaps I can convince Edith that we should go up to London tomorrow afternoon, instead of today."

"But you have tickets for the opera tonight," Charles reminded him. He smiled. "And no bride wants to postpone the ordering of her wedding ring. Take Edith to Bond Street, Bradford. The poor girl would be devastated if you suggested delaying your visit to the jewelers. She would think you didn't love her."

"Oh, I doubt that," Bradford said with an answering grin. "Edith is a confident young woman. But I'd rather not risk her displeasure." He breathed out a wreath of blue smoke. "I don't recall your telling us how you spent your morning, Sheridan."

"Ah, yes," Charles said. He reached into his pocket and took out a small envelope. "Since we have been speaking of jewelers, perhaps you should have a look at this."

He opened the envelope and spilled out a heavy gold ring, a sparkling diamond of immoderate size flanked by four large emeralds and set in an extravagantly ornate gold mounting. It was a ring fit for a queen—of some decades past.

Bradford picked up the ring to examine it closely. "I hope you're not suggesting that I buy something like that for Edith. She would much prefer a modern setting to something ornate and old-fashioned, like this. But it is rather unique. I don't think I've seen anything quite like it before."

Jack Murray took the ring from Bradford, turned it in his fingers, and put it back on the table. "I have," he said shortly. "Seen it before, that is."

Charles raised both eyebrows. "Have you, now?" he remarked with satisfaction. "I thought as much. Perhaps you would be so good as to tell us what you remember about it."

267

"The ring is one of several matching pieces that originally belonged to the Empress Eugénie. There was a necklace, as I recall, as well as a bracelet, a brooch, and a pair of earrings. The settings were all the same, heavy, ornate, ponderous. Not at all in the modern fashion—but highly memorable."

"And where did you see these pieces?" Charles asked.

"I saw only the brooch," Murray said regretfully. "It escaped the thief and was provided by the owner at my request, so that if I should locate one of the matching pieces, I might recognize the setting. The other pieces, you see, had been stolen."

"Ah," Charles said. "And from whom were they stolen?"

Murray was impassive. "They were taken from the vault of the Union Bank in Sloane Street, on the authority of a note bearing the forged signature of the owner."

"The Union Bank!" Bradford's eyes had widened. "Why, man, you must be talking about the theft of the Langtry jewels!"

"You were one of the detectives assigned to the case, were you not?" Charles asked.

"I was," Murray said. "I interviewed Mrs. Langtry several times after the theft and obtained from her a list of the missing pieces. Unfortunately, there was no independent inventory of the items in that famous tin box of hers, as the bank was careful to point out when she sued them for the full forty thousand pounds. We could only rely on Mrs. Langtry's memory."

"And her veracity," Charles remarked.

"Indeed," Murray said, somewhat sardonically. "However, with regard to this ring, might I point out that it bears the Empress's mark: that tiny pair of interlaced circles." He pointed with his fork to the mark. "There is no doubt in the world that it belongs to the stolen set." He glanced up at Charles. "If you would be so kind, sir, where did you obtain this ring?"

"Indeed, Sheridan!" Bradford exclaimed. "Where did you get it? From Mrs. Langtry?" He frowned. "But that's impossible, since the ring was stolen. Where *did* you get it?"

"In the safe at the home of Mr. Alfred Day, in Oxford Street."

"Alfred Day!" Bradford exclaimed. "Good Lord!"

Jack Murray whistled between his teeth. His eyes were gleaming. "So it was Badger who stole those jewels! Or fenced them," he added. He grinned. "I doubt if the Jersey Lily would have made a gift of the ring to Badger. And in those days, he had not yet taken up bookmaking, so she would not have owed him any money."

"But she has owed him money more recently," Charles remarked. "And he seems to have been anxious to collect." He took a note out of his other pocket. "This morning, I encountered Mrs. Hardaway just coming out of the butcher's shop. She urgently entreated me to accompany her to Hardaway House so that she could give me this note, which my wife enclosed in one of her own and sent to me yesterday afternoon." He unfolded the note, which bore evidence of having been crumpled. "Through a series of misadventures," he added regretfully, "I did not receive it quite as soon as Kate intended."

"It's like Kate," Bradford said with a smile, "to go about discovering intrigue. Who wrote the note?"

"The now-deceased Mr. Day," Charles replied. "Kate's maid Amelia found it in the fireplace in Mrs. Langtry's bedroom." He held up the note. "It escaped burning, as you can see, because wine was spilled on it—fortunately for us." He read the note slowly, pausing after each sentence so his hearers could understand its full import. When he had finished, he looked up.

"By Jove!" Bradford let out his breath. "What a crafty old conniver! So the Badger was blackmailing our Gilded Lily! And if he'd succeeded, she would lose her chance at young de Bathe."

"So it would seem," Charles agreed. "He also implies that he knows how Edward Langtry died and who stole the jewels—an insinuation confirmed by the ring in his safe, where he was no doubt keeping it in case it proved useful." He held up the ring so that the stones caught the light. "However, there is something quite interesting about this particular piece of jewelry."

"I'm sure there is, sir," Murray said. His eyes, unexpectedly, were twinkling. "Have you had it to a jeweler yet?"

"On my way here," Charles said. "I stopped to have it examined. And as you have guessed, Jack, the gems are paste."

"Paste!" Bradford gasped. "You must be joking! The Lily made her reputation on the authenticity of those gems!"

"It's no joke, sir," Murray said. "Those of us working the case theorized that the jewelry wasn't worth anything like what the lady claimed. Nobody but a fool would carry forty thousand pounds worth of diamonds and emeralds and sapphires on those Wild West tours of hers. And while she may not be much of a stage actress, Mrs. Langtry is no fool."

"But she is hungry for publicity," Charles said. "Her career depends upon her being constantly in the public eye. The jewels brought her that sort of attention—and plenty of customers. The cowboys and farmers and miners didn't come to appreciate her acting ability. They came to gawk at her, and at the jewels she wore. As far as she was concerned, the gems were merely stage props. On the other hand," he continued thoughtfully, "the fact that these jewels are fakes doesn't mean that *she* arranged for the substitution. The thief could have done so, and sold the genuine stones for full value."

"But why would a thief go to the trouble of replacing the real stones with paste?" Bradford said. "He'd simply sell the gems and be done with it. I cast my vote for the Lily."

"Right," Murray said. "Anyway, our theory was more or less confirmed when we were tipped by one of her acquaintances to the effect that the gems were worthless—which she denied, of course, when we questioned her about it. She was trying to get the bank to make good the loss at the full forty thousand pounds she was claiming. She settled, I think, for ten." He added, parenthetically, "If she knew the stuff was real, she'd have held out for more."

"So Badger either took the tin box from the bank, or was given the jewels to fence," Bradford said. "At which time, he discovered their true worth."

"I suspect there's more to it than that," Charles said.

"Such as Mrs. Langtry's staging the theft for the sake of publicity?" Murray asked. "Or to cover up the fact that she'd already sold the gems? Or to defraud the Union Bank?"

"It's all possible," Charles said. "It's also possible that someone else—someone she trusted, perhaps someone she loved—did it without her knowledge. Short of a confession from her or the person who committed the crime, I doubt we will ever know the truth, either about the jewels, or about Langtry's death."

Murray frowned. "D'you suppose Badger actually killed Langtry?"

"Anything is possible," Charles said. He looked up. "All of these possibilities, gentlemen, might add up to a motive for murder."

"Damn!" Bradford exclaimed. "So we're back to the Lily again! Did *she* kill Badger?"

"No, I don't think so," Charles replied. "And neither does Kate. In fact, it is her theory that Alfred Day was killed by a man whom Lillie calls by the nickname of Spider, who visited her on Monday afternoon." He looked at Murray. "Does that name strike any sort of chord with you, Jack?"

"Spider?" Murray frowned. "Not right off, I'm afraid. What makes Lady Sheridan believe that this Spider person killed Badger?"

"Kate told Bradford and me on Monday night that she had overheard a conversation between this man and Mrs. Langtry in which he alluded to a knowledge of the jewel theft and of Edward Langtry's death. The next day, Kate learned that a parlormaid had observed this same man in the act of opening the drawer where Mrs. Langtry's gun was kept—which has now turned up missing. The servants apparently know the man only by the name of Spider."

"Spider," Bradford said thoughtfully. "Members of the Marlborough Set take a great pleasure in giving one another nicknames. There's Billy Stomachache, for instance—Lord William Savernake, the Marquess of Aylesbury. And Harty-Tarty, Lord Hartington. And of course, Hugh Lowther, the Earl of Lonsdale, is Lordy to his friends."

"Can you think of anyone who might be called Spider?" Charles asked.

"I've never heard the name." Bradford frowned. "The only possibility that comes to mind is Reggie Hunt. He lost a great deal of money on his horse Tarantula, whom he fancied for the Derby. But I've never heard anyone call him Spider, and I can't think that he would've been involved with the Lily, for heaven's sake. He's so... ineffectual."

"Lord Hunt," Murray said slowly. "He's the owner of Gladiator, isn't he? He's here in Newmarket—I saw him yesterday."

Bradford shrugged. "Come to that, I seem to recall that Suggie de Bathe owned a racing yacht called *The Black Widow*—yet I don't quite see him stealing the Lily's gun to shoot Alfred Day. Anyway, Lillie Langtry's servants would surely know de Bathe." He appealed to Charles. "Don't we already have quite enough suspects without adding more to the list?"

"The trick is," Charles said soberly, thinking of Owen North, "to have the right suspect." He pulled out his watch and looked at it. "If you're going to catch the London train, I'm afraid that you'd best be on your way, Bradford. The lovely Edith wouldn't like to go without you."

37

Regal Lodge

A Palmist's Analysis of Lillie Langtry's Hand

"The hand would be beautiful, were it not for one
defect, the crookedness of the little finger. The long
thumb shows strong will, obstinate in youth. She
has a perfect passion for power which will later
be succeeded by a passion for luxury. A restless
disposition is shown and a love of social distinction,
the social instinct having increased with gratification.
She is a thorough woman of the world..."

The Palmist, 1898
Mrs. St. Hill, Editor

KATE HAD PASSED an uncomfortable night and morning.
She was anxious about the note she had sent to Charles
along with Alfred Day's letter, for Amelia had returned to
say that his lordship had been out and the message had
been left with Mrs. Hardaway. Kate had heard nothing
from Charles, so she could only trust that her message had
not somehow been lost or fallen into the wrong hands.

But if Kate was worried, Lillie was obviously much more deeply troubled. The morning post had brought a long letter from Suggie de Bathe—not a reassuring letter, judging from the expression on Lillie's face when she opened and read it at the breakfast table. In fact, she appeared so distressed that Kate thought she might even confide what her lover had written. But at that moment, Jeanne-Marie had come into the room, looking pale and drawn and with an obstinate set to her mouth. She avoided her mother's eyes, refused to answer her mother's queries as to her health, ate only a piece of dry toast, and drank only a cup of black coffee. Then she left the room, her back straight as a ramrod, her shoulders expressing her defiance. All the while she had said not a single word.

At midmorning, Lillie invited Kate for a tour of the Regal Lodge stables, where she kept the six or seven horses that were not in training with Jack Robinson in Wiltshire. Jeanne-Marie was twice summoned to go with them. She came downstairs at last and followed along behind Kate and Lillie, but while her mother was lively and vivacious, pointing out the merits of one horse and remarking on the difficulties of another, the girl resolutely said nothing. She did not even reply when Lillie made a great show of giving her a filly named Princess, to take back with her to Jersey. She was silent at luncheon, too, and while Kate made every effort to speak naturally, what little conversation there was seemed forced and awkward.

In the drawing room after luncheon, Lillie flung herself onto the sofa. "What *am* I to do with that horrid child!" she exclaimed petulantly. "I have apologized as well as I can, offered all the amends I can think of—even given her a horse of her own! And yet nothing satisfies her, nothing at all! What *can* she want of me?"

Kate felt such a deep surge of indignation that she

was struck momentarily dumb. That she could not bear children was a great and lasting heartache, and the idea that a mother could deny her maternity and then wonder why the child was unhappy almost took her breath away.

"I think," she managed at last, in as even a tone as possible, "that your daughter wants nothing but your public acknowledgment."

"Acknowledgment!" Lillie cried vexatiously. "If that's what the child hopes for, she will be sadly disappointed, for that is exactly what I *cannot* give her!"

"But why not acknowledge her?" Kate persisted. "It can no longer be a matter of Edward Langtry's possible intervention in Jeanne's life. And she is no longer a child—she would enjoy accompanying you on your tours. Surely—"

"It has nothing to do with Jeanne, actually," Lillie said in a sulky tone. "The truth is that Suggie's father is making a tremendous row about us, and poor Suggie is feeling utterly besieged on all sides. Discovering that he's about to inherit a stepdaughter only a few years younger than he might tip the balance in the wrong direction. And it would certainly give his father more ammunition with which to snipe at me." She sighed discontentedly. "It's not as if there aren't plenty of eligible young women madly flinging themselves at Suggie," she added, with an unconscious emphasis on *young*. "They all want to be Lady de Bathe."

"I'm sure you love one another," Kate remarked, "but is it all that important to be married? You can support yourself without leaning on his social distinction, such as it is. Surely, a woman of your experience of the world—"

"Dearest Beryl," Lillie said, with the patient air of one explaining something to a small child. "Marriage is not at *all* important—in fact, it usually gets in the way of satisfying one's needs and deepest desires. And indeed I can support myself, and I intend to. I am not interested in the de Bathe money, not a bit of it!"

"Well, then," Kate said, "why not claim Jeanne-Marie and let Suggie go. Surely—"

"Marriage is not important," Lillie said, "except in *this* instance. Marriage to Suggie offers me something I want much more than mere money. It offers me social distinction, a title, respectability. I love Jeanne-Marie, but she must be content with our little deception until I am safely married to Suggie. Then I will joyfully tell the whole wide world that she is my daughter." She spread her arms dramatically. "I will publish it in *The Times*, if she wishes, or proclaim it from the stage, if that will satisfy her! But for now—"

"No, Aunt Lillie," a voice said, clear and firm. "You will never publicly acknowledge that you are my mother. I forbid it."

Kate turned. Jeanne was standing in the drawing room doorway, dressed for travel, with a valise in one hand. Her face was pale, but there were two spots of color in her cheeks, and she had the look of a lioness.

"You don't mean that, Jeanne," Lillie said softly, holding out her hands. "Come to me, *ma petite chérie*. We will kiss and make up and everything will be right again."

"No!" Jeanne flung the word, fierce with indignation and pent-up anger, at the woman on the sofa. "I am going back to Jersey, where I at least know who I am. I will make my appearance in court, since His Highness has so kindly arranged it, but you are forbidden to attend. And I forbid you to claim me as your daughter. Do you hear? *Never!*"

"But I *want* to acknowledge you, Jeanne!" Lillie cried shrilly. "I want it so desperately! It is my deepest, truest heart's desire. But the world doesn't give us what we wish for, and we must be practical. I want—"

"You want to be Lady de Bathe far more desperately than you want to be my mother," Jeanne broke in. "Out of the thousands of lies you have told throughout your life, that, I believe, is the single truth." Her voice was strong and measured, her eyes magnificently defiant. "So now *I* repudiate *you*. Do you hear that, Aunt? You are not my mother and never will be. I repudiate you!"

And with that, she turned away, picked up her valise and was gone. A moment later, the crunch of wheels was heard in the drive.

Lillie's eyes were full of what Kate hoped were genuine tears. "Oh, dear," she said brokenly. "Have I lost her forever? Tell me, Beryl—have I lost her?"

Kate could not answer that question. The natural bond between daughter and mother was incredibly strong. But if a mother refused to acknowledge her child, how could she expect to claim that child's love? And perhaps it was better for Jeanne, after all, to learn to stand strong in her own right and for herself, rather than hoping against hope that her mother would declare who she was.

For a few moments, Lillie sat quietly, the tears streaming down her face. Then she took out a handkerchief and began to dab at her eyes. "I am sure Jeanne will think better of this in a few days," she said. Her voice became more firm as she continued: "She will see that as a stage actress I cannot do a great deal for her, or make her life easier in any important way. But as Lady de Bathe, I can help her to make an excellent marriage. In fact, I already have my eye on one or two young men, friends of Suggie's, who would be very fine candidates. One of them will inherit a baronetcy. The other has strong investments in—"

Kate cleared her throat. She could not say what she wished, but she had to say something, or she was afraid that she would scream. "I'm sure it will all work out in the end," she said, thinking how banal and clichéd the words sounded, and how false. But truth was not a valued commodity in this house.

"You're right, of course," Lillie said, tucking her handkerchief away. "It will all work out in the end. Jeanne is temperamental. By tonight, she will have forgotten all about our little contretemps." She looked up brightly. "Now, for this afternoon—I was thinking of taking a drive into Bury St. Edmunds to call on an old acquaintance there. Do you wish to accompany me—or would you prefer to spend time in the garden?"

Lillie's tone made it plain that she was not eager to take Kate calling, and Kate did not prefer either of the options she was offered. She stood.

"Thank you for the invitation. I think, though, that it might be time to bring my visit to an end. We've determined that we won't be staging *The Duchess*, and I believe we've concluded our interview. I'm quite sure I have enough material for an article." She arranged a smile on her face and forced herself to lie. "You have been a wonderful hostess, Lillie. I've enjoyed my visit very much."

"Oh, have you?" Lillie asked cheerily, cocking her head to one side. "I'm so very glad, Beryl! You *must* come again, and next time I promise that we shan't be bothered by any of my little domestic tragedies. But you must let me tell Williams to have the pony cart brought round to take you to Newmarket. You'll be catching the train?"

"Lord Charles is still in Newmarket," Kate said. "I think I shall stay over for a time, to see our young friend Patrick ride in Friday's race. But I would like the pony cart, thank you."

She went quickly up the stairs, meeting Amelia in the hallway. She grasped her hand and pulled her into the bedroom. "We're packing, Amelia," she said. "Hurry! I

279

want to be out of here just as soon as we can!"

"Has something gone wrong, my lady?" Amelia asked in surprise.

"I can't bear to stay in the same house with that awful woman for one more minute!" Kate exclaimed. "And don't bother with careful packing—just throw the things in." She went to the wardrobe and seized a dress. "Here—I'll help."

Between the two of them, packing took only ten minutes. Kate put on her hat and gloves and a short cloak over her green dress. Then Amelia went down the back stairs to get help with the luggage, and Kate, her purse in her hand, went down to the drawing room to say goodbye to Lillie. As she stepped into the room, however, she saw that the only occupant was a man standing by the window, gazing out, a brandy snifter in his hand. At the rustle of her skirts, he spoke without turning, his voice hard, unsoftened by even the slightest affection.

"What took you so long?" He put the snifter on the table. "You know that I do not like to be kept waiting." He turned. Seeing Kate, he colored. "Forgive me," he said with a slight bow. "I was expecting Mrs. Langtry."

"I am Lady Sheridan," Kate said, holding out her gloved hand. "Mrs. Langtry's houseguest. And you, sir, are—?"

"My dear Lady Sheridan." With a charming flourish, the man bent over her hand. He was impeccably dressed, nearing fifty, perhaps, and becoming stout. His hair was brown, his side-whiskers just going gray. He was quite a distinguished-looking man, Kate thought, but there was a certain quality of shrewdness beneath the surface, evident in his swift, measuring glance, as if he were seeing and calculating all her weaknesses so that he would know how to use them. There was something of the predator in him.

The French doors opened, and Lillie came in. "Ah,

Spider!" she said ebulliently, going to him with both hands out.

"Mr. Jersey, I presume," the man said playfully. He put his arms around her and bent to her throat for a familiar kiss. "Out seeing to your new horse, eh? Do you like him?" He smiled.

Lillie pushed the man back, but his arms tightened for a moment. Then, as if teasing her, he laughed and let her go.

"I *adore* him, Spider!" Lillie exclaimed. "And you are such a dear, such a very sweet and loving dear, for giving Tarantula to me. You must come out to the stable and tell me all about him." She caught a glimpse of Kate. "Oh, Beryl, I thought you had gone. Well, you must come too. Really, Tarantula is a most exciting horse! He has the look of a winner."

The man turned toward Kate with a slight smile. "Your charming guest and I were just getting acquainted."

"I don't believe I caught your name," Kate said.

"Oh, just call him Spider," Lillie replied playfully. "It's ever so much more descriptive than his own name." She tucked a hand through the man's arm and glanced at Kate. "Coming, Beryl?"

"I think I'd better be getting on my way," Kate said. "Williams will have loaded the luggage into the pony cart." She added, convincingly, she hoped, "I must thank you again for a most delightful visit."

"Oh, that's quite all right," Lillie said carelessly. She tugged the man toward the French doors. "Come along, Spider. And Beryl, my dear Beryl," she added over her shoulder, "I do hope you'll come back. You'll always be welcome at Regal Lodge."

And with that, the two of them made their exit center stage, through the French doors, to the tune of Lillie's vivacious chatter.

Kate turned as if to leave. But instead of going to the door, she took two swift steps to the table beside the window where the man had been standing when she came into the drawing room. She opened the table drawer, put in her gloved hand, and drew something out. Quickly, she dropped it into her purse and closed the drawer.

She had just stolen Lillie Langtry's silver-handled derringer.

And as an afterthought, she also scooped up the brandy snifter.

38

Newnham Grange

'"Our friend here is a wonderful man for starting a chase. All he wants is an old dog to help him to do the running down.'

'I hope a wild goose may not prove to be the end of our chase,' observed Mr. Merryweather gloomily.

'You may place considerable confidence in Mr. Holmes, sir,' said the police agent loftily. 'He has his own little methods, which are, if he won't mind my saying so, just a little too theoretical and fantastic, but he has the makings of a detective in him.'"

The Red-Headed League
ARTHUR CONAN DOYLE

NEWNHAM GRANGE WAS a late eighteenth-century house stuck all over with chimney pots and built on a branch of the River Cam about halfway between Foster's Mill and the Newnham Mill, on the outskirts of Cambridge near the Silver Street Bridge. By a great coincidence, Charles had actually visited the house some time before, for it was the residence of George Darwin, the second son of the famous evolutionist Charles Darwin. George Darwin, professor of astronomy at Cambridge, was well known in his own right, and his speculative interest in the movements of the moon and the tides happened to coincide with Lord Charles's. After the publication the previous year of Professor Darwin's book, *The Tides and Kindred Phenomena of the Solar System*, they had met several times to discuss these highly theoretical and rather fantastic topics, and Charles had once been asked to Newnham Grange to continue their conversation.

As Charles did not wish to make explanations to the Darwins (Mrs. Darwin was an American, a lovely woman but apt to make a fuss about things), he stopped the gig at Foster's Mill and gave the horse into the care of a boy who worked there. After some discussion, he and Murray agreed that Murray would go to the Grange kitchen and try to find out from the cook whether she knew the whereabouts of her brother. Charles would wait on the nearby Silver Street Bridge.

Murray went on foot down the drive and around to the tradesman's entrance. The kitchen door was opened by an aproned girl, and the odor of onions assaulted him. He snatched off his bowler hat. "Mrs. Thompson, please," he said humbly.

The girl took in his green bow tie, checked tweed suit, and bowler hat. "I s'pose ye're 'ere 'bout the oysters," she said enigmatically.

"Actually, I—" Murray said.

"Ye'd better come in, then, and face up to it." The girl opened the door. She turned and bawled, over her shoulder, "It's a man 'bout them bad oysters, Miz Thompson." She went into the scullery to carry on with the washing up, making a great show of banging the pots and pans.

Sally Thompson was a large woman with a round face and a cross expression. Her gray hair was curled like a large snail at the back of her neck, and her bulbous nose was red and covered with a spidery web of blood vessels. With a glower, she looked up from her work at the pine table, where she was elbow-deep in a tub of bread dough. The offending onions were cooking in a cast-iron fry pan on the coal range.

"I can't take the respons'bility fer them oysters," she said in a dark tone. "Ye'll 'ave to talk to Mrs. Darwin. She wuz terr'ble upset, 'cause there was fourteen t'dinner, including Perfessor Kelvin, 'oo is partic'lar fond of oysters." She gave him a knowing look. "I'm sure ye can guess wot 'appened after that."

Murray preferred not to think about it. "I'm very sorry about the oysters, Mrs. Thompson," he said contritely, "but that is not why I've come. I was sent by Mr. Thompson's cousin Angus." In the scullery, there was a lull in the banging of the pots.

Mrs. Thompson looked momentarily confused, as if she were having difficulty associating her dead husband's cousin and the misadventure of the oysters. Then her expression cleared. "Oh, Angus," she said, and turned a large lump of dough out of the tub onto the floury table. "'Ow is the old devil?"

"Oh, he's quite well, thank you." Murray added, inventively, "He asked to be remembered to you. With affection."

Mrs. Thompson put her head on one side and smiled reminiscently, raising her voice over the sound of pot-washing, which had once again resumed. "Angus was allus me fav'rite on that side of the fam'ly." She floured her hands and began to knead the dough with a vigorous push and pull. "Why'd 'e send ye?"

285

"He and I both are eager to get in touch with your brother," Murray said. "It's a matter of some importance, I'm afraid."

"Eddie?" Mrs. Thompson's eyes flickered. She frowned. "Wot's 'e done now?"

"Oh, nothing," Murray said hastily. "Nothing at all. But it is possible that he may have some information about an accident in Newmarket. Angus thought you might happen to know where he is."

Mrs. Thompson kneaded more vigorously. "Are ye from the p'lice?"

"No, ma'am. As I said, your cousin sent me. He is as anxious as I am to be in touch with Eddie."

"Well, it's no good talkin' to me," Mrs. Thompson said, wiping her nose with the back of her hand. "Ye're on a wild-goose chase." Into another pause in the washing-up clatter, she added, "I ain't seen Eddie since Boxing Day. 'E don't come 'ere much. We ain't been wot ye might call close since our poor dear mother died."

"Oh, dear," Murray said. "That really is too bad." The scullery remained silent. "You're sure you can't give me some clue to his whereabouts? It's awfully urgent, I'm afraid. A man's life may depend on his information." He paused. "I'd be glad to make it worth your while."

Mrs. Thompson turned the pliant dough and pummeled it as though it were the truant Eddie. "I ain't me brother's keeper," she snapped. "Off with ye now. If ye can't 'elp with the oysters, ye're no good to me."

Murray turned, catching the flash of an apron at the scullery door. "If you hear of him," he said, putting one of his cards on the table, "I can be reached at this address."

For answer, Mrs. Thompson only assaulted the dough more energetically. Murray put on his hat and went to the door. "Thank you," he said loudly. "I'll be off now."

He went out, leaving the door open a little behind him. Ten paces down the path, he stepped into the shrubbery and waited.

He didn't have to wait long. Inside two or three minutes, the surly girl had joined him. He put his hand in his pocket and felt for a coin.

"Where is he?" he asked in a low voice.

The girl looked at the coin and gave a scornful grunt. "Thought ye said 'twas a man's life."

Murray added a second coin.

"'E's down there," the girl said with a nod toward the river. "At the cottage on the bank, just down from the bridge. That's where she lives, the old witch. But ye'd better 'urry. 'E's leavin' today. 'E's goin' t'America."

"Thank you," he said. "Thank you very much."

But she was already striding off, back to the scullery and a sink full of dirty pots and pans.

Charles and Murray made their way down an over-grown path toward the river, which still smelled of sewage, although drains had recently been installed throughout the town. Charles half smiled, remembering the story of Queen Victoria, being shown over Trinity College many years before by its master, Dr. Whewell, and asking, when she walked over the bridge, about the pieces of paper that were floating down the river. Dr. Whewell, with extraordinary presence of mind, had replied: "Those, Your Majesty, are notices that bathing is forbidden."

The path dipped down to the riverbank. Ahead of them stood a small timber-framed Tudor cottage that might have been a bucolic addition to a romantic landscape painting, overhung as it was by a large weeping willow and fronted with a rose hedge in full bloom. Behind the cottage a small herd of cows was fording a shallow inlet on their way to their pasture at Sheep's Green, and out on the river proper Charles could see two rowing teams in their sculls.

But the damp situation and the occasional spring rises of the River Cam had not done the cottage any good, and whatever pastoral romance it might have offered to a harried city-dweller in search of a weekend rural retreat was obscured by its dilapidated reality. The plaster on the walls had sloughed off, exposing the lath underneath; the thatched roof was ragged and pocked; the plank door sagged at an angle; and the window frame gapped so widely that, open or closed, there must be no want of fresh air indoors, especially when the winter winds blew. Through the dirty glass, Charles saw that the ground floor was one small, dark room, like a cave, brick-floored, with a fireplace at one end and a ladder at the other, reaching up through the low ceiling into a loft. Mrs. Sally Thompson seemed not to have made a great success of life, at least so far as material possessions might testify, for the room contained only a bare table, three chairs, and a narrow bed under a gray wool coverlet, pushed against the back wall. There was no china on the mantel, no pots of geraniums on the sill, no braided rug on the floor, no cozy cat warming itself by the fire—although an old black-and-white dog lay under the willow tree. Two empty whiskey bottles in the dustbin outside the door suggested one possible reason for the lack of niceties and knicknacks. Mrs. Thompson was fond of her tipple.

Inside the cottage, a slender man in a light-blue checked suit was just descending the ladder from the loft, a blue tweed cap on his head and a portmanteau in one hand. He turned toward the door just as Charles stepped inside, followed by Jack Murray, who was followed in turn by the dog, who stood just inside the doorway, scratching. They seemed to fill the small room.

The man looked up, his face draining of color, his eyes wide with sudden fear behind thick-lensed glasses. Then, seeing men whom he did not recognize, his fear turned to nervous belligerence.

"Who're you?" he demanded thinly. "What do you want?"

"We've come to talk to you, Mr. Baggs," Charles said, wondering just who the man had feared might find him. The police, perhaps? Or someone else?

The man cleared his throat. "There's no Baggs here," he said indistinctly. "You've got the wrong house. Now, if you don't mind, I'll be off. I've a train to catch."

"It's Baggs, all right," Murray said in a low voice to Charles. "I saw him once, with Badger. No mistaking those glasses. He's blind as a bat without them." At the mention of Badger's name, the man pressed his lips together.

"Mr. Baggs," Charles said. "I am Charles Sheridan and this is Jack Murray. We are conducting a private investigation, commissioned by the Jockey Club, into the murder of your partner. We would like to ask you a few questions, please."

The dog growled low in his throat. Baggs put down his portmanteau and straightened his shoulders, the muscles in his jaw tightening. "A... private investigation?" he asked hesitantly.

"Right," Murray answered gruffly. "We ain't police." He booted the dog outside, closed the door, and shoved the bolt into place. The action was clearly a threat.

Baggs's chin began to quiver. "I... I don't know anything about Badger," he said plaintively. "I heard he'd been shot, but I'd already made plans to leave before that happened. I've been... I've decided to go into a different line of work, you see. In America. I'm looking for more opportunity."

"That's interesting," Charles said, as Murray began to

edge around the table. He gave Baggs an encouraging smile. "It is a natural thing to want more opportunity, and I congratulate you on your initiative. But what about your business in Newmarket? I've heard that it's thriving. I shouldn't think you'd want to leave it."

"Business?" Baggs asked uneasily, his glance shifting from Charles to Murray. He took a step backward, in the direction of the fireplace. "That's all over. Badger and I ended our partnership the week before, quite... quite amicably."

"Amic'bly, huh?" Murray snarled, now standing within an arm's length of Baggs. He spoke in a thick Cockney accent that made him seem larger and more menacing than he was. "That ain't wot Sobersides sez. 'E sez you threatened to kill Badger if 'e didn't lay off about the doping. 'E sez 'e'll swear to it in court. So wot about it, huh? You killed 'im, right? You killed Badger."

"No!" Baggs took another step backward. His eyes were wide and frightened behind his glasses, his mouth was working. "We... we may have had a few hard words. But—"

"When I said that your business was thriving, I was speaking of your connection with the Americans," Charles said mildly. "I understand from various sources that you have undertaken a new business arrangement with them, which was in part the reason for terminating your relationship with Mr. Day."

"That ain't all," Murray said menacingly. He thrust his face close to Baggs's and growled, "You 'ad a row wiv Badger at the Great Horse jes' before 'e was killed—a big row. You wuz seen, and 'eard, Baggs, so don't try to lie out of it."

Charles pulled out a chair from the table and sat down, crossing his legs. He leaned back. "I fear that Mr. Murray is correct," he said regretfully. "The proprietor will testify that you followed Badger out of the pub and didn't come back. I'm very much afraid that the police believe that *you* are the killer, Mr. Baggs. They're looking for you, you see. They will no doubt trace you, just as we did." He shook his head, the gesture seeming to say that it was a pity that such a promising career could be cut off by so dreadful a misunderstanding.

Baggs sagged against the fireplace mantel. "I... I'm not the man they're looking for," he whispered. His eyes were terrified. "I... I swear it."

Murray yanked the other chair forward. "Oh, yeah?" He put a thick hand on Baggs's shoulder and forced him into the chair. "You sure look like that man to me, Baggs, you do fer a fact. You and Badger 'ad a row, you followed 'im out in the alley, you shot 'im." He leaned over and shouted into Baggs's ear. "You did it. Didn't you?"

Baggs shook his head wordlessly, his eyes rolling.

Charles leaned forward. "Then who did?" he asked softly.

"I... don't know," Baggs said. He blinked rapidly, as if he were blinking back tears. "I... didn't see."

Murray reached down and snatched Baggs's thick glasses. "Lemme see them specs o' yers. Mebbe you need better lenses, huh? Mebbe that way, you can see."

"Give me back my spectacles!" Baggs cried, leaping up from the chair and grabbing at the air. "I can't see without them!"

Roughly, Murray pushed him back onto the chair. "But you couldn't see wiv 'em, now, could you, guv'nor? You couldn't see 'oo killed Badger, right? So they ain't much good to you, are they?" He held up the glasses with a grating laugh. "So mebbe I'll jes' step on 'em."

"No, no!" Baggs turned to Charles, begging. "Stop him,

291

please, sir!" He rubbed his eyes with the backs of both hands, like a schoolboy. "Make him give them back, sir!"

"I'm afraid that Mr. Murray is deplorably single-minded," Charles said sadly. "He has his own methods for getting information, and he does not take direction well. You will have to undertake to persuade him yourself."

Baggs was openly weeping now. "What... what do you want?"

Murray leaned close. "The truth!" he thundered. "'Oo killed Alfred Day?" He put the spectacles on the floor and raised one foot as if to crush them.

Faced with this terrifying loss, Baggs broke down completely.

39

At Hardaway House

"Search then the Ruling Passion: there, alone,
The wild are constant and the cunning known;
The fool consistent, and the false sincere...
This clue once found, unravels all the rest."

ALEXANDER POPE

"Call me a spider-catcher."

Love Tricks
JAMES SHIRLEY

KATE PUT AMELIA on the afternoon train back to Bishop's Keep; then, carrying one small portmanteau with her, took a hansom to Hardaway House, stopping along the way to buy a few things for tea. She lit the fire, put on the gas kettle, and had just sat down on the sofa to write in her journal when Charles entered the room, accompanied by a small man in a checked tweed suit, green bow tie, and bowler hat, smelling strongly of cigars.

"Kate!" Charles exclaimed. "What are you doing here?"

"Waiting for you, my very dear," Kate replied quietly.

She lifted her face for his welcoming kiss, glad to be out of the emotional storms which seemed to whirl around Lillie, glad to be back in the calm haven of her husband's presence.

"But why aren't you at Regal Lodge?" Charles asked. "I assumed that you would be staying another day, at the least." From his expression, Kate could see that he was both excited and troubled. He turned toward the other man. "Kate, this is Mr. Jack Murray, the Jockey Club's investigator and formerly of Scotland Yard. Mr. Murray, Lady Sheridan, my wife."

"Delighted, ma'am," Murray said, snatching off his hat.

"I am glad to meet you, Mr. Murray," Kate said. "Charles has spoken highly of your abilities and experience." She turned to Charles. "I left Regal Lodge," she said in answer to his question, "because I couldn't bear to stay. I fear that a little of Mrs. Langtry goes a very long way, at least for me." She glanced up. "Please pardon me if that seems a rude thing to say, Mr. Murray."

"I'm afraid I know just what you mean, my lady," Jack Murray said ruefully.

"Jack was one of the Scotland Yard men on the Langtry jewel theft case," Charles explained. "He had dealings with Mrs. Langtry then."

"More than I cared to, ma'am," Murray put in fervently, "begging your pardon."

"I understand," Kate said with a sympathetic smile. She could imagine the scene: Lillie a study in astonished horror and dismay; Lillie complaining melodramatically about the inability of the Yard to catch the criminals; Lillie indignant and betrayed when the police failed to return her jewels. And if she had been complicit in the theft, the whole thing would have been nothing more or less than a grand performance: Mrs. Lillie Langtry starring in the role of the beautiful and helpless victim of an appalling robbery.

The kettle was steaming. Kate got up, poured hot water into the tea pot, and set out three china cups she had found in the sideboard. As she assembled a tray of cheeses and purchased biscuits, she said, "I met Spider this afternoon."

"You *met* him?" Charles asked, with open excitement. "He came to Regal Lodge?"

"Yes," Kate said. "He gave Lillie a horse." She smiled as she added, over her shoulder, "A horse named Tarantula, of course. Exactly as one might expect from a Spider."

"Tarantula?" Murray frowned. "That's Lord Hunt's horse. The one he lost on so heavily last year."

"Lord Hunt?" Kate looked around sharply. "Is that Spider's real name?"

"You didn't get the man's name, then?" Charles asked.

Kate shook her head. "I asked, but both he and Lillie avoided answering, and I didn't like to press, for fear of seeming overly curious. The man had ridden a horse, so there was no driver I might ask." She put the tray on the small table in front of the sofa. "Will you be so kind as to pour the tea, Charles?" she added, going for her purse. "I have something to show you."

While Charles poured, Kate opened her purse and took out the derringer and the brandy snifter, each wrapped in a handkerchief. She put them on the table next to the tray and opened the handkerchiefs.

"By thunder!" Mr. Murray exclaimed, letting out his breath. "Is this—"

"The missing derringer," Charles said, with satisfaction. "Kate, my sweet, you are a treasure of treasures. Where in the world did you happen on it?"

"In the drawer in the drawing room," Kate said, sitting beside Charles on the sofa. "Spider was alone in the room

295

when I came in. It occurred to me that if he were indeed the man who took the gun, he might have taken the opportunity to return it. After he and Lillie went out to the stable, I looked in the drawer—and there it was."

Charles slipped his arm around her waist and hugged her. "Wonderful, Kate!"

"Excuse me, ma'am," Mr. Murray said, "but what about the brandy snifter?"

"The man called Spider was drinking from that glass," Kate said. "I thought you might like to see if his fingerprints are on it, Charles. To be compared to any you might be able to find on the gun," she added. "I was wearing gloves when I picked up both objects."

"Fingerprints?" Murray asked, surprised. He raised both eyebrows. "You're speaking of that dactyloscopy business that Edward Henry is pushing at the Yard?"

"Oh, you know about that, then, do you, Jack?" Charles asked, pleased.

Murray nodded. "A friend of mine, Sergeant Randal, has been taking fingerprints at Sir Francis Galton's South Kensington laboratory for some years, and he keeps me posted on the progress. According to Sergeant Randal, Henry has been using dactyloscopy in India with a great deal of success. He thinks there's a chance that the Anthropometry Bureau might be compelled to at least give the method a trial." His face became gloomy. "Although I personally doubt that will happen. The Home Secretary is convinced that anthropometry provides the best means of identification. Barking up the wrong tree, if you ask me," he added. "Measuring noses and ears isn't precise enough. Too much chance for error. And the record-keeping is preposterous."

"Fingerprint records aren't much of an improvement," Charles remarked. "And even if the Yard takes up fingerprinting, the courts will still have to accept it as evidence. And that is some distance in the future."

Kate frowned. "It's all well and good to have the fingerprints on the gun—they might be of some help. But isn't the first task to match the gun to the crime? How is that to be done without—"

"Without the fatal bullet?" Charles reached into his pocket and took out a bullet, putting it on the table. "Here it is, Kate. Taken yesterday from Badger's body by Dr. Stubbings. We'll fire a test round and see whether we can determine any similarities."

Murray was even more gloomy. "The experts at the Yard don't think ballistics evidence counts for much, either. And no court in England has ever been presented with a case involving such a thing. However, it won't hurt to give it a try. There's a first time for everything." He put down his teacup and stood. "I don't imagine any of us has a .41 caliber bullet handy for a test-firing, so I'll just pop around to the gun shop before it closes." He bowed to Kate. "Ma'am."

When Murray had gone, Kate turned back to her husband, feeling a surge of excitement. "Charles, this is wonderful! Now that you have these pieces of physical evidence, you can confront Lord Hunt and force him to confess to killing—"

"Lord Hunt?" Absently, Charles got up from the sofa to get his fingerprint kit out of his satchel. "But Reggie Hunt didn't kill Alfred Day."

"He didn't?" Kate frowned. "But I thought Mr. Murray said that Tarantula belonged to Lord Hunt. Charles, I am *very* confused."

His kit in his hand, Charles sat back down on the sofa. He seemed lost in thought. "Reggie Hunt owed a great deal of money to the man Mrs. Langtry calls Spider," he said slowly. "In payment of the debt, Spider took Hunt's estate and half his stable—including the horse, I suppose."

Kate stared at Charles, wide-eyed. "Then who *is* Spider? And how did you find him out?"

"We learned Spider's identity from Eddie Baggs," Charles replied. "Baggs followed Badger out of the pub and was standing in the shadows at the back of the Great Horse. He saw, and heard, the entire encounter from beginning to end."

"But that means that there's an eyewitness!" Kate exclaimed excitedly, "and that none of this fingerprint or ballistics evidence matters! With the testimony of an eyewitness, any jury in the land will convict the man. Who *is* he, Charles?"

"His name," Charles said soberly, "is Henry Radwick. He's a moneylender—and quite a successful one, at that, judging from those who patronize him. Half of the members of the Jockey Club have been in the man's debt at one time or another. Lord Hunt certainly isn't the only one who has owed him money."

"But why did he shoot Mr. Day?"

"According to Baggs, Radwick was in a violent temper. He had discovered that Badger was attempting to blackmail Mrs. Langtry. According to Baggs, as Radwick pulled the trigger, he shouted, 'She's mine, do you hear? I won't let you hurt her!'"

"So it was a crime of passion," Kate said, thinking of what she had heard through the drawing room window. Yes, the man who had declared that he would not let Lillie marry Suggie de Bathe *was* capable of killing someone in a fit of rage. She felt sure of that. There was something wrong with that scenario, though. The crime was committed with Lillie's gun, coolly and deliberately taken from the drawer in her drawing room.

Kate frowned. "Spider—Radwick, I mean—stole Lillie's gun. He anticipated using it. That doesn't sound like a crime of passion. It sounds quite deliberate."

"You're right, Kate," Charles replied. "By Radwick's own admission, which you overheard, he was involved in the jewel theft and in Edward Langtry's death. In fact, it's entirely possible that he masterminded both, with or without Lillie's prior consent. I'm conjecturing that Radwick knew something of Badger's threat—although perhaps not the entire scheme—and that he took Lillie's gun, anticipating its possible use. After all, if Radwick allowed Badger to blackmail her, how long would it be before Badger began making demands on him, as well?"

"But why Lillie's gun?" Kate persisted. "A man of Spider's resources—surely he could have found a different weapon."

Charles shrugged. "Perhaps he felt some sense of dramatic irony, using Lillie's gun to kill the man who threatened to betray her."

"Or perhaps he felt he might use it to gain some hold over her," Kate said quietly. "Perhaps he thought to keep her from marrying Suggie de Bathe, and persuade her to marry him instead. I wonder whether, after I left this afternoon, he boasted to Lillie that he murdered Alfred Day for her sake. Do you suppose he opened the drawer to show her the gun he used?"

Anticipating her next thought, Charles said, with a wry smile: "If he did, do you suppose he guessed that Lady Sheridan is now in possession of Mrs. Langtry's derringer?"

Kate gave a little shrug. "There's one thing I don't quite understand, Charles. Why was Radwick called Spider?"

"I've been thinking about that," Charles said. "There might be some kind of private association, of course. But the word 'spider' is also a perjorative term for moneylenders."

"Lurking in the corners, I suppose," Kate said thoughtfully. "Weaving webs to ensnare their innocent prey."

"Something like that," Charles said. "Although in this case, I suspect that the innocent are not quite as innocent as they might like to appear. Certainly Lord Hunt knew what he was doing when he laid his family's estate as a pledge against a gambling debt."

Kate pursed her lips. "When Radwick is tried, this whole ugly business is going to come out in the courts, isn't it? His motive, and so on, I mean. Lillie will be called as a material witness, won't she?" She paused, as the import of this idea began to sink in. "And then the whole thing will come out, won't it, Charles? The jewel theft, Edward Langtry's death—" Her eyes widened and her breath caught in her throat as she began to imagine all of the consequences of a murder trial in open court, with the press and the public looking on. "She'll be ruined, Charles! Utterly *ruined!* Everyone knows that she's still close to the Prince—it will be a terrible scandal."

With a sigh that was both regretful and ironic, Charles opened his fingerprint kit. "Somehow I doubt it will come to that, Kate. I doubt it very much."

40

At the Jockey Club

"If I were to begin life again, I would go to the Turf to get friends. They seem to me to be the only people who really hold close together. I don't know why; it may be that each knows something that might hang the other, but the effect is delightful and most peculiar."

LADY HARRIET ASHBURTON

"What need we fear who knows it, when none can call our power to account?"

Macbeth
WILLIAM SHAKESPEARE

CHARLES SPENT THE better part of an hour that evening writing a careful and fully detailed report to Admiral Owen North. When it was done, he sat for a long time thinking about the implications of what he had written, about what should happen next, and about what was likely to happen next. At last, with an ironic twist to his mouth, he sealed the envelope and sent it by Mrs. Hardaway's boy to the Jockey Club, where North was staying. That done, he and Kate, with Jack Murray, adjourned to the Stag Hotel for a passable dinner and a bottle of champagne, after which he and Kate retired alone to Hardaway House for their first private evening together in several days. It was a renewing respite that both of them cherished.

The next morning, their companionable breakfast was interrupted by a knock at the door and a message from the admiral: North had summoned both Charles and Kate to a meeting at the Jockey Club at eleven o'clock. Charles was not surprised, for he had expected to be called for a discussion of his report, nor was he surprised that the invitation included Kate, as well. By obtaining the physical evidence and by contributing what she had overheard of the conversation between Henry Radwick and Lillie Langtry, she had played a material role in the solution of the crime, and she knew as much as he and Murray knew about what had happened. Yes, of course she would be summoned.

Nor was Charles surprised when he and Kate entered North's office at the Club an hour later to find there, not just Admiral North and Jack Murray, but another man, as well, seated in the admiral's usual chair behind the desk: a supremely stout, gray-bearded man who graciously inclined his head as Kate made a deep curtsy and Charles bowed.

"Your Royal Highness," Charles murmured.

"Please sit down," the Prince said, gesturing to a trio of chairs in front of the desk, where Murray was already seated. Charles and Kate took their seats, Charles feeling like a schoolboy called before the headmaster for a reprimand. He crossed his legs, leaned back, and waited.

After a moment, the Prince of Wales took the cigar out of his mouth. "Well, then," he said, in his gruff, Germanic accent, "I understand that you have been playing the detective again. And very successfully, I must say. I have read your report, Sheridan. I am quite impressed." He looked from Charles to Kate to Jack Murray. "Quite impressed, both with your logical arguments and with the evidence you have assembled to support your accusation of Mr. Henry Radwick." He flicked his cigar ash into North's ashtray. "Fingerprints, ballistics, blackmail letter. Quite a barrage of evidence." He looked at Owen North. "What do you say to that, North? Aren't you impressed?"

"Oh, yes," North said hastily. "Oh, yes, indeed. Lord Sheridan and Mr. Murray have given us all the information we could have wished, Your Highness."

And somewhat more, Charles thought ironically. "Thank you," he said.

"Well, now." The Prince looked once again at Murray, then at Charles. "I am told that the Newmarket constabulary have not been involved in any way in this investigation. Is that correct, gentlemen?"

"Not entirely, sir," Charles said. "I took the liberty of asking Chief Constable Watson to provide interim private lodging in the Newmarket jail for Mr. Baggs. I did not, however, inform the chief constable of the reason for my request."

"Ah," the Prince said gruffly. "Mr. Baggs is the unfortunate eyewitness?"

"That is correct, sir," Charles said. "When Mr. Murray and I located him in Newnham, his valise was packed and he was preparing to leave for America. He was planning to take up a new line of work there."

"Very good, very good," the Prince said approvingly. He turned to North. "If Mr. Baggs has not yet purchased his boat ticket, Owen, see that he has one, will you? You might arrange to have him escorted to his departure point. And slip him a few pounds to help him begin his new career."

"Yes, sir," North said.

The Prince frowned. "Oh, and I should think you might want to have a word or two with him yourself, to be sure that he understands the situation."

"Of course, sir. I shall, sir."

Kate was leaning forward, frowning. "I'm not sure that *I* quite understand, Your Highness. Mr. Baggs is leaving the country? But what about his testimony at the trial? What about—"

"Yes, my dear," the Prince replied with a smile. His tone was condescending, as if he were speaking to a child. "Mr. Baggs will find it advantageous to pursue his original plan. It might be… awkward if he were to stay."

"I take it, then," Charles said ironically, "that there's no point in sending the chief constable round for Mr. Radwick?"

The Prince turned to North. "I believe that's the case, is it not, Owen?"

"Right, sir," the admiral said. "According to my information, Radwick was to have left before dawn this morning." He looked directly at Kate. "Urgent business, your ladyship. In South America."

The Prince regarded his cigar. "The Argentine, is it, Owen?"

"I believe so, sir. Some quite rural area, as I understand it."

"Argentina," the Prince said thoughtfully. "Always wanted to go there myself. Hear that they have some fine shooting in Argentina. Emu, or is it rhea? I forget." He looked at Charles. "Speaking of shooting, you *did* bring the gun with you, I trust?"

"Yes, sir," Charles said. He took the handkerchief-wrapped gun out of his pocket and placed it on the desk. The Prince picked it up and looked at it with a distasteful frown.

"I shall return it to Mrs. Langtry myself," he said. "For

some time, I have wanted an opportunity to caution her about her tendency to become involved with persons of low repute." He pursed his lips and exhaled a round O of blue cigar smoke. "You did telephone Suggie de Bathe in London, did you not, Owen?"

"I did, sir," North said. "He asked me to tell you that he would be able to reach Regal Lodge by teatime."

"Good." The Prince frowned. "Does he understand what is wanted?"

"I believe so, sir," North said. He coughed. "Unfortunately, he anticipates that his father will be upset by the marriage. He rather hopes that you—"

"I'll speak to old Lord de Bathe myself," the Prince said. "I'm sure I can bring him around. And I'll speak to Lillie about her association with those Americans." The frown became a scowl. "Wishard and Clark are the worst, if you ask me. The Stewards ought to think about doing something, Owen. Not this year, perhaps, for we don't want to call too much attention to the matter. But the next, or the year after that. If we don't do something, the Americans will rob us all blind."

"Of course, sir," North said reassuringly. "We're working on it, sir."

"And I'll have a word with Squire Mannington about his objection. I'm sure he can be persuaded to see reason." The Prince put the derringer down on the desk and looked at Charles and Kate. "One might think," he said in a conversational tone, "that I have used my influence to enable a guilty man to escape the consequences of his actions. However, I assure you that Mr. Radwick's lifetime exile from England is a punishment far greater than any that might have been meted out by our courts. Especially when you consider that he has been forced to leave his fortune behind."

"As you say, sir," Charles said dryly. Beside him, Kate was angrily straining to hold her tongue. At the other end of the row, Murray was muttering something he could not quite catch.

The Prince stood and looked sternly down his nose. "I trust that I have your word that you will not speak with anyone else about what has transpired in the past few days." He turned his gaze directly upon Kate. "I am very much afraid that I shall require Beryl Bardwell's word on that as well, Lady Charles. I should not like to pick up *Blackwell's* magazine and read a story entitled *Death at Newmarket.*" He smiled gravely. "I know the importance you Americans place on the freedom of your speech. However, now that you have married into one of the most aristocratic of our British families, I'm sure you have noticed that an obligation to Her Majesty places limits on her subjects' abilities to speak and act as they might like."

"Indeed I have noticed it, Your Highness," Kate said. Charles winced at her defiantly sardonic tone, but the Prince did not seem to hear it.

"Very good, then," he said. He picked up the gun and dropped it into his pocket, glancing at the clock. "Now, if you will excuse me, I am off to Regal Lodge for luncheon with Mrs. Langtry. Good day, gentlemen. Good day, Lady Charles."

"Good day, sir," they echoed dutifully.

When the Prince had left, there was a long silence. Finally, Kate said something, half to herself. Charles looked questioningly at her. Owen North said, "I'm sorry, Lady Charles. I didn't quite catch that. What did you say?"

Kate lifted her chin. "I said," she replied distinctly, "'What need we fear who knows it, when none can call our power to account?'"

41

15 September, 1899

Bishop's Keep

"Certain of our esteemed contemporaries have applied their lack of wits arduously to the problem whether Mrs. Langtry acts better or worse than she used to. Such a discussion is both tedious and unnecessary. Mrs. Langtry never did act and she does not act now."

Review of The Degenerates

KATE PUT DOWN the newspaper and turned her face up to the late morning sun, feeling a twinge of sympathy for Lillie. Her most recent play, *The Degenerates*, which had opened at the beginning of the month, had not been received kindly by the drama critics, who thought it was ugly, immoral, and, yes, degenerate. But judging from the news that had traveled from London, Kate reflected that Lillie—now the wife of Hugo de Bathe—probably did not care about the critics. Her new husband had left for the Continent immediately after the wedding and had been seen there in the affectionate company of a young blond French actress. But the play had been sold out every night and was showing a weekly profit of something like twelve hundred pounds.

"Hello, my love," Charles said, coming onto the terrace to join her. "Anything of interest in *The Times*?"

"Only more criticism of the second Dreyfus court-martial," Kate replied, knowing that Charles would not be very curious about Lillie's reviews. "The French seem to be taking it coolly enough, but there is world-wide unhappiness with the second guilty verdict. It is said that President Loubet will likely pardon him next week and set him free."

Charles sat down, his face grave. After a long moment, he spoke. "The pardon doesn't erase the unjust conviction. Captain Dreyfus should never have been tried, let alone convicted—and convicted twice! The French Army was only trying to cover up its own misdeeds."

"Of course," Kate said with asperity, "the British never do anything like that. They just let the guilty leave the country and start a new life somewhere else."

Charles regarded her with a thoughtful look. "I received a post from Owen North a few minutes ago," he said. "He has heard from sources in Argentina that Henry Radwick is dead."

Kate stared at him, dumbfounded. "Dead! How? How did he die?"

"He was shot in some sort of tavern brawl," Charles replied evenly, "in the village where he had gone to live. The report North received apparently wasn't very specific as to details. It seems that the men who shot him—there were two or three of them—got away." There was a thin smile on his lips. "It's not clear whether there actually was a brawl or whether the whole thing was staged. However it happened, there seems to have been some sort of justice at work, carving out a punishment that could not be imposed within the system of our law. I thought you ought to know about it."

Kate sat back, pondering what Charles had told her. "Did you know?" she asked at last. "Did you know Radwick would be... executed?"

"I thought he might be," Charles replied. "The evidence we gathered—the ballistics, the fingerprints, the eyewitness testimony—was strong enough for any jury of reasonable men to have convicted him." He touched her arm. "Even the Prince, who certainly wished to sweep the whole matter under the rug, had to acknowledge the validity of the accusation and the strength of the evidence. I felt it likely that HRH would arrange for the cause of justice to be served, somehow or another. And if there had been enough evidence against Lillie Langtry—evidence of her complicity in her husband's death, for instance—I believe he would have imposed some sort of sentence upon her, as well."

"Perhaps he has," Kate said quietly. "He has given her a husband, to replace Mr. Langtry. He has made her... respectable."

"Respectable," Charles repeated wryly. A smile lit his eyes. "Yes, indeed. Well, I rather think that she and Hugo deserve one another." He stretched out his legs. "Speaking of the newly married, did I understand correctly that Bradford and Edith are coming for dinner tonight?"

Kate nodded. "I'm looking forward to seeing both of them. Edith will no doubt have word from Mr. Rhodes, and his version of the latest news from the Transvaal." She frowned, thinking of the report from South Africa that filled the front page of *The Times*. "Do you think it will come to war?"

"I think certain British interests believe that war would serve their purposes," Charles said dryly. "But they may well underestimate their enemy. The Boers are well trained. If there's war, they'll be well armed by their supporters in Germany. And they are fighting on their own territory, for their homes and for their way of life. Defeating them won't be as easy as Whitehall thinks." He looked grave. "I hope the conflict is resolved before Patrick is of an age to serve."

"Oh, but surely it could never drag on that long," Kate exclaimed. "I don't want to think about his going to war."

At that moment, Patrick, on Gladiator, trotted past the terrace. His red hair glinted in the sunlight and Kate saw that he was wearing his new silks—white with red and blue stripes. He threw them a happy wave. "I have to rub him down before I come to lunch," he called. "Don't wait for me."

"Of course we'll wait," Kate called back. "Take as long as you like." To Charles, she said, with an almost inexpressible feeling of quiet joy, "I'm so glad you bought the horse for him, Charles. And I'm so very happy that he's here."

"After he dared to disappoint Pinkie and Lord Hunt by riding Gladiator to win that ten-furlong handicap at Newmarket, it was clear that the boy had no future at the Grange House Stables," Charles said. "But George Lambton is delighted to take him on as an apprentice next year, and to have Gladiator in training as well."

"I do wish we could come to some conclusion about school though," Kate replied. "Patrick needs an education if he is to be happy in the world."

"Well, no decision need be made just yet. In another week or two, I'll suggest that Paddy start doing maths and science with me and reading and writing with you, and we shall see how he gets along."

With a sigh of pleasure, Kate reached for Charles's hand.

"I'm in no hurry to send him off anywhere. I'm content just to have him here with us, for now." She looked off into the distance, thinking how much her life had changed in the last few years. She was married to the man she loved, they had a child to love and care for together, and she had good work to do, work she loved as much as she loved Charles and Patrick. For a moment, she thought of Lillie Langtry, whose daughter had rejected her and who had married a man for his title. But it was not a thought on which she wanted to linger. Nor did she have to, since she had promised the Prince that Beryl would not write a story called *Death at Newmarket* and had informed the editor of *The Strand* that she would not, after all, be submitting an article about Mrs. Langtry. She would need to think of a new writing project. But that would not be at all difficult—and in the meantime, Mrs. Grieve would be there that afternoon to meet the students and begin the course on herbs.

Kate put aside the newspaper and stood up. "I'll be in the garden," she said. "You can call me there when you and Patrick are ready for lunch."

AUTHORS' NOTES

"To give an accurate description of what has never occurred is not merely the proper occupation of the historian, but the inalienable privilege of the man of arts."

OSCAR WILDE

Bill Albert writes:

Racing is the oldest national sport in England, and the late Victorian and Edwardian periods were brilliant chapters in its history. Led by the Prince of Wales, himself one of the most respected racehorse owners of the time, the social elite embraced racing as its favorite entertainment and made the race meetings at Epsom, Ascot, Newmarket, and Goodwood important events in the social calendar. With plenty of leisure time on their hands and with what was left of their family fortunes in their pockets, aristocratic owners indulged extravagently in buying, breeding, and training horses—and, not least, in gambling. It was a time when, after the reforms of the 1870s and 1880s, racing had become respectable.

But there were some particularly ugly aspects of racing in this period, and we have used them as the background for this book. The Brits have always been sensitive about American invasions of one sort or another (remember the

World War II joke about GIs that included the phrases "over-sexed" and "over here"?). We have been factual about the British attitude toward such well-heeled American gamblers as John Drake and Bet-a-Million Gates, hard-riding jockeys like Todhunter Sloan and the Reiff brothers, and trainers like Enoch Wishard; and about their fear of the horse doping that Wishard had brought from American tracks to the richer courses of England. For five racing seasons, the Stewards of the Jockey Club wrung their hands helplessly, debating what to do. Finally, in 1903, they declared doping an illegal practice. Even then, the main impetus seems not to have been a concern for the health of the horses or for good sportsmanship, but for the cost to the gambling establishment (and hence to the economy): conservatively estimated, British bookmakers had lost over two million pounds to the enterprising Americans, something like seventy million pounds in today's currency, close to one hundred and twenty-five million dollars.

In the same year that the British Jockey Club outlawed doping, its French counterpart forbade the practice as well, but doping had already caught on among French trainers. Within a half-dozen years, it had spread across Europe, and a variety of substances were being used: caffeine, strychnine, and morphine, as well as cocaine. Finally, in 1910, the Austrian racing authorities hired a Russian chemist named Bukowski to develop a test for the presence of drugs in horse saliva. In 1912, a horse named Bourbon Rose was disqualified in France because it tested positive for dope. The owners sued and lost, and testing became an accepted practice.

If you've ever tried to learn the nuances of a complicated sport like football or tennis from a source who either had an imperfect knowledge of the game or was so perfectly versed in it that he assumed that everyone knew as much as he did, you can grasp the problems we faced when we began to do the research for this book. We had a great deal to learn, not only about horseracing and training, but about the underworld of doping and cheating—most of which is only obliquely addressed in the primary sources of the period. As a consequence, we've relied more heavily than usual on secondary sources, chief among them George Plumptre's splendidly anecdotal book on Edwardian racing, Professor Thomas Tobin's scholarly work on the doping of racehorses, and (for the characters of Henry Radwick and Alfred Day), on Henry Blyth's study of the Henry Hastings scandal, *The Pocket Venus*. In fact, it probably wouldn't have occurred to us to write about this obscure and difficult subject if it hadn't been such a significant factor in the life and times of Lillie Langtry. It was an interest in her that snared us into the complex milieu of nineteenth-century racing.

Susan Albert writes:
I can think of only two women of our time who might be compared to Lillie Langtry: Madonna, the Material Girl; and Marilyn Monroe—Hollywood superstar, voluptuous sex queen, and lover of a president. In her time, Langtry commanded the same kind of public adulation and public censure that Madonna and Monroe have commanded, and for many of the same reasons. She was more widely known on both sides of the Atlantic than any other woman of her day (with the possible exceptions of Queen Victoria and Princess Alexandra), certainly more widely photographed, and probably more widely written about.

And yet, despite the words and pictures that convey Langtry's image to our time, despite the "autobiography" that conceals far more than it reveals, the real Lillie Langtry remains a fascinating enigma. She was a brief sensation on the London social scene in the late 1870s; she gave birth to a daughter whose paternity can only be guessed at (good guesses are Prince Louis of Battenberg and the Prince of Wales); she spent two decades as a mediocre actress whose figure, face, costumes, and jewelry excited far more attention and approval than did her acting or the plays she produced; and she relied for much of her financial support upon the generosity of a string of wealthy lovers. She married Hugo de Bathe in a private ceremony in July of 1899 (the only congratulations came from the Prince of Wales, who telegraphed to Mr. Jersey his compliments not on her marriage but on Merman's winning of both the Goodwood Plate and the Goodwood Cup) but she had to wait eight long years for old Lord de Bathe to die so that his son could inherit his baronetcy. Long before Mrs. Langtry became Lady de Bathe, however, Hugo had found other entertainments; although they remained married through Langtry's lifetime, the two lived together for less than a year. She outlasted the glamour of the theater and the glitter of the Edwardian period; nearly twenty years after King Edward VII died in 1910, she was living alone and embittered in a villa in Monte Carlo. "If the world could see the turmoil going on in my heart," she said to a friend, "it would be startled beyond words. I have lost my daughter, the only thing that is dear to me. My life is sad indeed." She died of pneumonia in 1929, at the age of seventy-six, and was buried on the Isle of Jersey.

But while these facts of Lillie's life are known, the mysteries we have portrayed in this book remain unsolved. What *did* happen to the jewels—worth more than two million dollars in today's currency—that were taken from the Union Bank in 1895? How *did* Edward Langtry die? What *was* her relationship with Jeanne-Marie?

We don't know the answers to these questions. Nobody does. But a study of Langtry's life certainly suggests that she was the kind of woman who might have converted her jewels to ready cash and had the paste copies stolen to cover up the substitution. To gain her freedom, she might also have connived at Ned Langtry's death; he was an alcoholic and relatively easy to dispose of—and the circumstances of his death in Chester Lunatic Asylum, where he was taken after being involved in some sort of accident at Chester Station, were certainly mysterious enough. And while we can't know for certain that Jeanne actually renounced her mother, we do know that Lady de Bathe was not given an invitation to Jeanne's wedding (in 1902, to the Honorable Ian Malcolm) and had to plead with a policeman to admit her. We also know that Jeanne promised the Malcolm family, before her marriage to Ian, that she would sever all relations with her mother.

Like Marilyn Monroe, like Madonna, Lillie Langtry was as notorious as she was famous and as scorned as she was praised. But whatever else she was, she remains an intriguing subject for fiction.

REFERENCES

Here are a few books that we found helpful in creating *Death at Epsom Downs*. Other background works may be found in the references to earlier books in this series. We hope that the next time you travel to England, you will take time to visit the National Horseracing Museum, in the High Street, Newmarket, Suffolk, where you'll find Lillie Langtry's boots on display. If you can't go to Newmarket, visit the Museum's website at http://www.nhrm.co.uk/body_index.html. If you have comments or questions, you may write to Bill and Susan Albert, P.O. Box 1616, Bertram, TX 78605, or email us at china@tstar.net. You might also wish to visit our website, where you will find additional information about the life and times of Lillie Langtry: http://www.mysterypartners.com.

The Annual Register 1899. London: Longman, Green and Co., 1900.

Blyth, Henry. *The Pocket Venus: A Victorian Scandal*. New York: Walker and Company, 1966.

The British Journal Photographic Almanac & Photographer's Daily Companion. London: Henry Greenwood, 1899.

Brough, James. *The Prince and the Lily: The Story of Lillie Langtry—The Greatest International Beauty of Her Day*. New York: Coward, McCann & Geoghegan, Inc., 1975.

Cannadine, David. *The Decline and Fall of the British Aristocracy*. New Haven: Yale University Press, 1990.

Dudley, Ernest. *The Gilded Lily: The Life and Loves of the Fabulous Lillie Langtry.* London: Odhams Press Ltd., 1958.

Fairfax-Blakeborough, JMC. *Paddock Personalities: Being Thirty Years' Turf Memories.* London: Hutchinson & Co. Ltd., 1936.

Hunn, David. *Epsom Racecourse: Its Story and Its People.* London: Davis-Poynter, 1973.

Onslow, Richard. *The Squire: A Life of George Alexander Baird, Gentleman Rider 1861–1893.* London: George G Harrap & Co. Ltd., 1980.

Plumptre, George. *The Fast Set: The World of Edwardian Racing.* London: André Deutsch Ltd., 1985.

Tuchman, Barbara W. *The Proud Tower: A Portrait of the World Before the War 1890–1914.* New York: The Macmillan Co., 1962.

Tobin, Thomas. *Drugs and the Performance Horse.* Springfield Illinois: Charles C Thomas Publishers, Ltd., 1981.

Welcome, John. *Neck or Nothing: The Extraordinary Life and Times of Bob Sievier.* London: Faber and Faber, 1970.